Known for her darkly violent, stunningly erotic Anita Blake, Vampire Hunter novels, #1 New York Times bestselling author Laurell K. Hamilton reveals new dimensions of her talent in these fantastical fairy tales, lush parables, and Anita Blake, Vampire Hunter stories. Share her vision as she welcomes you to the far corners of her "fertile imagination" (Diana Gabaldon) . . .

From a woman who marries into a family of volatile wizards to a couple fleeing a gang of love-hungry cupids, from a girl who seeks sanctuary in the form of a graceful goose to the disgruntled super-hero Captain Housework, you'll revel in the many twists and turns of fortune in these unique, sometimes surreal visions. Even hardened vampire hunter and zombie animator Anita Blake gets blindsided by the disturbing motives of her clients in the new story "Those Who Seek Forgiveness" and in "The Girl Who Was Infatuated with Death."

Sweet and spicy, the stories in *Strange Candy* are a treat for longtime fans and newfound readers—and will leave you with a craving for more.

PRAISE FOR
LAURELL K. HAMILTON'S
ANTIA BLAKE, VAMPIRE HUNTER NOVELS

DANSE MACABRE

"[A] fabulously imagined series." —*Publishers Weekly*

continued . . .

MICAH

"An exciting, erotic, and evocative paranormal romantic suspense thriller that will thrill her fans and send new readers scrambling for her backlist."　　　　　　　　　　　　　　　*—The Best Reviews*

"Highly palatable...equal portions of hot sex and supernatural crime fighting—with a dollop of old-fashioned male-female melodrama."　　　　　　　　　　　　　　*—Publishers Weekly*

"A tightly plotted, fast-paced romp."　　　　　　*—Romantic Times*

"Fantastic...provides further depth to her characters...would make a wonderful introduction to the series...a kick-butt heroine."
—A Romance Review

INCUBUS DREAMS

"Hamilton maintains a terrific pace with suspense, revenge, and heart-pounding endings."　　　　　　　　*—Detroit Free Press*

"Gruesome, action-packed scenes and episodes...Hamilton really does come off like the genre's answer to Henry Miller."
—The Denver Post

"[A] thrill ride."　　　　　　　　　　*—St. Louis Post-Dispatch*

"There's plenty of life (and undeath) left in this series, and Hamilton's imagination is apparently as inexhaustible as her heroine's supernatural capacity for coupling."　　　　　*—Publishers Weekly*

"[A] gutsy, no-nonsense female unafraid to take on anything that the preternatural world throws her way."　　　　*—Library Journal*

"The 'it' girl for bloodsuckers, werewolves, wereleopards, and assorted undead types."　　　　*—The Fort Meyers (FL) News-Press*

CERULEAN SINS

"One of the most fascinating fictional heroines since Scarlett O'Hara—and a hell of a lot more fun than most...hot stuff...the best Blake yet." —*Publishers Weekly* (starred review)

"Hits the ground running and doesn't let up...erotic."
—*St. Louis Post-Dispatch*

"Good, clean (or bloody) fun—meant for those who like their page-turners with a little bite to them." —*Austin American-Statesman*

"Fresh and fun." —*Metropole*

"Hamilton's complex, enthralling world is utterly absorbing, and Anita's many fans will be thrilled to see her back in action." —*Booklist*

"Antia's uncontrollable sexual energy has its amusing (not to mention arousing) moments...this manages to go over-the-top while remaining a really compelling read." —*Locus*

NARCISSUS IN CHAINS

"Laurell K. Hamilton's sexiest book...*Narcissus in Chains* hits the ground running and never stops...Hamilton just keeps getting better and better." —*St. Louis Post-Dispatch*

"In [this novel] tough, sarcastic Anita Blake...torn between her inner vamp and wolf makes a final mating choice that no fan will expect...Better pounce." —*Kirkus Reviews*

"Interesting...compelling." —*Locus*

"Amorous." —*Publishers Weekly*

Anita Blake, Vampire Hunter novels by Laurell K. Hamilton

GUILTY PLEASURES

THE LAUGHING CORPSE

CIRCUS OF THE DAMNED

THE LUNATIC CAFE

BLOODY BONES

THE KILLING DANCE

BURNT OFFERINGS

BLUE MOON

OBSIDIAN BUTTERFLY

NARCISSUS IN CHAINS

CERULEAN SINS

INCUBUS DREAMS

MICAH

DANSE MACABRE

THE HARLEQUIN

STRANGE CANDY

STRANGE CANDY

LAURELL K. HAMILTON

BERKLEY BOOKS, NEW YORK

THE BERKLEY PUBLISHING GROUP
Published by the Penguin Group
Penguin Group (USA) Inc.
375 Hudson Street, New York, New York 10014, USA
Penguin Group (Canada), 90 Eglinton Avenue East, Suite 700, Toronto, Ontario M4P 2Y3, Canada
(a division of Pearson Penguin Canada Inc.)
Penguin Books Ltd., 80 Strand, London WC2R 0RL, England
Penguin Group Ireland, 25 St. Stephen's Green, Dublin 2, Ireland (a division of Penguin Books Ltd.)
Penguin Group (Australia), 250 Camberwell Road, Camberwell, Victoria 3124, Australia
(a division of Pearson Australia Group Pty. Ltd.)
Penguin Books India Pvt. Ltd., 11 Community Centre, Panchsheel Park, New Delhi—110 017, India
Penguin Group (NZ), 67 Apollo Drive, Rosedale, North Shore 0745, Auckland, New Zealand
(a division of Pearson New Zealand Ltd.)
Penguin Books (South Africa) (Pty.) Ltd., 24 Sturdee Avenue, Rosebank, Johannesburg 2196,
South Africa

Penguin Books Ltd., Registered Offices: 80 Strand, London WC2R 0RL, England

Copyright © 2006 by Laurell K. Hamilton
For a listing of copyright details for previously published stories, please see page 289.
Cover art by Craig White
Cover design by Judith Murello
Text design by Tiffany Estreicher

PRINTING HISTORY
Berkley hardcover edition / October 2006
Berkley trade paperback edition / June 2007

Berkley trade paperback ISBN: 978-0-425-21521-0

Library of Congress has cataloged the Berkley hardcover edition as follows:

Hamilton, Laurell K.
      Strange candy / Laurell K. Hamilton. — 1st ed.
         p. cm.
      ISBN 0-425-21201-7
   1. Supernatural—Fiction.   I. Title.

   PS3558.A443357S76 2006
   813'.54—dc22

                                      2006021153

PRINTED IN THE UNITED STATES OF AMERICA

10   9   8   7   6   5   4   3   2

This one is for all those editors who took a chance on me when I was an unknown. To everyone who bought my stories when putting my name on the front of their magazine, or in their anthology, didn't guarantee them more sales. Thanks for taking a chance on me.

ACKNOWLEDGMENTS

To my husband, Jonathon, who knew me first through my stories, and now knows me better than anyone. He loves me still—the dark and light of me. To Darla and her husband, Jack, who were two of the four people who used to show up at my signings, when no one knew who I was. To Andrew, best man at our wedding, and the fourth of that long-ago four that kept me company at all those empty signings. You guys can truly say you knew me when, and the fact that you all still know me now is even better.

This one is also for the other readers who first discovered me not through the Anita Blake series, or the Meredith Gentry series, but through my short stories. Thanks also to all those fans who have asked over the years when am I going to do the sequel to *Nightseer*. Here, at least, are stories set in the same world—not the same characters, sorry about that, but the world and the magic system are here. I hope you enjoy seeing other parts of Keleios's world.

Thanks to Richard Nichols, who for the first time helped edit. Also, as I write this, he is turning thirty. Happy Birthday, Richard. Mark and Sarah Sumner, who were my next-door neighbors when many of these stories were written. Good neighbors, good friends. Rett MacPherson, one of the bravest women I know. Marella Sands, I look forward to your new world finding its footing and its fans. Deborah Millitello, who was there, almost from the beginning, and saw most of these stories in some rough form or another. Thanks for the encouragement. There were days when your support kept me from giving up. Sharon Shinn, for gripe sessions and an understanding ear. Tom Drennan, a quiet, comforting presence at all the meetings of the Alternate Historians. To Jannie Lee Simner, who had the audacity to move all the way to Arizona a few years back and abandon us all. Congrats on all your books. N. L. Drew, who also got to see some of these stories in rougher form. Robert K. Sheaf, who was with us early, and now is with us no longer. Are you writing stories up in Heaven, Bob? For you, and your so-firm faith, God bless. For my faith, blessed be.

Contents

INTRODUCTION

Welcome to the parts of my imagination that don't get much play at book length. Some people see short stories as a way to further their book career. The last story, "The Girl Who Was Infatuated with Death," was commissioned by my publisher for a collection of pieces with other of their supernatural writers. So I guess that one was designed to further my reading audience and those of the other writers with me in the anthology. But as for the rest of the stories, these are ideas I was compelled to write by nothing but my sometime peculiar imagination and a desire to play. Short stories for me are like vacations. You know, those trips you take to new places to do things you don't normally get to do in your work-a-day life. These stories, with a few exceptions, are worlds where most of you have never been with me. Several of these are set in the same world as my first book, *Nightseer*. So for those of you who keep writing in, or asking at signings, when will I finish that series, here are at least a few more pieces of that world—though with different characters and countries. I thought once I would write only heroic fantasy like a mix of Tolkien and Robert E. Howard. But the bottom fell out of the heroic fantasy market and I was left scrambling to find a vision that the publishers would buy. I had a few stories that were different, set in modern day with fantastic elements. One was the first Anita Blake short story, "Those Who Seek Forgiveness." Another was "The Edge of the Sea"—which is still an idea that intrigues me. You have also my only completed science fiction story, "Here Be Dragons." You also get the only story I've ever written in Anita's world that has none of the main characters in it, "Selling Houses."

I have dozens of other short story ideas, and most of them are very unlike Anita and Merry's adventures. My unwritten short ideas are vacations of the mind. The last thing you want to do on vacation is your normal job. So how does a girl get to a point where normal is vampire hunting, fairie princesses and private detectives, and some of the most erotic relationships on paper? Just lucky, I guess.

THOSE WHO SEEK

FORGIVENESS

This is the first time Anita ever walked onto paper for me. The cemetery in this story is based on the cemetery where my mother is buried. It was a place I knew very well, because my grandmother, who raised me, took me often. I guess it was inevitable that I would write about the dead; my childhood was haunted by death. Not real ghosts, but the ghosts of memory and loss. Anita raises the dead in this story, which was all I had planned on her doing. The idea of her being a legal vampire executioner actually didn't hit my radar until quite late in trying to write the first book. Originally this story represented what I thought Anita would do: raise zombies. How different things would have been if I'd stuck to my original plan. No Jean-Claude, no Richard, not much of anybody except Anita. What a bleak world it would have been, with just Anita and me in it.

"DEATH is a very serious matter, Mrs. Fiske. People who go through it are never the same."

The woman leaned forward, cradling her face in her hands. Her slim shoulders shook quietly for a few minutes. I passed another box of tissues her way. She groped for them blindly and then looked up. "I know you can't bring him back, exactly."

She wiped at two tears, which escaped and rolled down flawless cheekbones. The purse she clutched so tightly was reptile, at least two hundred dollars. Her accessories—lapel pin, high heels, hat, and gloves—were all black as her purse. Her suit was gray. Neither color suited her, but they emphasized her pale skin and hollow eyes. She was the sort of woman that made me feel too short, too dark, and gave me the strange desire to lose ten more pounds. If she hadn't been so genuinely grief-stricken, I could have disliked her.

"I have to talk to Arthur. That's my husband . . . was my husband." She took a deep breath and tried again. "Arthur died suddenly. A massive coronary." She blew delicately into a tissue. "His family did have a history of heart disease, but he always took such good care of himself." She finished with a watery hiccup. "I want to say good-bye to him, Miss Blake."

I smiled reassuringly. "We all have things left unsaid when death comes suddenly. But it isn't always best to raise the dead and say it."

Her blue eyes stared intently through a film of tears. I was going to discourage her as I discourage every one of my clients, but this one would do it. There was a certain set to the eyes that said *serious*.

"There are certain limitations to the process." My boss didn't allow us to show slides or pictures or give graphic descriptions, but we were supposed to tell the truth. One good picture of a decaying zombie would have sent most of my clients screaming.

"Limitations?"

"Yes, we can bring him back. You came to us promptly. That helps. He's been buried only three days. But as a zombie your husband will only have limited use of his body and mind. And as the days go by, that will grow worse, not better."

She stood up very straight, tears drying on her face. "I was hoping you could bring him back as a vampire."

I kept my face carefully blank. "Vampires are illegal, Mrs. Fiske."

"A friend told me that . . . you could get that done here." She finished in a rush, searching my face.

I smiled my best professional smile. "We do not do vampires. And even if we did, you can't make an ordinary corpse into a vampire."

"Ordinary?"

Very few people who came to us had even a remote idea of how rare vampires were, or why. "The deceased would have to have been bitten by a werewolf, vampire, or other supernatural creature, while alive. Being buried in unconsecrated ground would help. Your husband, Arthur, was never bitten by a vampire while alive, was he?"

"No," she half laughed, "he was bitten by my Yorkshire terrier once."

I smiled, encouraging her turn of spirits. "That won't quite do it. Your husband can come back as a zombie or not at all."

"I'll take it," she said quietly, all serious and very still.

"I will warn you that most families find it advisable to lay the zombie to rest after a time."

"Why?"

Why? I saw the happy family embracing their lost loved one. I saw the family sick, horrified, bringing the decaying corpse to be put down. The smiling relative reduced to a shambling horror.

"What exactly do you want Arthur to do when he arises?"

She looked down and shredded another tissue. "I want to say good-bye to him."

"Yes, Mrs. Fiske, but what do you want him to do?"

She was silent for several minutes. I decided to prompt her. "For instance, a woman came in wanting her husband raised so he could take out life insurance. I told her most insurance companies won't insure the walking dead." She grinned at that. "And that is what Arthur will come back as—the walking dead."

Her smile faltered, and tears came again. "I want Arthur to forgive me." She hid her face in her hands and sobbed. "I had an affair for several months. He found out, had a heart attack, and died." She seemed to gain strength from the words, and the tears slowed. "You see that I have to talk to him one last time. I have to tell him I love him, only him. I want Arthur to forgive me. Can he do that as a . . . zombie?"

"I've found that the dead are very forgiving of the living, when they die of natural causes. Your husband will have ample brainpower to speak. He will be himself at first. As the days progress, he will lose memory. He will begin to decay, first mentally, then physically."

"Decay?"

"Yes, slowly, but after all, he is dead."

The relatives didn't really believe that a fresh zombie wasn't alive. Knowing intellectually that someone smiling and talking is the walking dead is one thing. Emotionally, it is very different. But they believed as time passed and as he or she began to look like a walking corpse.

"It's temporary then?"

"Not exactly." I came from behind the desk and sat next to her. "He could stay a zombie possibly forever. But his physical and mental state would deteriorate until he was not much better than an automaton in tattered flesh."

"Tattered . . . flesh," she whispered.

I touched her hand. "I know it's a hard choice, but that is the reality." *Tattered flesh* didn't really touch the white sheen of bone through rotting flesh, but it was a term our boss allowed.

She gripped my hand and smiled. "Thank you for telling me the truth. I still want to bring Arthur back. Even if it's just long enough to say a few words."

So she was going to do it, as I had known she would. "So you don't want him for weeks, or days, only long enough to talk."

"I think so."

"I don't mean to rush you, Mrs. Fiske, but I need to know before we set up an appointment. You see, it takes more time and energy to raise and then lay to rest, one right after another." If she laid and raised quickly enough, Mrs. Fiske might be able to remember Arthur at his best.

"Oh, of course. If possible I would like to talk for several hours."

"Then it's best if you take him home for at least the evening. We can schedule putting him back for tomorrow night." I would push for a quick laying to rest. I didn't think Mrs. Fiske could take watching her husband rot before her eyes.

"That sounds good." She took a deep breath. I knew what she was going to say. She looked so brave and resolute. "I want to be there when you bring him back."

"Your presence is required, Mrs. Fiske. You see, a zombie has no real will of its own. Your husband should be able to think on his own at first, but as time wears on, the zombie finds it very difficult to decide things. The person, or persons, who raised it will have control over it."

"You and I?"

"Yes."

She paled even more, her grip tightening.

"Mrs. Fiske?" I got her a glass of water. "Sip it slowly." When she seemed better, I asked, "Are you sure you're up to this tonight?"

"Is there anything I need to bring?"

"A suit of your husband's clothes would be nice. Maybe a favorite object, hat, trophy, to help him orient himself. The rest I'll supply." I hesitated, because some of the color had crept into her face, but she needed to be prepared. "There will be blood at the ceremony."

"Blood." Her voice was a breathy whisper.

"Chicken, I'll bring it. There will also be some ointment to spread over our faces and hands. It glows faintly and smells fairly strange, but not unpleasant." Her next question would be the usual.

"What do we do with the blood?"

I gave the usual answer. "We sprinkle some on the grave and some on us."

She swallowed very carefully, looking slightly gray.

"You can back out now but not later. Once you've paid your deposit, it can't be refunded. And once the ceremony begins, to break the circle is very dangerous."

She looked down, thinking. I liked that. Most who agreed right away were afraid later. The brave ones took time to answer. "Yes." She sounded very convinced. "To make peace with Arthur, I can do it."

"Good for you. How is tonight?"

"About midnight," she added hopefully.

I smiled. Everyone thought midnight was the perfect time for raising the dead. All that was required was darkness. Some people did put a great deal of stock in certain phases of the moon, but I had never found it necessary. "No, how about nine o'clock?"

"Nine?"

"If that will be all right. I have two other appointments tonight, and nine was left open."

She smiled. "That will be fine." Her hand shook as she signed the check for half the fee, the other half to be delivered after the raising.

We shook hands, and she said, "Call me Carla."

"I'm Anita."

"I'll see you at nine tonight at Wellington Cemetery."

I continued for her, "Between two large trees and across from the only hill."

"Yes, thank you." She flashed a watery smile and was gone.

I buzzed our receptionist area. "Mary, I'm booked up for this week and won't be seeing any more clients, until at least next Tuesday."

"I'll see to it, Anita."

I leaned back in my chair and soaked up the silence. Three animations a night was my limit. Tonight they were all routine, or almost. I was bringing back my first research scientist. His three colleagues couldn't figure out his notes, and their deadline, or rather grant, was running close. So dear Dr. Richard Norris was coming back from the dead to help them out. They were scheduled for midnight.

At three this next morning I would meet the widowed Mrs. Stiener. She wanted her husband to clear up some nasty details with his will.

Being an animator meant very little nightlife, no pun intended. Afternoons were spent interviewing clients and evenings raising the dead. Though we few were very popular at a certain kind of party—the sort where the host likes to brag about how many celebrities he knows, or worse yet, the kind who simply want to stare. I don't like being on display and refuse to go to parties unless forced. Our boss likes to keep us in the public eye to dispel rumors that we are witches or hobgoblins.

It's pretty pitiful at parties. All the animators huddled, talking shop like a bunch of doctors. But doctors don't get called *witch*, *monster*, *zombie queen*. Very few people remember to call us animators. For most, we are a dark joke. "This is Anita. She makes zombies, and I don't mean the drink." Then there would be laughter all around, and I would smile politely and know I'd be going home early.

Tonight there was no party to worry over, just work. Work was power, magic, a strange dark impulse to raise more than what you were paid for. Tonight would be cloudless, moonlit, and starred; I could feel it. We were different, drawn to the night, unafraid of death and its many forms, because we had a sympathy for it.

Tonight I would raise the dead.

Wellington Cemetery was new. All the tombstones were nearly the same size, square or rectangle, and set off into the night in near-perfect rows. Young trees and perfectly clipped evergreen shrubs lined the gravel driveway. The moon rode strong and high, bathing the scene clearly, if mysteriously, in silver and black. A handful of huge trees dotted the grounds. They looked out of place among all this newness. As Carla had said, only two of them grew close together.

The drive spilled into the open and encircled the hill. The mound of grass-covered earth was obviously man-made, so round, short, and domed. Three other drives centered on it. A short way down the west drive stood two large trees. As my car crunched over gravel, I could see someone dressed in white. A flare of orange was a match, and the reddish pinpoint of a cigarette sprang to life.

I stopped the car, blocking the drive, but few people on honest business visit cemeteries at night. Carla had beaten me here, very unusual. Most clients want to spend as little time as possible near the grave after dark. I walked over to her before unloading equipment.

There was a litter of burned-out cigarettes like stubby white bugs about her feet. She must have been here in the dark for hours waiting to raise a zombie. She either was punishing herself or enjoyed the idea. There was no way of knowing which.

Her dress, shoes, even hose, were white. Earrings of silver flashed in the moonlight as she turned to me. She was leaning against one of the trees, and its black trunk emphasized her whiteness. She only turned her head as I came up to her.

Her eyes looked silver-gray in the light. I couldn't decipher the look on her face. It wasn't grief.

"It's a beautiful night, isn't it?"

I agreed that it was. "Carla, are you all right?"

She stared at me terribly calm. "I'm feeling much better than I did this afternoon."

"I'm very glad to hear that. Did you remember to bring his clothes and a memento?"

She motioned to a dark bundle by the tree.

"Good, I'll unload the car." She didn't offer to help, which was not unusual. Most of the time it was fear that prevented it. I realized my Omega was the only car in sight.

I called softly, but sound carries on summer nights. "How did you get here? I don't see a car."

"I hired a cab, it's waiting at the gate."

A cab. I would love to have seen the driver's face when he dropped her off at the cemetery gates. The three black chickens clucked from their cage in the backseat. They didn't have to be black, but it was the only color I could get for tonight. I was beginning to think our poultry supplier had a sense of humor.

Arthur Fiske was only recently dead, so from the box in the trunk I took only a jar of homemade ointment and a machete. The ointment was pale off-white with flecks of greenish light in it. The glowing flecks were graveyard mold. You wouldn't find it in this cemetery. It only grew in graveyards that had stood for at least a hundred years. The ointment also contained the obligatory spider webs and other noisome things, plus herbs and spices to hide the smell and aid the magic. If it was magic.

I smeared the tombstone with it and called Carla over. "It's your turn now, Carla." She stubbed out her cigarette and came to stand before me. I smeared her face and hands and told her, "You stand just behind the tombstone throughout the raising."

She took her place without a word while I placed ointment on myself. The pine scent of rosemary for memory, cinnamon and cloves for preservation, sage for wisdom, and lemon thyme to bind it all together seemed to soak through the skin itself.

I picked the largest chicken and tucked it under my arm. Carla stood where I had left her, staring down at the grave. There was an art to beheading a chicken with only two hands.

I stood at the foot of the grave to kill the chicken. Its first artery blood splashed onto the grave. It splattered over the fading chrysanthemums, roses, and carnations. A spire of white gladioli turned dark. I walked a circle sprinkling blood as I went, tracing a circle of steel with a bloody machete. Carla shut her eyes as the blood rained upon her.

I smeared blood on myself and placed the still-twitching body upon the flower mound. Then I stood once again at the foot of the grave. We were cut off now inside the blood circle, alone with the night, and our thoughts. Carla's eyes flashed white at me as I began the chant.

"Hear me, Arthur Fiske. I call you from the grave. By blood, magic, and steel, I call you. Arise, Arthur, come to us, come to me, Arthur Fiske." Carla joined me as she was supposed to. "Come to us, Arthur, come to us, Arthur. Arthur, arise." We called his name in ever-rising voices.

The flowers shuddered. The mound heaved upward, and the

chicken slid to the side. A hand clawed free, ghostly pale. A second hand and Carla's voice failed her. She began moving round the gravestone to kneel to the left of the heaving mound. There was such wonder, even awe, in her face, as I called Arthur Fiske from the grave.

The arms were free. The top of a dark-haired head was in sight, but the top was almost all there was. The mortician had done his best, but Arthur's had been a closed-casket funeral.

The right side of his face was gone, blasted away. Clean white bone shone at jaw and skull, and silver bits of wire where the bone had been strung together. It still wasn't a face. The nose was empty holes, bare and white. The skin was shredded and snipped short to look neater. The left eye rolled wildly in the bare socket. I could see the tongue moving between the broken teeth. Arthur Fiske struggled from the grave.

I tried to remain calm. It could be a mistake. "Is that Arthur?"

Her hoarse whisper came to me. "Yes."

"That is not a heart attack."

"No." Her voice was calm now, incredibly normal. "No, I shot him at close range."

"You killed him, and had me bring him back."

Arthur was having some trouble freeing his legs, and I ran to Carla. I tried to help her to her feet but she wouldn't move.

"Get up, get up, damn it, he'll kill you!"

Her next words were very quiet. "If that's what he wants."

"God help me, a suicide."

I forced her to look at me instead of the thing in the grave. "Carla, a murdered zombie always kills his murderer first, always. No forgiveness, that is a rule. I can't control him until after he has killed you. You have to run, now."

She saw me, understood, I think, but said, "This is the only way to be free of guilt. If he forgives me, I'll be free."

"You'll be dead!"

Arthur freed himself and was sitting on the crushed, earth-strewn flowers. It would take him a little while to organize, but not too long.

"Carla, he will kill you. There will be no forgiveness." Her eyes had wandered back to the zombie, and I slapped her twice, very hard. "Carla, you will die out here, and for what? Arthur is dead, really dead. You don't want to die."

Arthur slid off the flowers and stood uncertainly. His eye rolling around in its socket finally spotted us. Though he didn't have much to show expression with, I could see joy on his shat-tered face. There was a twitch of a smile as he shambled toward us, and I began dragging her away. She didn't fight me, but she was a dead, awkward weight. It is very hard to drag someone away if they don't want to go.

I let her sink back to the ground. I looked at the clumsy but de-termined zombie and decided to try. I stood in front of him, block-ing him from Carla. I called upon whatever power I possessed and talked to him. "Arthur Fiske, hear me, listen only to me."

He stopped moving and stared down at me. It was working, against all the rules, it was working.

It was Carla who spoiled it. Her voice saying, "Arthur, Arthur, forgive me."

He was distracted and tried to move toward her voice. I stopped him with a hand on his chest. "Arthur, I command you, do not move. I who raised you command you."

She called one more time. That was all he needed. He flung me away absentmindedly. My head hit the tombstone. It wasn't much of a blow, no blood like on television, but it took everything out of me for a minute. I lay in the flowers, and it seemed very important to hear myself breathe.

Arthur reached down for her, slowly. His face twitched, and his tongue made small sounds that might have been, "Carla."

The clumsy hands stroked her hair. He half fell, half knelt by her. She drew back at that, afraid.

I started crawling over the flowers toward them. She was not going to commit suicide with my help.

The hands stroked her face, and she backed away, just a few inches. The thing crawled after her. She backpedaled faster, but he came on surprisingly quick. He pinned her under his body, and she started screaming.

I half-crawled, half-fell across the zombie's back.

The hands crept up her body, touching her shoulders.

Her eyes rolled back to me. "Help me!"

I tried. I tugged at him, trying to pull him off her. Zombies do not have supernatural strength, no matter what the media would like you to think, but Arthur had been a large, muscular man. If he could have felt pain, I might have pulled him off, but there was no real way to distract him.

"Anita, please!"

The hands settled on her neck and squeezed.

I found the machete where it had dropped to the ground. It was sharp, and did damage, but he couldn't feel it. I chopped at his head and back. He ignored me. Even decapitated, he would keep coming. His hands were the problem. I knelt and sighted at his lower arm. I didn't dare try it any closer to her face. The blade flashed silver. I brought it down with all the strength in my back and arms, but it took five blows to break the bone.

The separated hand kept squeezing as if it were still attached. I threw the machete down and began prying one finger at a time from her neck. It was time consuming. Carla stopped struggling. I screamed my rage and helplessness at him and kept prying up the fingers. The strong hands squeezed until there was a cracking sound. Not a sharp pencil break like a leg or an arm, but a crackling as the bones crushed together. Arthur seemed satisfied. He stood up from the body. All expression left him. He was empty, waiting for a command.

I fell back into the flowers, not sure whether to cry, or scream, or just run. I just sat there and shook. But I had to do something about the zombie. I couldn't just leave him to wander around.

I tried to tell him to stay, but my voice wouldn't come. His eye followed me as I stumbled to the car. I came back with a handful of salt. In the other hand I scooped the fresh grave dirt. Arthur watched me without expression. I stood at the outer edge of the circle. "I give you back to the earth from which you came."

I threw the dirt upon him. He turned to face me.

"With salt I bind you to your grave." The salt sounded like sleet on his suit. I made the sign of a cross with the machete. "With steel I give you back."

I realized that I had begun the ceremony without getting another chicken. I bent and retrieved the dead one and slit it open. I drew still-warm and bloody entrails free. They glistened in the moonlight. "With flesh and blood I command you, Arthur, return to your grave and walk no more."

He lay down upon the grave. It was as if he had lain in quicksand. It just swallowed him up. With a last shifting of flowers, the grave was as before, almost.

I threw the gutted chicken to the ground and knelt beside the woman's body. Her neck flopped at an angle just slightly wrong.

I got up and shut the trunk of my car. The sound seemed to

echo, too loud. Wind seemed to roar in the tall trees. The leaves rustled and whispered. The trees all looked like flat black shadows, nothing had any depth to it. All noises were too loud. The world had become a one-dimensional cardboard thing. I was in shock. It would keep me numb and safe for a little while. Would I dream about Carla tonight? Would I try to save her again and again? I hoped not.

Somewhere up above, nighthawks flitted. Their cries came thin and eerie, echoing loud. I looked at the body by the grave. The whiteness of it stained now with dirt. So much for the other half of my fee.

I got in the car, smearing blood over the steering wheel and key. There were phone calls to make; to my boss, to the police, and to cancel the rest of my appointments. I would be raising no more dead tonight. There was a taxi to send away. I wondered how much the meter had run up.

My thoughts ran in dull, frightened circles. I began to shake, hands trembling. Tears came hot and violent. I sobbed and screamed in the privacy of my car. When I could breathe without choking, and my hand was steady, I put the car in gear. I would definitely be seeing Carla tonight and Arthur. What's one more nightmare?

I left Carla there alone, with Arthur's forgiveness, one leg lost in the flowers of his grave.

A LUST OF CUPIDS

I feel like we need a depth chamber between this and the preceding story. We're moving from almost as dark as I get as a writer, to almost as light as I get. I got a lot of nice rejection slips on this story. Editors loved it, but not enough to buy it. One editor at one of the top-paying magazines at the time actually told me the truth: that since they published only one piece of fiction in each issue, I wasn't a big enough name to help their magazine sales. But she adored the story. When I became a big enough name to make a difference, I did not send the story back to her for another chance. One, I was too busy with novels to think about it. Two, I'm petty. It's the same story; the only thing that changed was that now I was a name. I rarely give second chances.

I WAS walking along Market Street on my lunch hour, wishing I hadn't worn high heels today, or a skirt. Pantyhose were no protection at all against the icy winter air. I was minding my own business when I saw them. They floated by the streetlight at the corner like gigantic moths attracted to the cold electric light. Half a dozen small naked children with cotton-candy wings and curly ringlets, mostly blond. They were also carefully neuter, smooth as a Barbie doll.

Cupids. Shit. That was all I needed. I looked for a door, a shop, anything that I could take refuge in. The brick building stretched smooth and doorless. There was a small shop across the street, but I'd never make it, too open, no cover. I began to walk sideways, back down the street. One hand on the wall to make sure I didn't trip. If I could just make the far corner, maybe I could run for it.

But it was too late; they had spotted me. One of the chubby pink things strung his tiny golden bow and began to sift through his quiver for an arrow. His shiny little eyes never left me. I wasn't close enough to see his eyes, but I knew what color they were. All Cupids have sky-blue eyes, like Easter eggs, or baby blankets.

I didn't wait to see what color of arrow it chose, I turned and ran. My high heels seemed to echo the narrow street. They'd find me. Damn it!

I made it around the corner and found every building as blank and smooth as the Cupids themselves. I had just walked down this street. There should have been doors, shops, people. I had heard that Cupids could cloud your mind, but I had never believed, until now.

I darted a look behind me. Nothing. I wasn't sure if that was a good sign, or a bad one. They either had given up, or were so sure of me that they didn't need to hurry. Or, they were right above me and I just couldn't see them, like the doors that should have been here. I wanted to scream and rant and stomp my feet, but that wouldn't help. Think, Rachel, think.

If I couldn't see the doors, maybe I could feel them. Cupids wouldn't follow me inside. I had walked this street a hundred times, surely I could remember where one door was, any door.

My hands slid over cold, blank bricks. If there was something there, I couldn't feel it. The Cupids flew around the corner. There were six of them, hovering, soft pastel wings fluttering like lazy butterflies. The look in their eyes wasn't soft, it was cold.

I flattened myself against the wall and screamed, "Leave me alone, you overweight cherubs!"

They glanced at each other; maybe I had offended them. I

hoped so. A Cupid with soft pink wings drew an arrow from behind his back. The rest of them hovered like chubby vultures.

A man yelled, "In here!"

I glanced to my right and found a door open and a man motioning to me. "Run for it," he said.

I ran for it. I was almost to the door when my heel broke and sent me sprawling on the sidewalk. Something whirred over my head and thunked into the door. The white arrow vibrated in the door. White, the color of true love. Shit!

A hand grabbed my arm and pulled me inside. I scrambled inside the shop on hands and knees, no time to be ladylike. A tall, broad-shouldered man closed the door and asked, "Are you all right?"

I nodded, still sitting on the floor, staring at the arrow. It was already beginning to evaporate. In a few minutes it would be gone. No danger of us mere mortals getting hold of one of the arrows of love. Once fired they just didn't last.

"What did I do to deserve white?" I asked, not really expecting an answer.

"Are you over thirty?" the man asked.

I thought that was a rather rude question from a stranger, but he had saved me. "Why do you ask?"

"Because once you're over thirty the little things get pesky. I'm thirty-five and never been married. Something in a Cupid just can't stand that."

I smiled. "Thirty-three, never married, never want to be."

He offered me a hand up. I took it. His hand was big like him and nearly swallowed my hand to the wrist. His eyes were perfect brown like polished chestnut. Curly brown hair was cut short and had never seen the inside of a styling salon.

I couldn't stand straight with only one heel so I took the shoes off. "It was lucky I wore heels today."

"Damn straight. How many of 'em are after you?"

"Six."

He gave a low whistle. "They want you bad."

I nodded. He was right. One Cupid was standard, maybe even two; they didn't seem to like to be alone much. But a lust of Cupids was a damn posse. All for little ol' me. Had I offended someone? I had an awful thought, an uncharitable thought. Had my mother paid them off, slipped one of the little winged horrors some sweets? Cupids didn't need money, but they loved candies and desserts. It was frowned upon, but everyone knew it happened. Corrupt Cupids with a sweet tooth.

"I'm Tom Hagan," the man said.

"Rachel Carrdigan." We shook hands again and his hand was warm and callused. There was something oddly appealing about his square face. If I hadn't known better, I'd have wondered if a pink arrow had gotten me. Pink for infatuation.

"Were you out to lunch?" he asked.

"Yes."

He smiled. "Well, it isn't much, but I'll split mine with you. Cupids don't have much patience. They'll wander off if you can hide long enough."

"You sound like an expert."

"Hey, I'm two years older than you. They've been after me longer."

I laughed. "All right, if you're sure it's not trouble."

"It isn't like the shop is busy today."

I glanced around the warm interior of the shop for the first time. Hand-carved wood was everywhere. Small furniture, shelves, animals. All the folksy wooden things the tourists bought in droves, but it was winter now and the tourists were gone. I always wondered how some of the shops made it through the off-season. One of the good things about being a lawyer, crime was always in season.

Tom brought a rocking chair he'd made himself to sit beside his own chair. He gave me a lap-size linen napkin to spread over my business skirt and shared a huge roast beef sandwich and apple pie. The pie was delicious and I said so.

"Made it myself." He seemed embarrassed but pleased. Since I couldn't boil soup without burning it, I was impressed.

I called my office and said I'd be later without explaining the reason. We spent a very pleasant time drinking fresh coffee and talking about small things. Nothing major or earth shattering, but comfortable.

Tom glanced at the clock. "I hate to say it, but it's probably safe for you to leave."

"My God, it's two. I had no idea it was that late." I smiled. "Maybe I'll be needing a wooden shelf or two for my condo, soon."

He grinned and, I swear, blushed. "I'd like that."

There was a little click down in my solar plexus, pleasure. Who needed Cupids? I limped in my high heels, one heel on, one heel off, but it was better than going barefoot on freezing cobblestones.

Tom let me out the back door, just in case. We both looked up and down the alley. Nothing, empty, home free. "Thanks for everything, Tom." I shook his hand and felt that warm tingle as our skin met. Probably nothing would come of it, but it was nice anyway.

I turned just before I rounded the corner and waved. He waved back, smiling, then his face changed and he was running for me. "Behind you!"

I whirled. The Cupids were flying in at my back. I flung myself onto the ground. A white arrow buried itself into the cobblestones near my head. Tom was running toward me, shouting.

A white arrow took him through the chest. He staggered back, eyes wide and surprised. He stumbled back a few steps, then fell backward onto the cobblestones. I screamed, "Tom!" I heard the whir of wings above me. I turned, slowly, and stared into shining blue eyes. A small feminine mouth smiled at me. The little gold bow pulled back, a white arrow pointing at me.

A second Cupid with slightly paler hair and baby-blue wings floated off to the left, bow trained on me. I wasn't getting away this time.

"Get it over with, you ugly little harpies," I yelled. I threw my shoe at them, the one with the broken heel. The Cupid dodged effortlessly. How could something that chubby be so graceful? I saw the arrow leave the bow, then felt a sharp pain in my chest, over my heart. Then nothing but darkness.

TOM and I woke in the alley and did the only thing we were able to do, fall in love. It was a nice wedding as weddings go. Our mothers sat in the front rows beaming at us. Both of them admitted to having bribed the Cupids, but it had all worked out for the best, they said, smiling smugly.

We smiled back; what else could we do? Arrows of true love had hit both of us. We were in love, married, happy, vengeful.

My mother is a widow. Tom's mother is divorced. All we need now is a corrupt Cupid, with a sweet tooth.

THE EDGE OF THE SEA

This is another story that I wrote when I lived in California for a few years. It's the only time in my life that I've lived near the water. I've almost drowned four times. At one point I had my dive certificate. I thought it would help me overcome my phobias. Then I had a diving accident, and now I'm claustrophobic on top of being afraid of water. Oh, well. This is a very sensual story, and was the first peek of that side of me as a writer. But it is a melancholy story. The idea of it—that fear and longing that the ocean fills me with—will be visited at more length in an upcoming Anita book. Some of the characters introduced in Danse Macabre *will be helping me explore some of the themes of this story in more loving, and even more frightening, detail.*

ADRIA woke to the sound of the sea. She lay under the cool wash of sheets, wondering what had woken her. Moonlight spilled through the white curtains. The rushing hush of the sea poured underneath the balcony. It filled the bedroom with an intimate whispering noise. What had woken her? There was a sense of urgency, as if she had forgotten something.

She sat up, brushing strands of dark hair away from her face. She called out, not really expecting an answer, "Rachel?"

The only sound was ocean, a purring roar along the sand.

Adria slipped on a pair of jeans that lay rumpled by the bed. Her nightshirt flapped almost to her knees, a man's extra large. She padded barefoot over scattered fitness magazines and clothes. The living room stretched perfectly neat, like a magazine cover, where no one lived. Rachel's neat and tidy hand was visible everywhere.

Adria's hand brushed the music box on the end table. It sang a few forlorn notes. The music boxes were Rachel's hobby. She called them her vice.

Adria walked across the thick white carpet to the short hall. It led to the bathroom and Rachel's bedroom. The door stood ajar, moonlight spilling into the black hallway. Adria froze, pulse thudding against her throat. The urgency she had woken with turned to fear. They had shared the house for almost two years. In all that time Rachel had never left her door open. She had a habit of listening to music as she fell asleep. The sound would leak through the house if the door were open.

No sound. The rushing sea seemed muted in the hall. Adria paused, almost touching the door. "Rachel?" Silence. "Rachel, can you hear me?"

Adria touched the door; it swung inward. The bed was rumpled, pale sheets turned to silver by the moonlight. Rachel's clothes lay neatly folded on the back of the room's only chair. Even her shoes were toes out, heels touching, just waiting to be put on again.

The drapes flapped in the wind, cord slapping the screen. Adria jumped then laughed, but the laughter sounded wrong. So quiet. She walked to the window. There was always a chance Rachel had gone outside, though that was more something Adria would do than Rachel.

The beach was a narrow whiteness, heavy and pale under the moon. The ocean rolled gray and silver, white foam riding the waves, as it whisper-roared, eating away at the shore. Rocks gleamed dull black as the surf swirled and blew white spray up into the air. During the day Adria had jogged every inch of the beach but moonlight made it an alien place.

Adria heard something, a moan, a muffled cry. She wasn't

sure if it was the sound of pleasure or pain. Adria smiled to herself. If she went out there and Rachel had a boyfriend on the beach . . . Adria turned back to the room. No, there were no other clothes. If Rachel had undressed, so would he.

Rachel had only brought two men home in as many years. Both times, she had given Adria advance warning. Rachel was not a casual person in her surroundings or her relationships.

Adria checked the open bathroom, but she knew, could feel, how empty the house was now. She was alone, alone with the sea. And Rachel was out there somewhere. Adria began listening to her own heartbeat. It was impossibly loud. Something was very wrong.

She slipped on a pair of deck shoes and opened the sliding glass door that led down to the beach. She left it open behind her; a vague thought that she wanted someone to know where she had gone.

The night air was cool; she shivered in the thin shirt. She debated on going back and getting a sweatshirt, but no, she needed to find Rachel.

Rachel's footprints started at the bottom of the steps. They led down near the surf, where the sand was firm, wet, and easier to walk in. Water swirled shockingly cold around Adria's ankles. The water was crumpling the edges of the tracks, sweeping them away. Adria began to jog, hoping to trace the prints before the sea took them. She fell into a familiar easy stride, arms pumping, breath deep and even. It felt good. Her fear faded in the face of something so ordinary.

The only sounds were the rush of waves and the slap of her feet as she ran. Moonlight gleamed along the shore, showing everything in stark shadows and silver light. The footprints ended at the rocks. Adria touched a cold boulder and began to clamber over them. She slipped on a strand of seaweed and fell hard on one knee. The sharp pain forced her to lean against the damp rock and wait for the knee to move again. She could see over the rocks now, to the beach beyond. They were there.

Rachel's long blond hair was spilled out across the sand. He lay on top of her, his nude body made up of muscle, pale flesh, and shadows.

Adria felt foolish, surprised, and relieved. She meant to turn away, to leave them to their privacy, but something stopped her. A wave curled up the beach and tugged Rachel's hand up and down, loose, limp, unresisting. Adria watched for a few minutes, embarrassment swallowed up by fear. Rachel never moved, not a hand, not her head, not her leg. There was a limp quality to her as the man rode her that was more terrifying than any struggle.

The man buried his face in the sand, baring Rachel's face to the sky. The face was totally slack, nothing.

Adria couldn't breathe for a moment, couldn't think. She screamed, "Rachel!"

The man looked up, startled. Adria had an impression of dark eyes, impossibly large, a sculpted face. *Beautiful* was the word that flashed in her mind. She scrambled down the rocks, not sure what she would do if he didn't run. Had to try. She was screaming as she came. Someone would hear; someone had to hear.

He stood, and there was a tension to him. Adria stopped, panting, and stared at him across the sand, across Rachel's body. She had seen a wolf once, while hiking in the mountains. It had turned startled eyes to her. There had been nothing human in its eyes. There was nothing human now.

A light flashed on at the nearest house. He jumped, startled, and ran, not up the shore, but toward the sea. He ran into the surf, and it cut him across the waist and he dived between the waves, clean and neat, vanished. She watched his head surface and then his arms as he stroked for deeper water.

Then he dived, and what splashed after him was the curving lines of a tail, like a whale, or a dolphin. He vanished under the waves.

Adria stood there for a heartbeat. She couldn't have seen it. Could she? Adria glanced back at Rachel. She lay unmoving, horribly still.

Adria knelt in the wet sand. Her shaking hands couldn't find a pulse. She pressed her ear to the chest and held her own breath. Adria had expected to hear a heartbeat. Even though she had thought death, she wasn't prepared for silence. She pressed her cheek against Rachel's slack mouth, nothing, no breath. "Oh, God, oh God."

A man's voice called from the house where the light had flashed on. "Is everyone all right down there?"

Adria couldn't answer for a minute, couldn't think, then she yelled, "Get an ambulance, and get the police. It's an emergency! Hurry!"

"I'll call, don't worry." He rushed back inside.

Tears threatened hot and close. "No!" She tilted Rachel's head back, pinched off the nostrils, and began breathing for her. The chest rose and fell, four breaths, four rises. Adria stopped. "Breathe, Rachel, breathe."

Surf rushed in and tugged at her body. "Damn it, Rachel, damn it!" Adria breathed and then cupped her hands over the chest and pumped, counting, "One one thousand, two one thousand, three one thousand." She crawled back to Rachel's head and breathed. Then pumped the chest. "Rachel, breathe, damn it, breathe. Oh, God! Help me!" Tears choked her, trying to steal her own breath away. She couldn't cry yet. Not yet!

A man was there in his pajamas and bathrobe. He knelt in the wet sand. "I called the ambulance and the cops."

Adria looked at him. She couldn't think what to say. "Help me."

"I'll pump the heart, if you breathe."

She really looked at him for the first time, younger than she had thought. She nodded and breathed three quick breaths. He pumped the heart, like he knew what he was doing.

"Rachel, please, please." Breathing, breathing until she felt light-headed. She looked at the man as he worked to start Rachel's heart. His eyes held hopelessness. Adria shook her head, tears tracing like fire down her cheeks.

"Don't worry," he said, "I won't give up until you do."

"Then we won't give up."

They were still trying to breathe life into Rachel when the ambulance came. Adria sat in the rising surf, watching as they worked on Rachel. They punched needles into her arm, set up an IV of some clear liquid. They did what Adria and the man had done, but nothing worked.

Adria noticed the world looked flat, one-dimensional. There was no depth to anything. And all the noises seemed distant, dreamlike. She stared at her own hand and couldn't figure out what was wrong. Why had everything changed?

They strapped Rachel to a gurney and began to carry her up the steps to the road. The police came in a flash of red and blue lights, a kaleidoscope against the darkness. There were men asking questions, but Adria couldn't concentrate on it, she couldn't hear them. Someone had thrown a jacket over her shoulders; it was too big and sleeves flapped in the wind as she followed the gurney to the ambulance.

A tall man with a gold shield clipped to his coat stopped her, putting a hand on her shoulder. "We'll need to ask you a few questions."

She nodded. "I understand, but later." She looked up at him. "I have to go to the hospital, for Rachel."

"I understand. Just tell us where he went. You are our only witness."

She nodded, "He swam out to sea."

The detective frowned. "Are you sure?"

"He swam out to sea."

"Thank you."

A second detective pushed close and looked ready to ask other questions, but there must have been something in her face that stopped him. "We'll talk to you tomorrow then, miss."

She nodded and crawled into the ambulance. Adria made herself as small as possible riding in the corner, not crying anymore. Everything seemed so distant, unreal, dreamlike. The world wasn't meant to be flat, like cardboard.

The sirens blared to life, and they were out on the highway in a spill of gravel and brakes. She looked up at the paramedic as he checked Rachel one more time. He met Adria's eyes once and then wouldn't look at her again. Wasn't it a bad sign when they wouldn't look at you?

"She's a doctor."

He glanced at Adria. "What?"

"Dr. Rachel Corbin, that's her name." It seemed important that he know she was a doctor. Adria wasn't sure why, but if anything made Rachel who she was, it was that. She was a doctor.

He whispered, "Oh, God." And shouted something through the window to the driver.

Rachel's hospital was the nearest one, so very close. They would take Rachel to Rachel's hospital, Rachel's emergency room.

* * *

THE police drove Adria back home as dawn was easing through the clouds. She stood in her own living room, looking out the sliding glass door. The sea was an immense blue, rolling out and out until it touched the sky.

The sun was rising and Rachel wasn't rushing out to her car. Adria would still be in bed. The vague roar of Rachel's car was one of the sounds of morning. But not today.

The doctors had given her something to take. They said she was in shock. She hadn't taken the pills yet, and if this was shock, it didn't feel so bad. It didn't feel like anything. Adria felt distant, light, as if a strong wind would blow her away, shatter her into slivers of glass. She knew Rachel was dead, but it was a distant knowing, as if all of last night had happened to someone else.

If she walked into the other room, Rachel's things would be there waiting. But Rachel would never come for them. Adria tried to make last night a lie as she stared out at the sea. So bright and blue, so inviting.

The dark-haired detective said, "Ms. Reynolds, do you feel up to answering questions now? I wouldn't ask, but you are our only witness, and the sooner we start, the sooner we can catch him."

She answered without turning around, staring out the window. "Yes, I understand."

"Tell me what happened last night; take your time."

Adria took a deep breath and let it out. Her voice belonged to someone else. She listened to some other person tell about waking up and going out to look for Rachel. The voice that was hers and not hers told everything, even glimpses of something impossible.

The second detective had gold-framed glasses that didn't

quite hide his eyes. "Excuse me, Ms. Reynolds. Would you repeat that, please?"

"Repeat what?"

"The part starting, *I watched him swim out to sea, and then he dived, flashing a length of tail, like a whale or a dolphin.* Is that what you meant to say, Ms. Reynolds?"

Adria thought about that for a minute, cheek pressed against the cool glass. "I didn't mean to mention it to you, no. It's what I thought I saw." She shook her head, forehead against glass. "I don't know."

"Ms. Reynolds." His voice was condescending, humor the poor hysterical witness. "You're saying the perpetrator was a mermaid?"

She turned to stare at him, a small flash of anger making her feel more like herself. "Not a mermaid—a merman, a triton. A male equivalent."

His face showed what he thought of that theory.

"I don't know, detective. I don't know if I saw it, or dreamed it, or hallucinated. I'd just found my best friend murdered, brutalized. I don't know. Is there anything else? I'm very tired." She wanted his condescension, his pity, out of her house, out of their house.

The dark-haired detective stood. Adria thought he frowned at his partner. "Ms. Reynolds, you had a very traumatic experience last night. There's nothing wrong with seeing things under that kind of stress."

"I suppose not." She hesitated and asked, "Do other murder witnesses see monsters?"

He folded his notebook up and put it in his coat pocket. "In a manner of speaking, yes, they do."

She turned away from his eyes, kind, sad eyes that had seen too much until Rachel's death was just one more, among too many.

"We'll want you to come down and talk to a sketch artist when you're ready. I don't mean to rush you. I know how hard this is on you."

She started to accuse him of not understanding, but his eyes wouldn't let her. They had seen more death than Adria would ever see, if she was lucky.

"Get some rest, Ms. Reynolds. Use those pills the doctor gave you. That's what they're for."

Adria turned back to the window.

"Let's go, Frank. We've got all we need for a while." The detective with the gold-framed glasses seemed ready to argue, but he followed his partner.

"We'll leave a patrol car outside for a day or two. Don't be alarmed."

"I'm not." The thought that the killer might come back to hurt her didn't seem real or possible, not in the broad light of day.

The door shut, and she was alone. She took a long, hot shower and two of the pills the doctor had given her. Adria tracked water across the carpet. Rachel wouldn't care. She would never fix her famous apple omelets for them late at night. No more popcorn and sad movies. No more anything.

Adria choked back a sob. If she started crying, she felt as if she would split into pieces and fall down a long black hole. She collapsed on the unmade bed, hair wet, wrapped in towels. A deep, dreamless sleep pulled her under.

She woke to late-day sunlight. She had slept nearly twelve hours. The first thought was, *Rachel is dead.* The knowledge was a leaden emptiness. It was as if a great hole had opened up inside her. And the hole was full of pain, and rage and helplessness.

Rachel was the third victim of what the newspapers were now calling "The Beach Rapist." The only thing the victims had in common was where they had been killed, at the edge of the sea. Two victims hadn't been newsworthy. Three seemed to be the magic number. There was a serial killer loose.

What had Rachel been doing out on the beach? Why Rachel? Adria needed answers, but there was no one to ask.

She checked her watch, not for time, but for what day it was. It seemed like it had taken weeks for Rachel to die, the hospital. Days at least, but her watch said it was Sunday. Only hours had passed. Only hours and Rachel was gone, just like that.

Adria dressed and tried to comb the tangles from her hair, but it didn't seem to matter all that much. The numbness shredded, falling away. Tears choked at the back of her throat. She took another little pill, just one. She didn't want to sleep, but she wanted the pain to go away. Had she really told the detective the murderer was a triton? Had she really seen a tail? Adria closed her eyes and saw it, flashing in the moonlight, wet and slick, and attached to the man. Could she have made it up, to make the brutality more understandable? Like a child, saying a monster did it, instead of Daddy.

Adria shook her head. It didn't help to call the man a triton. It raised more questions. Why would she hallucinate the man was a merman?

Co-workers from the health club came in the next few hours, to cry, offer comfort, and be comforted. Adria didn't want any of them, didn't want to grieve in a group. It cheapened it to share memories and sob on each other's shoulders. None of them had really known Rachel. She refused to exercise. She was five-nine and had never gained weight. Adria was nine inches shorter. Adria had to work at staying in shape. She could never convince Rachel to go to the club.

Adria asked all the people to go away. Their kind intentions, their helpfulness, their sorrow, it was all more than Adria could deal with. She needed to be alone, wanted to be alone. She wasn't ready for company, no matter how well intentioned.

Adria told no one about her delusion. There was no such thing as mermaids, or mermen. She didn't want to see pity and knowing looks among their friends.

When the flock of mourners had been chased away, Adria lay down on the couch and waited for the tranquilizer to give her sleep.

She woke, gasping in the darkness, strange dreams vanished. Nightmares fading. She had vague images of ocean and strong hands trying to drown her.

Darkness lay pressed against the sliding glass doors. Moonlight shivered through the closed drapes. Adria sat up, abrupt, and felt dizzy and awkward. She couldn't remember closing the drapes. Her head felt like cotton, her throat horribly dry. Too many pills, she felt detached, the rush of fear dying under the dregs of the tranquilizer.

A shadow fluttered against the drapes. Adria stood, a little unsteady. Was it a man's shadow? She touched the drapes, soft, cool. Fear was back, adrenaline chasing the tranquilizer away. The sound of her own heart was obscenely loud. Adria shoved the drapes back, sudden, and he was there. He stood naked and beautiful on the other side of the glass. She tried to scream but couldn't, not while looking into his eyes, dark and peaceful.

He put a hand against the glass, spread it flat. There was webbing between his fingers like a frog's. Adria touched fingertips to the glass. The webbing began to shrink, smaller and smaller, until it melted away, like a moonlit dream. He smiled then, and she felt his need like a physical touch. His hand touched the door lock. Adria jerked back, startled, frightened, awake. The drapes fell shut—the moonlight gleamed empty.

Adria peeked round the drapes, hand shaking. There was nothing there. Had she dreamed it? She had been dreaming of him, of strong hands pushing her under the water. Adria stared at the empty deck. Moonlight glittered off something. She knelt against the glass and stared. There was a puddle of water on the deck. There was no rain this time of year.

Adria was halfway to the phone to call the police when she stopped. What could she say? "I saw webbing between his fingers, and it melted away." They wouldn't believe her, and he had known they wouldn't. He had come to taunt her, or to kill her. Adria remembered the feel of him inside her mind, slick, and cold and warm, like nothing she had ever felt. She wondered what he could have done if she hadn't been on the pills, half dead to the world. If he had opened the door . . .

Adria knew now how he had gotten Rachel down on the beach. He had called her, lured her, with himself as bait. The police wouldn't find him, because he could go places they couldn't, places they would never dream of going.

Adria knew the truth, but no one would believe her. It was crazy. If she'd had her gun tonight she could have given him a surprise. Would bullets hurt a triton? They didn't hurt vampires, did they?

Adria couldn't remember any stories about how to kill a mermaid. Just fairy tales.

The morning paper showed another victim, miles from Adria. Adria drank morning coffee with a gun lying on the table. She had bought it years ago when her ex-husband had traveled a lot and left her alone. It was cleaned, oiled, and loaded. The hammer rested on an empty chamber. If five bullets weren't enough . . . well, Adria didn't think it would matter.

The triton didn't come back, but he killed two more women.

The police were baffled, looking for lifeguards, triathletes. They weren't even close.

Adria stayed safe and warm and dry. And another woman died. He was killing almost every other night. The police were frantic; everyone on the beach was terrified.

When Rachel had been dead almost four weeks, Adria dreamed of the triton again. Strong webbed hands caressed her skin; she swam under water and breathed. She woke halfway across her bedroom floor. Her feet were tangled in a pair of discarded old jeans. Almost tripping had woken her. Adria swallowed, tried to breathe, tried to think. She heard his song then, inside her head. Music that cried and wept, that rolled and roared, lonely as the sea, vast and deep, promising miracles. She stood frozen for a moment, listening.

Adria stumbled back to her bed and sat on the edge of the rumpled sheets. She could not go to him, should not, would not. The song sighed and eased her mind, until she was standing. His need was in the music, strong and deep, careless as the ocean itself, and as unstoppable. She picked up her robe from the floor and slipped it on. It felt real and soft. She picked up the gun from the bedside table and put it in the robe pocket. It hung heavy and awkward, bumping her leg as she walked. She could not deny him, but she might be able to surprise him.

The moon rode high and almost full, shimmering silver on the rolling waves. The sea whispered, adding to the triton's song. Music and ocean hissed and roared until Adria could not be sure who was singing to her. Was it the sea? Did the sea itself want to touch her, to hold her? Yes, the sea wanted her. It was not love the sea offered, but violent need, a need so great it filled the world with crying.

She walked at the edge of the wet sand, as the lips of curling waves sloshed over her ankles. High tide was spilling inland.

She waded ankle deep to the rocks, the water soaking the edge of her robe, pulling, tripping. The song said, *Leave it*. But Adria climbed the rocks with the heavy robe still on. She didn't remember why it was important to keep it on, but there was a reason. The beach was bigger on the other side; part of it stayed dry. She thought of Rachel, and fear, grief filled her mind, but the sea took her terror and her sorrow and wove it into its song. Her throat was tight with fear, heart threatening to choke her. She slipped down to dry sand and waited, waited for the sea to come.

A chill wind blew off the ocean. She shivered, and the song took the thread of her chill, for the singer had never been cold. There was something heavy in her pocket that pressed against the damp robe, but it didn't matter. Nothing mattered but the sea.

Something bobbed out in the surf, dark and small, a sea lion maybe. The head disappeared and surfaced closer to shore. It wasn't a seal.

The triton let the waves sweep him up on shore, tumbling. His upper half was the muscular paleness she remembered, except for the long dark hair. Below the waist, he was a soft grayish black, abrupt against the white skin, as if somebody had pieced together two different creatures. There was a small ridge along his spine like a whale's humped back. His tail flukes whipped up and down, a dull half moon. He lay on his stomach in the surf and watched Adria with eyes so huge and luminous, they seemed to have a light of their own.

Tail began to melt, like wax exposed to heat, the tail flukes became blunt, the main trunk began to shrink, growing tight, and the shadow of legs pressed against the shrinking skin.

His face flickered in pain, and that fed into his song. It hurt to change over. Adria felt his pain, crumbling to her knees, staring, waiting, needing.

He stood, nude, and human, his dark hair hanging in wet curls round his face. He called out to her, inside her head, the music sliding and seducing. She went to him.

He was tall. She came only to the middle of his chest. When he reached for her, moonlight glistened through the webbing on his hands. Adria took a step back, away. He frowned, and the song roared inside her until she could hear only that. She watched him come closer. He undid her robe, pushing it open. She shivered as the wind blew against her nightshirt. His hands cupped her breasts, water soaking through the shirt, cold. His face bent over her, eyes huge and drowning deep. Terror flashed through her; she shook her head, violently, tried to step back. He grabbed her, pressing her against the hard cold of his body. The song roared in her head, but her fear rode the waves. The sea had come to drag her down, and she was afraid.

His mouth closed over hers, probing. His lips nibbled down her neck. Adria tried to scream, but she couldn't. She was afraid, afraid of the song, afraid of the sea, afraid of this thing touching her, but she could not scream, could not move. He spilled her back onto the sand. Strong hands tore her nightshirt, leaving her gasping and half naked. Waves rushed in, spilling over her breasts, curling between her legs. He knelt over her, staring down, arrogant, no pity, no doubts, the sea made flesh. She meant nothing to him, the song clanged through her mind, a roaring violence, a vast unknowing guiltless thing.

She whispered, "No."

He lowered himself on top of her, skin cold, so cold. Waves splashed over his back and spilled into her face. He still kissed and bit along her skin. The hardness of him rested against her panties.

"No." Still only a whisper. She needed to shout, to scream. "No." Then she remembered the gun.

His hands ripped away her damp panties. He lowered his hips, eyes distant.

The gun clicked on the empty chamber. Adria pulled the trigger again. The gun fired through the robe pocket. The shot seemed to explode, so loud. His body jerked, eyes staring at her, seeing her for the first time. She pulled the trigger again. He jerked and then slumped over her.

The song ended abruptly, jarring. Adria's breath came in ragged gasps. She tried to push him off her, but couldn't. He was too heavy. She panicked, beating at his arms and chest. His blood flowed warm onto her skin. She took a deep breath that quavered, and let it out. "I'm all right. I'm all right." She began to crawl out from under him, his body dragging along her skin as she wiggled free. She was crying now, sobbing. She began screaming, low tiny screams. The screams frightened her because she couldn't stop them.

She crawled free of him and clawed through the sand until she was free of the water. She sat in the dry sand, letting it cake the wet robe. She held the gun in her hand, loosely.

A wave washed over him, and his hand waved limp, moved by the water. An image of Rachel flashed through her mind. She put a shaking hand against her mouth to stop the awful whimpering screams.

His hand clenched. Adria stopped breathing for a moment. He raised his head. She felt his mind reach out for her. It was like the slow drag of the sea when you're tired and it would be better, easier to rest, to let the water take you down. He got to his feet.

Adria raised the gun two-handed. Blood flowed from two wounds in his stomach, but he never hesitated; the sea did not acknowledge death. Blood blossomed in his chest. He staggered, but kept coming. Adria fired, watching the bullets explode into his chest, ears ringing with the noise. He fell to his knees and then slid to one side, slowly so slowly.

He lay on his side in the dry sand, staring at her. His dark eyes were patient as the sea, nothing in them that she could read, or understand. He didn't seem to be able to move. His chest was a bloody mess. He lay only an arm's length from her. She watched his life pour out into the sand. He blinked. Adria pointed the gun at those eyes and squeezed the trigger. The gun bounced in her hands. A neat red hole appeared in his forehead, blood leaking into his eyes. His eyes stared sightless, the light gone out of them.

Adria did not check his pulse to make sure he was dead. She backed off, the empty gun still in her hand and began running for home. She looked back once from the top of the rocks. The body lay pale and dark, shadow patched. Nothing moved.

Adria ran.

She heard police sirens a long way off. The strobe lights flickered outside her windows, colored shadows against the curtains. The police found blood on the sand but no body.

"The Beach Rapist" did not strike again. Was he really dead? Or had he just started hiding the bodies, letting the ocean take the evidence away? Adria couldn't sleep with the sea whispering outside her window anymore.

She sold the house for a nice price, even with the murders. Beachfront property was dear. Adria moved inland, far from the sea. But there are nights when the rustle of leaves outside her window becomes the rushing of the sea. And there is an echo in her head, a hiss of distant music.

Adria is looking for some place out of state. Some place where the sea does not touch the land for hundreds of miles on any side. Surely, there she will be safe.

A SCARCITY

OF LAKE MONSTERS

I have a degree in biology. Wildlife biologist was one of the few other careers I dreamed about besides writing. This story comes out of wondering if the monsters of fable existed, then how would we deal with them? What if lake monsters were real? It's another example of my continuing theme of taking the fantastic and dropping it into the middle of the real.

I WAS dreaming of sea monsters when the phone rang. I dragged the phone under the sheets with me and said, " 'Lo."

"Did I wake you, Mike?"

Why does everyone ask that when the answer is obviously yes? And why do we lie automatically? "No, no, what's up, Jordan?"

"It's your damn lake monster. He broke through the barricade again."

I groaned. "What's he doing?"

"Chasing speedboats, what else?"

"We'll be right there."

"Make it quick, Mike. The skiers are about to wet their pants."

I hung up the phone and sat up, pushing back the covers. Susan was still deeply asleep. Her shining black hair lay in a fan across the pillow. Her face was an almost perfect triangle. The firm jaw was the only hint a person had that this pretty, delicate-seeming woman was one of the toughest people I'd ever met. She was a fanatical champion of lost causes. Right now, it was lake monsters, and our monster was loose.

I touched her tanned shoulder gently. "Come on, wife, duty calls."

She muttered something unintelligible, which meant she wasn't awake at all. She's the only person I know who hates morning more than I do.

"Come on, Susan, Irving broke out of his barricade and is terrorizing the tourists."

She turned over, blinking at me. "He won't hurt them," she said thickly.

"No, but they don't know that."

She laughed, a rich, dark sound like good wine. "Do you think they'd believe he was a vegetarian?"

"Not with all those teeth," I said. "Come on, we gotta go herd Irving back inside and repair the barricade."

"You know," Susan said, "Irving used to be almost exclusively nocturnal, but lately he's active at all hours. I wonder why?"

I shrugged and ran a comb through my hair. "Unknown," I said.

Unknown, a good word for lake monsters. Nobody knew much about them, and now they were endangered, nearly extinct. Two lake monsters had died in the last fifteen years, both killed by pollution. To make the tragedy worse, both monsters had been pregnant. The babies had been fully formed, but the pollution had gotten them, too. Lake monsters need nearly pristine conditions, and as man spreads out, pristine gets pretty rare.

The question that no one could answer was, how had the two dead females gotten pregnant? Sexual reproduction is a little hard without a mate. There are wonderful theories about secret tunnels connecting the lakes, but no one had found any tunnels. Another idea was that male lake monsters look so different from females that they had been classed as some sort of fish or . . . something. But Irving, and two other monsters, had male genitalia. Irving didn't look anything like a fish.

Susan had come here three years ago to study Irving, the lake monster. I was a forest ranger with a master's degree in cryptozoology, a nice degree if you work in the Enchanted Forest National Park. I was assigned to help Dr. Susan Greco, noted cryptozoologist, look into a possible breeding program for our lake monster. A female lake monster in New England was being studied as well. The idea was to transport her to Irving, maybe. There was always the chance that the two monsters would fight and kill each other. No one had ever seen two monsters together.

Three years later, married to each other for almost two years, and we still didn't know a damn thing about the sex life of the greater lake monster. Whether there was such a thing as a lesser lake monster was a matter of great debate. Were the two small monsters in other states just younger greater lake monsters, or were they a separate species? How long did lake monsters live? We could reach up and rub Irving between the eye ridges, and we still didn't know how old he was.

Twenty minutes later we were bouncing across the lake in a small boat. The sky was milky blue with cumulus clouds like white cotton candy. The water was the usual mirror brightness, reflecting the straight cones of pines, and the distant rise of mountains. Two boats passed us at full throttle; the passengers waved and yelled. I caught one word: "Monster!"

Jordan guided our boat. He was one of the junior rangers. He looked like his name: blond, handsome in a California surf-boy kind of way. Susan said he was cute. If Jordan hadn't been such a hardworking nice guy, I could have disliked him. Jordan drove the boat so Susan and I could slip into diving gear. If you've ever tried to get into a wet suit while riding full tilt in a small boat, *slip* is not quite the word—*struggle* maybe. When I was encased in latex from ankle to neck, I took a quick peek through binoculars at our lake monster.

Irving looks like a cross between a Chinese dragon, an eel, and an oil slick. His head is the most dragonlike, with slender horns and rubbery spikes bristling around very square jaws. Most of his thirty-foot length is all slick and slightly flattened; eel, not land snake. His fringelike dorsal fin extends nearly the length of his body. Overall, his color is black, but he glistens in sunlight like an oil slick; rings of color flash and melt along his skin. The rainbow only shows up at close range, though. Most people aren't much interested in how pretty he is when they're that close.

Irving's head was keeping pace with the last water-skier. It was a man in a bright orange ski vest. Though through my binoculars his tanned face looked bloodless. Irving's mouth was half open, exposing a dazzling display of teeth. The boat was going full out, motor screaming. The skier was riding the white foam of the wake like his life depended on it.

The faster the boat went, the faster Irving swam, but quiet, no foaming wake for the lake monster. He could glide at incredible speeds nearly silent and waveless. The only reason we saw so much of Irving was because he liked people. He wanted to be seen. Most lake monsters gave a new definition to the word *shy*.

The skier fell into the water. He bobbed to the surface, trapped in his life vest. I could see him screaming and waving his arms.

The lake monster blew bubbles at him, then stretched his

neck up ten feet and gave a great honking sound. It's his version of human laughter.

If Irving had been human, he'd have been your obnoxious Uncle Ned—the one who makes really bad jokes, wears loud plaid, and slips you twenty dollars when your parents aren't looking. Irving had a good heart, but his sense of humor was a little sadistic.

Susan waved and called, "Irving!"

His great head swiveled and looked at our boat. He gave a loud snort and dived under the water. The skier started to paddle frantically for his boat.

Irving surfaced about five feet from us. Jordan cut the motor and let us drift while the monster moved up alongside. I struggled with my diving gear while Susan coaxed Irving. He finally let her rub the bristles on his chin and then snorted into her wet suit, splashing her with water and making a happy *humph* sound. She laughed and rubbed his eye ridges.

Jordan started the boat again, and we began moving slowly toward the barricade and Irving's part of the lake. Our walkie-talkies squawked to life. Someone was calling me. Jordan took it because I was still fastening air tanks into place. It was hard to hear anything over the whine of boat and happy monster noises.

"It's Priscilla. She and Roy are at an abandoned campsite. A whole troop of Girl Scouts plus two of their leaders are missing."

"How long have they been missing?"

"Unsure."

"Damn. Any signs of a struggle?"

Jordan asked, then shook his head. "Looks like they just walked away."

"Where were they camped?"

"Near Starlight Ridge."

"What genius let them camp that far up?"

"You know how it is, Mike, they pick their own campsite."

"But it's June," I said.

Jordan just frowned at me, but Susan let out a slow whistle.

"What?" asked Jordan.

"No all-female groups are allowed to camp above Bluebell Glade between May thirteenth and June thirtieth."

"But . . ." Then the light dawned. "Oh, shit."

I nodded. "Satyr rutting season. Have them check Satyr Glade. And find out who the hell OK'd the campsite."

Susan said softly, "Somebody's going to get sued over this one."

All I could do was nod. I wasn't usually in charge of anything but the monster. Unfortunately, our chief ranger was on the injured list for at least three weeks. I was acting chief ranger at the height of the tourist season.

The barricade stretched across the most narrow part of the lake, from pine-covered shore to rocky outcrop. It was a deluxe steel net, enough give and no sharp edges so Irving wouldn't be able to break it. The barricade had been the single most expensive item of the Lake Monster Breeding Program.

The net stretched smooth and unbroken, which meant the damage had to be below the water line. Irving had learned that if he damaged the visible part of the net, we'd discover his escape sooner, but underwater we wouldn't notice the breakout until we spotted him.

The water was cold even in June, not uncomfortable but cool, and it closed around me on all sides. Air may be all around you on land, but it doesn't have the invasive push of water. Water lets you know it's there. On a good day the visibility is twenty feet. Today wasn't a good day.

A swirl of water and Irving coiled through the silver trail of my air bubbles, the thickness of his body looped against my back. I brushed a hand down his side as he eased past me. I expected monsters to feel like dolphins, rubbery and somehow unreal, or snakes with their dry, soft brush of scales, but monsters feel like . . . monsters. Slick, wet but soft like pressed velvet. And underneath it all, even when you can't see most of him, just a glimpse of shining, black coils, there is the feeling of immense power. Even if you can't see him, you know he's big. You know he could flatten you if he wanted to, but Irving is like some of the great whales. He seems to know he's big and that you're small. He's careful around us.

The lake monster swam in and out of the wavering sunlight that pierced the water. Susan and I stayed within touching distance of each other. At twenty-five feet, we lost all light. Only my grip on the net let me know which way was up. I've been in caves where it was so dark you could touch your own eyeball and not see your finger. It was like that down here except the water gave the darkness weight and movement as if it were something alive. The water swirled, and something large rubbed against me. It had to be Irving, but my breathing seemed very loud. Even, deep breaths, that's it. I'm not afraid of water, and I'm not afraid of the dark, but combine the two and I am not a happy camper.

I switched on my flashlight and Susan followed suit. Her beam flashed into my eyes and I gave her the OK sign. She returned it, and we continued down into the blackness. I had to let my flashlight swing on the little loop around my wrist so I could use both hands to hold the net and feel for looseness. The light swung bizarrely, a slow-motion liquid dance of light and darkness.

The net wobbled under my hands, loose. I waved my light at Susan, and she swam over to me. Together we found the hole that Irving had pushed under the net, tearing out two mooring lines. He was thirty feet long, but he had a snake's ability to squeeze through the darnedest holes. I would have bet a month's pay he couldn't have slipped through the opening. After we fixed one, we'd make sure there were no others, but usually it was just one. Irving is a lazy monster and doesn't do more work than he has to.

First, of course, we had to get Irving back through that little hole.

Susan swam through the hole, raising a cloud of silt that floated like a brownish fog in the flashlight's beam. Now even with the light I couldn't see anything. But Irving's smooth bulk eased past my leg. Nothing else in the lake could displace water like our monster. He stopped and I put a hand on his side. I still couldn't see, or feel his tail end. With a convulsive wriggle, Irving began to back out of the hole. It stopped almost as soon as it began, and I knew Susan was bribing him with some of the fish we'd brought. The way to a lake monster's heart is through his stomach.

Two hours later, the barricade was temporarily secure. We were making our last dive and had stopped at fifteen feet for our decompression stop. If you go up too fast, the air in your lungs doesn't have time to adjust to the pressure as you swim toward the surface. Swim directly up with no decompression stop, and you'll get "the bends"—decompression sickness. The nitrogen in your blood will bubble like soda pop, causing, among other things, unconsciousness and death. That is the worst case, of course. Susan says I dwell too much on the things that can go wrong when you dive. I prefer to think of it as being cautious.

Irving butted me gently in the ribs, blowing bubbles at me. It's hard to laugh with a regulator in your mouth, but Irving will make you do it. Sunlight hovered in the water at this depth, making the monster's coils shimmer. He wrapped us both in his velvet muscled body, not tight, but to let us know he had us. Then he was gone swimming away into dimness.

Susan's fingers brushed mine, and I took her hand. We kicked for the surface, turning slowly together, caught in the soft, hovering brightness of light and water.

We spent the rest of the afternoon searching for the lost Girl Scout troop. We found them asleep, drugged with music. They were curled around a sign that said, "No All-Female Groups Beyond This Point. Satyr Breeding Area." Satyrs have a peculiar sense of humor.

I had found the orders for their campsite. They hadn't camped where we told them. The park was not liable for their mistake. Honest.

That night Susan, as usual, was asleep first. She lay on her side, half curled against my stomach. My face was buried in the back of her neck. She smelled of shampoo and perfume and warmth. Nothing felt as good as going to sleep with Susan's body pressed against mine. The soft rise and fall of her breathing was one of my top three favorite sounds in the world. The second is her laugh, and the first is the little sound she makes, deep in her throat, when we make love. It is a personal sound, just for us, no sharing. I've never been in love. Does it show?

The phone rang and Susan stirred in her sleep, but didn't waken. I rolled over and grabbed the receiver. "Hello."

"Mike, it's Jordan again . . ." His voice trailed off.

"What's wrong?" I asked.

"It's Irving. A couple of drunks dragged their boat into his part of the lake. Said they just wanted to swim with the monster."

I pushed the cover back and crouched on the edge of the bed. "What happened, Jordan?"

Susan touched my shoulder. "What's wrong?"

I shook my head. "Jordan, talk to me."

"They hit Irving with the propeller. It looks bad. I already called the vet. He's out on a call, but he'll get here as soon as he can."

We drove in silence toward the lake. The sky was black and glittered with the cold light of stars. So many stars. Susan's tanned face was pale, her lips set in a tight angry line. Her eyes turn nearly black when she is really angry. They glittered like black jewels now.

I just felt sick. It was too ridiculous, too stupid for words, that all our work was going to be screwed up by some drunks in a boat. How bad was he hurt? The questions kept running through my head like a piece of song. How bad was he hurt?

It was Roy who met us with a boat. His thinning brown hair was rumpled; he'd forgotten to comb it. There was a smear of something on his glasses, too dark to be mud. We struggled into the diving gear while Roy talked above the roar of the engine. "Priscilla's in the water with Irving. She swims like a fish. She's keeping him at the surface. Jordan's got our two drunks on the shore."

"How bad is it?" I asked.

"Bad, Mike, real bad."

Susan looked at me. I could see her jaw tighten by starlight. I felt the first warm flush of anger gliding up from my stomach to tighten my throat. Moonlight lay in a shining silver line across the lake. It was all so damn beautiful, so peaceful.

As the boat got close to the barricade, Jordan yelled, "He's sinking. Priscilla can't hold him!"

"Cut the motor, Roy. We'll go in over the barricade," I said.

The boat drifted against the netting with a soft bump. Susan and I pushed regulators into our mouths and grabbed for the barricade. Climbing netting while wearing fins is nearly impossible, but Susan spilled over the top first, using just her arms. I followed, plunging into the night-black water.

I couldn't see Susan's flashlight. I couldn't see anything, then I heard it, an echoing tap. The sound repeated, and I began to work my way toward it. Susan was tapping her air tank with the flashlight, guiding me to her.

Irving's body loomed out of the darkness first. She'd found him. I stroked my hand on his side and felt him shiver. My hand found a gash in his side. His dorsal fin had been half cut away, and I realized that part of what was making the water dark was blood. I swallowed hard around my regulator and swam toward Irving's head.

Susan was cradling his great head, and Irving leaned against her. She was rubbing his eye ridge. The whole left side of his face had been ripped open. The left eye was gone in a mass of meat and exposed bone. I swam up so Irving could see me out of his good eye. He nuzzled his nose against my chest and blew a thin stream of bubbles. There was a backwash of air and blood from his exposed jaw and underneath his body. I swam down to find a rip just in back of his head. His spine gleamed pale and unreal in the beam of my light. There was another rip in back of it. His stomach was half hanging into the water. At least, I thought it was his stomach.

There was no way the boat could have just hit him once. The first blow had to have been the head, stunned him, but the rest . . . They had to have driven back and forth over him, slicing him over and over.

I started to swim back to Susan when the stomach twitched. I shone my light on it and found a tiny lake monster moving inside a membranous sack. Irving was about to give birth!

The sack split and spilled about four feet of baby lake monster into the water. I cradled the little monster to my chest and swam for the surface. Irving was an air breather; it meant the baby probably was too. We were almost to the surface when I realized I had no idea how far down we'd been. Did I need a decompression stop? The little monster began to thrash in my arms. I let it go, and it popped to the surface. Decompression or not, it was too late. I said a silent prayer and surfaced.

The little monster made a loud happy snort as it gasped in air. It blinked at me; tiny bristling horns covered a dragonlike head. It was a perfect replica of Irving. Susan surfaced near me and just stared for a minute.

I wasn't in any pain, no tightness of chest, no muscle cramping; no decompression sickness, lungs okay. We couldn't have been down more than forty feet for a few minutes. Maybe I worry too much.

I rubbed my hand along the baby's back, like wet silk. I reached up to scratch a miniature eye ridge. The monster bit me, sinking needle teeth to the bone. I screamed around the regulator that was still in my mouth. The baby vanished into the water, gone.

Susan stared at the spot where it had been, then said, "Irving's dead. His body started to float down. How the hell did he get pregnant?" She lowered her mask to hang like a necklace. "My God, do you realize we've just seen the first birth of a lake monster ever?" Her voice held that hushed awe that you reserve for cathedrals and hospitals.

I held my bleeding hand up out of the water and didn't know

quite how to feel. Irving was dead, and the way he died was awful, but I had held a newborn monster in my arms. I would have the scars to prove that. Even if we couldn't find the baby to get pictures, the bite radius would prove how small it was. I laughed then, spitting out my regulator. Sometimes I think I've been around Susan too long. It hadn't even occurred to her yet that I was hurt.

Something else had occurred to her, though. She turned in the black water, looking toward shore. The humor, the awe had left her face. Her face was stiff and pale with anger, eyes like black holes.

"Susan," I said, reaching out to her, trying to touch her shoulder. She moved out of reach, with a smooth flow of ripples. "Susan, what are you going to do?"

She turned onto her back as much as the air tanks would allow, kicking backward. "I'm going to hurt them."

"You can't do that," I said.

"Watch me."

I started paddling after her, but she was going to get to shore first. My adrenaline rush was over: Irving's death, the birth, and the bite wound. Blood was running down my hand, and with the blood, pain. I was tired. Susan was still running on rage.

She was sitting down in the shallows taking off her flippers. Priscilla, the other junior ranger, moved over to help Susan take off the tanks.

Priscilla towered over Susan, heck, she towers over me. Priscilla is six foot one and has the strength to match the size.

Susan was free of the tanks and going toward the prisoners. I yelled, "Stop her!"

Priscilla looked toward me, but didn't move.

"Stop her! Susan!"

Priscilla laid the tanks on the ground and moved toward my wife.

I lay panting in the shallows, struggling one-handed to get out of my diving gear. The shot echoed, loud enough to make me jump. I twisted around, one flipper on and one off.

Susan had Jordan's rifle. She was pointing it at the two men. Another shot rang out, and the men started screaming. She was shooting into the ground, right next to them.

Jordan was trying to talk to her, but she motioned him away with the rifle.

Priscilla knelt beside me in the water, undoing the last strap of my equipment. "Talk to her, Mike. Somebody's going to get hurt."

I nodded, shrugged out of the buoyancy vest, and walked toward Susan. She was firing into the ground, in a pattern around them. So far, I don't think she had hit either of them, but only skill and plain luck had saved them. Luck would run out. Part of me wanted them bleeding, hurt. Maybe we could hang their dead bodies near the entrance to the park with a sign: "These Men Killed One of Our Animals." Yeah, maybe that would convince the tourists to behave.

"Susan, give the rifle back to Jordan."

"They killed him, Mike. They killed Irving."

"I know."

One of the men said, "She's crazy."

"Shut up," Susan said.

"I'd do what she says, mister," I said.

The man huddled against his companion. Both of them looked white in the moonlight. They stank of beer and urine.

"They slaughtered him," Susan said.

"Give me the rifle, Susan, please."

"What's going to happen to them? If I don't hurt them, what will the law do?"

"A hundred-thousand-dollar fine, or a mandatory ten-year prison sentence."

"Do either of you have a hundred thousand dollars?" she asked.

The men looked at each other, then at me. "Answer her," I said.

"Hell, no. We haven't got that kind of money."

"Susan gave a thin, tight smile, and handed the rifle to Jordan. "You better pray you get ten years apiece, because if you don't . . ." She knelt beside them. "I'll hunt you down and shoot you both."

"Hey, lady, it was just an animal."

I grabbed Susan and pulled her to her feet before she could slug him.

Jordan said softly, "I'll let you have the rifle again."

Susan leaned into me. "You're bleeding."

"A present from Little Irving."

She held my hand in her smaller ones, but I knew she wasn't trying to stop the blood flow; she was looking at the bite radius. My wife the scientist.

I missed Irving when we went down to the barricade. No happy snorts, no bubble blowing, no dragon head butting your ribs. It was lonely. Baby Irving is like most of the monsters, shy. The best picture we have is a night shot of ripples on the water. My bite mark did prove our point. Pictures of my hand will make up part of Susan's report.

Susan now thinks that all lake monsters are capable of cloning themselves by parthenogenesis. The clone is born at the death of the parent. That would explain why no one has ever seen more than one lake monster at a time. It also explains why both lake monsters that had been autopsied in the past had unborn babies. Pollution killed them all. Irving died from injuries, so his baby lived.

The problem is that cloning leads to mutation and genetic drift. You need sexual reproduction in a vertebrate to keep the species healthy. Maybe centuries ago the lakes were all connected, but as the land closed in and isolated the monsters, they had to survive long enough to reproduce, so they cloned themselves. The individual genotypes were saved, but there is no known natural way for lake monsters to find mates. Without help from man, lake monsters are probably a dead end. If we don't kill them off first, that is.

Little Irving's birth put a stop to the Lake Monster Breeding Program. Susan was out of a job, but since she is already living in the Enchanted Forest National Park and has full cooperation of the park service, she has a good shot at new grant money. If she gets it, we'll be studying the sex life of the red-bearded leprechaun. The real question is, are there any female leprechauns? No one has ever seen one. This problem sounds vaguely familiar.

Susan is happy off on another project to save yet another endangered creature. But I miss Irving, and though Susan would laugh at me probably, I like to think that Irving is somewhere chasing angelic speedboats, or maybe he's got his own wings. Surely, even God needs a laugh now and then, and Irving is a funny guy, for a monster.

SELLING HOUSES

This story is set in Anita's world, but Anita isn't in it. None of the main or even minor characters are in it. One day I wondered: What are people with less dangerous jobs doing in Anita's world now that vampires are legally alive? How has it changed other jobs? For instance, real estate . . .

THE house sat in its small yard looking sullen. It seemed to
squat close to the ground as if it had been beaten down.
Abbie shook her head to clear such strange notions from her
mind. The house looked just like all the other houses in the sub-
division. Oh, certainly it had type-A elevation. Which meant it
had a peaked roof, and it had two skylights in the living room and
a fireplace. The Garners had wanted some of the extra features.
It was a nice house with its deluxe cedar board siding and half
brick front. Its small lot was no smaller than any of the other
houses, except for some of the corner lots. And yet . . .

ABBIE walked briskly up the sidewalk that led through the
yard. Daffodils waved bravely all along the porch. They were a
brilliant burst of color against the dark-red house. Abbie swal-

lowed quickly, her breath short. She had only talked to Marion Garner on the phone maybe twice, but in those conversations Marion had been full of gardening ideas for their new home.

It had been Sandra who had handled the sell, but she wouldn't touch the house again. Sandra's imagination was a little too thorough to allow her to go back to the place where her clients were slaughtered.

Abbie had been given the job because she specialized in the hard-to-sell. Hadn't she sold that monstrous rundown Victorian to that young couple who wanted to fix it up, and that awful filthy Peterson house? Why, she had spent her days off cleaning it out so it would sell, and it had sold, for more than they expected. And Abbie was determined that she would sell this house as well.

She admitted that mass murder was a very black mark against a house. And mass murder with an official cause of demon possession was about as black a mark as any.

The house had been exorcised, but even Abbie, who was no psychic, could feel it. Evil was here like a stain that wouldn't come completely up. And if the second owners of this house fell to demons, then Abbie and her Realtor company would be liable. So Abbie would see that the house was cleansed correctly. It would be as pure and lily-white as a virgin at her wedding. It would have to be.

The real problem was that the newspapers had made a horrendous scandal of it all. There wasn't a soul for miles around that didn't know about it. And any prospective buyer would have to be told. No, Abbie would not try to keep it a secret from buyers, but at the same time she wouldn't volunteer the full information too early in the sales pitch either.

She hesitated outside the door and said half aloud, "Come on, it's just a house. There's nothing in there to hurt you." The words rang hollow somehow, but she put the key in the lock and the door swung inward.

It looked so much like all the other houses that it startled her. Somehow she had thought that there would be a difference. Something to mark it apart from any other house. But the living room was small with the extra vaulted ceiling and brick fireplace. The carpet had been a beige-tan color that went with almost any décor. She'd seen pictures of the room before. There was bare subflooring, stretching naked and unfinished.

The flooring was discolored, pale and faded, almost like a coffee stain, but it covered a huge area. Here was where they had found Marion Garner. The papers said she had been stabbed over twenty times with a butcher knife.

New carpeting would hide the stain.

The afternoon sunlight streamed in the west-facing window and illuminated a hole in the wall. It was about the size of a fist and stood like a gaping reminder in the center of the off-white wall. As she walked closer, Abbie could see splatters along the wall. The cleanup crew usually got up all the visible mess. This looked like they hadn't even tried. Abbie would demand that they either finish the job, or give back some of the deposit.

The stains were pale brown shadows of their former selves, but no family would move in with such stains. New paint, new carpeting; the price of the house would need to go up. And Abbie wasn't sure she could get anyone to pay the original price.

She spoke softly to herself, "Now what kind of defeatist talk is that? You will sell this house." And she would, one way or another.

The kitchen/dining room area was cheerful with its skylight and back door. There was a smudge on the white door near the knob but not on it. Abbie stooped to examine it and quickly straightened. She wasn't sure if the cleanup crew had missed it or just left it. Maybe it was time to hire a new cleaning crew. Nothing excused leaving this behind.

It was a tiny handprint made of dried blood. It had to belong to the little boy; he had been almost five. Had he come running in here to escape? Had he tried to open the door and failed?

Abbie leaned over the sink and opened the kitchen window. It seemed stuffy in here suddenly. The cool spring breeze riffled the white curtains. They were embroidered with autumn leaves in rusts and shades of gold. They went well with the brown and ivory floor tiles.

She had a choice now, about where to go next. The door leading to the adjoining garage was just to her right. And the stairs leading down to the basement next to that. The garage was fairly safe. She opened the door and stepped onto the single step. The garage was cooler than the house, like a cave. Another back door led from the garage to the backyard. The only stains here were oil stains.

She stepped back in and closed the door, leaning against it for a moment. Her eyes glanced down the stairs to the closed door of the basement. Little Brian Garner's last trip had been down those stairs. Had he been chased? Had he hidden there and been discovered?

She would leave the basement until later.

The bedrooms and bath stretched down the long hallway to the left. The first bedroom had been the nursery. Someone had painted circus animals along the walls. They marched bright and cheerful round the empty walls. Jessica Garner had missed her second birthday by only two weeks. Or that's what Sandra said.

The bathroom was across the hall. It was good-sized, done mostly in white with some browns here and there. The mirror over the sink was gone. The cleanup crew had carted away the broken glass and left the black emptiness in the silver frame. Why replace anything until they knew for sure the house wasn't being torn down? Other houses had been torn down for less.

The wallpaper was pretty and looked undamaged. It was ivory with a pattern of pale pink stripes and brown flowers done small. Abbie ran her hand down it and found slash marks. There were at least six holes in the wall, as if a knife had been thrust into it. But there was no blood. There was no telling what Phillip Garner thought he was doing driving a knife into his bathroom wall.

The master bedroom was next with its half bath and ceiling fan. The wallpaper in here was beige with a brown oriental design done tasteful and small. There was a stain in the middle of the carpet, smaller than the living room's blood. No one knew why the baby had been in here, but it was here that he killed her. The papers were vague about exactly how she had died, which meant it was too gruesome to print much of it. Which meant that Jessica Garner had glimpsed hell before she died. There was a pattern of small smudges low along one wall. It looked like tiny bloody handprints struggling. But at least here the cleanup crew had tried to wash them away. Why hadn't they done the same in the kitchen area?

The more Abbie thought about it, the madder she got. With something this awful, why leave blatant reminders?

The little bathroom was in stainless white and silver, except for something dark between the tiles in front of the sink. Abbie started to bend down to look, but she knew what it was. It was blood. They had gotten most of it up, but it clung in the grooves between the tiles like dirt under a fingernail. She'd never seen the cleanup crew so careless.

The boy's bedroom was in the front corner of the house. The

wallpaper was a pale blue with racing cars streaking across it. Red, green, yellow, dark blue, the cars with their miniature drivers raced around the empty walls. This was the only carpeting in the house that had some real color to it; it was a rich blue. Perhaps it had been the boy's favorite color. The sliding doors to the closet were torn, ripped. The white scars of naked wood showed under the varnish. One door had been ripped from its groove and leaned against the far wall. Had Brian Garner hidden here and been flushed out by his father?

Or had Phillip Garner only thought his son was in here? For it was certain the boy had not died here. There were no bloodstains, no helpless handprints.

Abbie walked out into the hallway. She had walked into hundreds of empty houses over the years, but she had never felt anything quite like this. The very walls seemed to be holding their breath, waiting, but waiting for what? It had not felt this way a moment before, of that Abbie was sure. She tried to shake the feeling but it would not leave. The best thing to do was finish the inspection quickly and get out of the house.

Unfortunately, all that was left was the basement.

She had been reluctant to go down there before, but with the air riding with expectation she didn't want to go down. But if she couldn't even stand to inspect the house, how could she possibly sell it?

She walked purposefully through the house, ignoring the bloodstained carpet and the handprinted door. But by ignoring them she became more aware of them. Death, especially violent death, was not easily dismissed.

Rust-brown carpet led down the steps to the closed door. And for some reason Abbie found the closed door menacing. But she went down.

She hesitated with her hand almost over the doorknob and then opened it quickly. The cool dampness of the basement was unchanged. It was like any other basement except this one had no windows. Mr. Garner had requested that, no one knew why.

The bare concrete floor stretched gray and unbroken to the gray concrete walls. Pipes from upstairs hung from the ceiling and plunged out of sight under the floor. The sump pump in one corner was still in working order. The water heater was cold and waiting for someone to light it.

Abbie pulled on all three of the hanging chains and illuminated all the shadows away. But the bare lightbulbs cast shadows of their own as they gently swung, disturbed by her passing. And there in the far corner was the first stain.

The stain was small, but considering it had been a five-year-old boy, it was big enough.

There was a trail of stains leading round the back of the staircase. They were smeared and oddly shaped as if he had bled and someone dragged him along.

The last stain was in the shape of a bloody pentagram, rough, but recognizable. A sacrifice then.

There was a spattering on one wall, high up without a lower source. Probably where Phillip Garner had put a gun to his head and pulled the trigger.

Abbie turned off two of the lights and then stood there with her hand on the last cord, the one nearest the door. That air of expectation had left. She would have thought that the basement where the boy was brutalized would have felt worse, but it didn't. It seemed emptier and more normal than upstairs. Abbie didn't know why but made a note of it. She would tell the psychic that would be visiting the house.

She turned off the light and left, closing the door quietly behind her. The stairs were just stairs like so many other houses had. And the kitchen looked cheerful with its off-white walls. Abbie closed the window over the sink; it wouldn't do to have rain come in.

She had actually stepped into the living room when she turned back. The handprint on the back door bothered her. It seemed such a mute appeal for help, safety, escape.

She whispered to the sun-warmed silence, "Oh, I can't stand to leave it." She fished Kleenex from her pocket and dampened them in the sink. She knelt by the door and wiped across the brownish stain.

It smeared fresh and bloody, crimson as new blood. Abbie gasped and half-fell away from the door. The Kleenex was soaked with blood. She dropped it to the floor.

The handprint bled, slowly, down the white door.

She whispered, "Brian." There was a sound of small feet running. The sound hushed down the carpeted stairs to the basement. And Abbie heard the door swing open and close with a small click.

There was a silence so heavy that she couldn't breathe. And then it was gone, whatever it was. She got to her feet and walked to the living room. *So there's a ghost*, she told herself, *you've sold houses with ghosts before*. But she didn't pick up the soggy Kleenex and she didn't look back to see how far down the blood would go before it stopped.

She was out the door and locking it as fast as she could and still maintain some decorum. It wouldn't help things at all if the neighbors saw the real estate agent running from the house. She forced herself to walk down the steps between the yellow flowers. But there was a spot in the middle of her back that itched as if someone were staring at it.

Abbie didn't look back, she wouldn't run, but she had no desire to see Brian Garner's face pressed against the window glass.
Maybe the cleanup crew had done the best they could. She'd have
to find out if all the marks bled fresh.

The house would have to be re-blessed. And probably a
medium brought in to tell the ghost that it was dead. A lot of
people took it as a status symbol to have a ghost in their house.
Certain kinds of ghosts, though. No one liked a poltergeist, no
one liked bleeding walls, or hideous apparitions, or screams at
odd times in the night. But a light that haunted only one hallway,
or a phantom that walked in the library in eighteenth-century
costume, well, those were call for a party. The latest craze was
ghost parties. All those that did not have a ghost could come and
watch one while everyone drank and had snacks.

But somehow Abbie didn't think that anyone would want
Brian's ghost in their house. It was romantic to have a murdered
sixteenth-century explorer roaming about, but recent victims and
a child at that. . . . Well, historic victims are one thing, but a
ghost out of your morning paper, that was something else en-
tirely.

Abbie just hoped that Brian Garner would be laid to rest easily. Sometimes the ghost just needed someone to tell it that it was
dead. But other times it took more stringent measures, especially
with violent ends. Strangely, there were a lot of child ghosts running around. Abbie had read an article in the Sunday magazine
about it. The theory was that children didn't have a concept of
death yet, so they became ghosts. They were still trying to live.

Abbie left such thinking up to the experts. She just sold
houses. As soon as the car started Abbie turned on the radio. She
wanted noise.

The news was on and the carefully enunciated words filled

the car as she pulled away from the house. "The Supreme Court reached their verdict today, upholding a New Jersey court ruling that Mitchell Davies, well-known banker and real estate investor, is still legally alive even though he is a vampire. This supports the so-called Bill of Life, which came out last year, widening the definition of life to include some forms of the living dead. Now on to sports . . ."

Abbie changed the station. She wasn't in the mood for sports scores or news of any kind. She had had her own dose of reality today and just wanted to go home. But first she had to stop by her office.

It was late when she arrived and even the receptionist had gone home. Three rows of desks stretched catty-corner from one end of the room to the other. Most of the overhead lights had been turned off, leaving the room in afternoon shadows. A thin strip of white light wound down the center and passed over Sandra's desk. Sandra sat waiting, hands folded in front of her. She had stopped even pretending to work.

Her blue eyes flashed upward when she saw Abbie come in. The relief was plain on her face and in the sudden slump of her shoulders.

Abbie smiled at her.

Sandra made a half smile in return. She asked, "How was it?"

Abbie walked to her desk, which put her to Sandra's left, and two desks over. She started sorting papers while she considered how best to answer. "It's going to need some work before we can show it."

Sandra's high heels clicked on the floor, and Abbie could feel her standing behind her. "That isn't what I mean, and you know it."

Abbie turned and faced her. Sandra's eyes were too bright, her face too intense. "Sandra, please, it's over, let it go."

Sandra gripped her arm, fingers biting deep. "Tell me what it was like."

"You're hurting me."

Her hand dropped numbly to her side and she almost whispered, "Please, I need to know."

"You didn't do anything wrong. It wasn't your fault."

"But I sold them that house."

"But Phillip Garner played with the Ouija board. He opened the way to what happened."

"But I should have seen it. I should have realized something was wrong. I did notice things when Marion contacted me. I should have done something."

"What, what could you have done?"

"I could have called the police."

"And told them that you had a bad feeling about one of your clients? You aren't a registered psychic, they would have ignored you. And Sandra, you didn't have any premonitions. You've convinced yourself you knew beforehand, but it isn't true. You never mentioned it to anyone in the office." Abbie tried to get her to smile. "And get real, girl, if you had news that important, you couldn't keep it to yourself. You are the original gossip. A kind gossip, but still a gossip."

Sandra didn't smile, but she nodded. "True, I don't keep secrets very well."

Abbie put her arm around her and hugged her. "Stop beating yourself up over something you had nothing to do with. Cut the guilt off; it isn't your guilt to deal with."

Sandra leaned into her and began to cry.

They stayed there like that until it was full dark and Sandra was hoarse from crying.

Sandra said, "I've made you late getting home."

"Charles will understand."

"You sure?"

"Yes, I have a very understanding husband."

She nodded and snuffled into the last Kleenex in the room. "Thanks."

"It's what friends are for, Sandra. Now go home and feel good about yourself, you deserve it."

Abbie called her husband before locking up the office, to assure him that she was coming home. He was very understanding, but he tended to worry about her. Then she escorted Sandra to her car and made sure she drove away.

IT was weeks later before Abbie stood in the newly carpeted living room. Fresh hex signs had been painted over the doors and windows. A priest had blessed the house. A medium had come and told Brian Garner's ghost that it was dead. Abbie did not know, or want to know, if the ghost had been stubborn about leaving.

The house felt clean and new, as if it had just been built. Perhaps a registered psychic could have picked up some lingering traces of evil and horror, but Abbie couldn't.

The kitchen door stood white and pure. There were no stains today, everything had been fixed, everything had been hidden. And wonder of wonders, she had a client coming to see it.

The client knew all about the house and its history. But then Mr. Channing and his family had been having difficulties of their own. No one wanted to sell them a house.

But Abbie had no problem with selling to them. They were people, after all; the law said so.

She had turned the lights in the living room and kitchen on. Their yellow glow chased back the night. Charles had been unhappy about her meeting the clients alone, at night. But Abbie knew you couldn't sell to people if they didn't think you trusted and liked them. So she waited alone in the artificial light, trying not to think too much about old superstitions. As a show of great good faith, she had no protection on her.

At exactly ten o'clock the doorbell rang. She had not heard a car drive up.

Abbie opened the door with her best professional smile on her face. And it wasn't hard to keep the smile because they looked like a very normal family. Mr. and Mrs. Channing were a young handsome couple. He was well over six feet with thick chestnut hair and clear blue eyes. She was only slightly shorter and blond. But they did not smile. It was the boy who smiled. He was perhaps fourteen and had his father's chestnut hair, but his eyes were dark brown, and Abbie found herself staring into those eyes. They were the most perfect color she had ever seen, solid, without a trace, falling. A hand steadied her, and when she looked, it was the boy who touched her, but he did not meet her eyes.

The three stood waiting for something as Abbie held the door. Finally, she asked them in. "Won't you please come inside?"

They seemed to relax and stepped through the door with the boy a little in front.

She smiled again and put a hand out to Mr. Channing and said, "It's a pleasure to meet you, Mr. Channing."

The three exchanged glances and then polite laughter.

The man said, "I'm not Channing; call me Rick."

"Oh, of course." Abbie tried to cover her confusion as the woman introduced herself simply as "Isabel."

It left Abbie with only one other client, but she offered her hand and her smile. "Mr. Channing."

He took it in a surprisingly strong grip and said, "I have looked forward to meeting you, Ms. McDonnell. And please, it's just Channing, no Mr."

"As you like, Channing. Then you must call me Abbie."

"Well then, Abbie, shall we see the house?" His face was so frank and open, so adult. It was disconcerting to see such intelligence and confidence in the eyes of a fourteen-year-old body.

He said, "I am much older than I appear, Abbie."

"Yes, I am sorry, I didn't mean to stare."

"That's quite all right. It is better that you stare than refuse to see us."

"Yes, well, let me show you the house." Abbie turned off the lights and showed the moon shining through the skylights. The brick fireplace was an unexpected hit. Somewhere Abbie had gotten the idea that vampires didn't like fire.

She did turn on the lights to show them the bedrooms and baths. They might be able to see in the dark, but Abbie didn't think it would impress them if she tripped in the dark.

The female, Isabel, spun round the master bedroom and said, "Oh, it will make a wonderful office."

Abbie inquired, "What do you do?"

The woman turned and said, "I'm an artist, I work mostly in oils."

Abbie said, "I've always wished I could paint, but I can't even draw."

The woman seemed not to have heard. Abbie had learned

long ago that you didn't make conversation if the client didn't want to talk. So they viewed the house in comparative silence.

There was one point in the master bathroom, when the three had to crowd in to see, that Abbie turned and bumped into the man. She stepped away as if struck and to cover her almost-fear she turned around and nearly gasped. They had reflections. She could see them just as clearly as herself. Abbie recovered from the shock and went on. But she knew that at least Channing had noticed. There was a special smile on his face that said it all.

Since they had reflections, Abbie showed them the kitchen more thoroughly than she had been intending. After all, if one myth was untrue, perhaps others were; perhaps they could eat.

The basement she saved for last, as she did in most of her houses. She led the way down and groped for the light pull cord but did not turn on the lights until she heard them shuffle in next to her. She said, "You'll notice there are no windows. You will have absolute privacy down here." She did not add that no sunlight would be coming down because after the mirror she wasn't sure if it was pertinent.

Channing's voice came soft and low out of the velvet dark. "It is quite adequate."

It wasn't exactly unbridled enthusiasm, but Abbie had done her best. She pulled on the light and showed them the water heater and the sump pump. "And the washer and dryer hookups are all set. All you need is the machine."

Channing nodded and said, "Very good."

"Would you like me to leave you alone for a few moments to discuss things?"

"Yes, if you would."

"Certainly." Abbie walked up the stairs but left the door

open. She went into the living room so they would be sure she wasn't eavesdropping. She wondered what the neighbors would think about vampires living next door. But that wasn't her concern; she just sold the house.

She did not hear them come up, but they stood suddenly in the living room. She swallowed past the beating of her heart and said, "What do you think of the house?"

Channing smiled, exposing fangs. "I think we'll take it."

The smile was very genuine on Abbie's part as she walked forward and shook their hands. "And how soon will you want to move in?"

"Next week, if possible. We have had our down payment for several months, and our bank is ready to approve our loan."

"Excellent. The house is yours as soon as the papers are signed."

Isabel ran a possessive hand down the wall. "Ours," she said.

Abbie smiled and said, "And if any of your friends need a house, just let me know. I'm sure I can meet their needs."

Channing grinned broadly at her and put his cool hand in hers. "I'm sure you can, Abbie, I'm sure you can."

After all, everyone needs a house to call their own. And Abbie sold houses.

A TOKEN FOR CELANDINE

This story is set in the world of my first novel, Nightseer. *It's set on a continent hundreds of miles away, but it's still the same world with the same magic system. Marion Zimmer Bradley rejected the story by saying that I'd done a pastiche of Tolkien, and elves really should be left to him, but do send another story and try again. I disagreed about elves being left to Tolkien and sent the story out again. It sold next time out, to* Memories and Visions. *And I would send Ms. Bradley my next story, and have the pleasure of her buying it. No elves in that one.*

THE prophet was an old man crazed with his own visions. He crouched against the dark wood of an elm. His fingers dug into the bark as if he would anchor himself to it. He gasped and wheezed as he drew in the morning air.

We had been chasing him through these woods for three days. And I was tired of it. If he ran this time, I was going to put an arrow in his leg. Celandine could heal him of the wound, and she could finally ask her question. I had not mentioned my plan to the healer. I thought she might object. The old man looked into a bar of dazzling sunlight. The glow showed his eyes milky with the creeping blindness of the very old and the very poor.

He was sick, blind, and crazy, and he had eluded me for days.

His prophecy protected him or perhaps the voices he called out to told him I was near. He turned his head to one side as if he were listening. I heard nothing but the wind and a small animal scuttling in the brush.

He turned his blind eyes and looked directly at me. The flesh along my back crawled. He could not see me, but I knew he did.

His voice was an abused cackle that never seemed to finish a thought completely. I had listened to him rant, but now he spoke low and well. "Ask," he said.

It was Celandine's question, but while he was in the mood to answer, I asked. Not all prophets are able to answer direct questions. Those that do tend to answer only one question for each person. "How do I find the token which Celandine the Healer seeks?"

"The black road must take. Demons help you. Fight in darkness you will."

I heard the whisper of cloth that announced the healer.

She came up beside me, white cloak huddled round her body.

Without taking my eyes from the old man I asked, "Did you hear what he said?"

"Yes."

"Ask him something."

"Where is the token I seek?"

"Demon, demon inside." He coughed, his body nearly doubled over with the violence of it. Bloody foam flecked his chin. Celandine stepped forward. "Let me heal you."

His eyes went wide. "Death want, death seek, no heal." And he was gone, vanishing into the underbrush noiseless as a rabbit.

Celandine stood there, tears glistening in her eyes. "He'll die."

"He wants to die."

She shook her head, and one teardrop slid from crystalline blue eyes down a flawless white cheek. "He doesn't know what he's saying."

I touched her arm. "Celandine, no healer can cure the madness of prophecy."

She nodded and pulled the cloak's hood to hide her face. A strand of black hair trailed across the white cloth like a stain.

I said, "This is the seventh prophet, Celandine. We must trust the information and act upon it."

She spoke in a low voice that I had to strain to hear.

"Aren't you afraid, Bevhinn?"

I debated with myself whether she wanted truth or for me to be strong for her. I decided on truth. "I fear the black healers of Lolth. I fear being a female trapped behind their dark border."

"And yet you will go?"

"It is where our quest takes us. We must go."

She turned to me, face framed in shadowed hood. "It is death by torture for me if I am caught."

I had heard the stories of what Loltuns did to white healers. They were tales to curdle the blood round winter fires.

"I will die before I let them take you. You have my word."

She spun round as if she would find an answer in the spring morning. "I have your word." She turned back to me, blue eyes hard. "What good is your word? You aren't human. You don't worship the Goddess that I serve. Why should I trust you to give your life for me?"

I clamped a six-fingered hand round my sword hilt. Five months I'd traveled with her. Five months of living off the land, killing that we both could eat. I had slain winter-starved wolves and fought bandits. I had guarded her back while she healed the sick. I had been wounded twice, and twice she had healed me. And now this.

I let the anger flow into my face. I stared at her with my alien purple eyes, but I kept my voice low with menace. I had no desire to shout and bring men or a wild beast upon us. "Your fear makes you foolish, Celandine. But do not fear. Your father paid me well to guard you on this exile's quest."

"You sell yourself for money like some harlot."

I slapped her hard, and she fell to the ground. She looked startled. I had never offered her violence before. "Your father bought my sword, my magic, and my loyalty. I will lay down my life to protect you, but I will not be insulted."

"How dare you. I am a white healer . . ."

I finished for her, "And bastard daughter of the King of Celosia. I know all that. He hired me, remember."

"You are my bodyguard, my servant."

"I'm not the reason we're out here in this godforsaken wilderness. You killed a man. You took that pure white gift of yours and twisted it. You used black healing and took a life."

She was crying now, softly.

"The only way to end this exile is to follow the prophet's advice and go to Lolth."

"I'm afraid."

I grabbed her upper arms, pulling her to her feet. "I'm afraid, too, but I want this over with. I want to go back to Meltaan. I want a bed and a bath and decent food. I want someone to guard my back for a change." I let her go, and she stumbled back, sobbing.

"I will not let your fear keep me out here forever. Your father didn't pay me that much."

"You can't leave me."

"I could, but I won't. But tomorrow we travel the dark road."

Morning found us on the bank of Lake Muldor. A blue cloak to match her eyes replaced the healer's cloak Celandine usually wore. She kept it pulled close around her though it was very warm for spring.

The sun was warm on my face. The light shattered diamond bursts off the lake water and the silver of my armor. I had bound my breasts tight under the scale mail. I was counting on the fact that most humans think male Varellians look effeminate. And that they would look at sword and armor and think me male.

Celandine would simply go as my wife. It was rare, but it was done. That would explain my exile. The problem was that we both stood out. We could not simply blend with what few travelers there were.

Celandine was too aware of her royal heritage to play the common wife. She had no talent for lying or being false. I could have wasted magic to disguise myself as human, but it wouldn't have been safe. I was earth-witch, not illusionist, and disguise was not one of my better spells. So I rode as a Varellian. My hair was spun snow with a purity of color that few humans achieved. The hair could have been dyed, the odd-shaped ears hidden, but a sixth finger was something else. It was considered a mark of good fortune in Varell but not among the humans. And, of course, my eyes gave me away. Purple as a violet, the color of a grape.

We were not your usual traveling couple. I rode a unicorn, which was very hard to hide. The unicorns of Varell are as big as a warhorse. They were the mounts of royalty and of the royal guard. Once a unicorn and a rider are bound, it is a lifelong binding. So through no fault of his own, Ulliam shared my exile among the humans and the horses.

But he also shared my magic, though he can only feel it and not perform it. His great split hooves danced on the damp meadow grass. The earth-magic of spring was calling. My power was tied to the ground and that which sprang from it. Every meadow flower, every blade of grass, was hidden power for my magic. My power called to other things. I shared the joy of the swallow as it turned and twisted over the lake. I froze in the long grass with the rabbit waiting for our horses to pass. Spring was one of the most powerful times for an earth-witch, as winter was one of the worst. And Ulliam danced with me on his back, feeling the power. I hoped I would not need it.

Celandine rode silently, blue cloak pulled over a plain brown dress. Visions of torture still danced behind her eyes. Her fear was an almost palpable thing. She rode one horse and carried the lead for a second. She would need a fresh mount if we were to make good time. I would have liked to rest Ulliam, but warhorses were not easily found in the wild lands. I would not ride less. You could not fight off the back of a normal riding horse. The clang of metal, the swinging shield, even drawing bow and arrow, could send a horse racing in fright. And you couldn't afford that in battle. A war steed had to be trained to it from birth; there was just no other way. Ulliam and I had been trained together. No other mount could have known my mind as he did.

I had used magic to make him less noticeable. Most would see a great white horse and nothing more. If a wizard concentrated, then perhaps he would see past the glamour, but it was the best I could do. In Lolth they sacrificed unicorns to Verm and Ivel.

I asked Celandine, "Have you ever worshipped Ivel?"

She made the sign against evil, thumb and little finger extended near her face. "Don't use her full name."

"As you like. Have you ever worshipped Mother Bane?"

"Of course, you must not ignore any of the three faces of the Great Mother."

I didn't argue theology with her. We had found we did not

agree on matters of worship. "You've never spoken of Mother Bane as one of your Gods."

"Because it is not wise to do so."

"Why do the Loltuns sacrifice women to Her altar?"

"It is a matter of theological interpretation."

"Interpretation?"

"Yes." She seemed reluctant to speak further, so I let the subject drop. Celandine was not happy that I could argue her into a corner using her own sacred tomes. The black road erupted from the damp meadow grass without marker or warning. It seemed to be made of solid rock, black as if the earth had bled. Legend said that Pelrith of the Red Eye forged the road. And seeing it lying there on the shore of the lake, I believed in demigods calling things forth from the earth. I urged Ulliam forward.

The moment his hooves hit the road, I felt it. The road was dead; no earth-magic sang through it. The horse Celandine was leading shied at the black surface. I moved Ulliam to calm it before the horse she was riding could bolt as well. We rode into Lolth three abreast, with the skittish horse in the middle.

I noticed bumps in the smooth surface of the road, but there was no pattern to them. I dismounted and walked Ulliam until I came to a bump that seemed higher than the others. I knelt and ran a mailed hand over the blackened lump. My eyes could not puzzle it out at first, then suddenly, it was clear. A human skull gaped from the road, barely covered in the black rocklike stuff. And I could not force the image from my mind.

Celandine called, "What is it?"

"Bones. Human bones."

She made the sign against evil again.

I mounted Ulliam, and we rode on. My eyes were drawn with

a horrible fascination to each half-hidden shape as we rode. We traveled on the burial mound of hundreds.

We came to the border guard then. There were only four of them, but two shone magic to my eyes. And I knew that I shone as well. But there was nothing illegal about being a wizard; at least I didn't think there was. A female wizard might have been stopped, but healers do not shine like wizards. Celandine would seem merely a woman until she healed someone. When she laid hands, she glowed like the full moon.

One man came from behind the wooden gate. He stood in front of me. "Well, you must be an ice elf."

It was a rather rude way to begin, but I had been prepared for that. It was a killing insult in Varell, but I had been five years from there. It wasn't the first time someone had called me elf to my face. It would not be the last. "I am Bevhinn Ailir, and this is my wife, Celandine."

His eyes turned to the healer, and he said, "Oh. She's a beauty." He walked over to her and put a hand on her knee, massaging it. Celandine glared at him.

The hand began to creep up her thigh, and she yanked her horse backward. It bumped the man, and he backed away smiling. He said, "You could make money off this one. She would bring a fair price every night you stay in our country."

"She is a wife, not a whore."

He shrugged. "There isn't that much difference, now, is there?"

"There is where I come from."

"Yes, the Varellians and their reverence for females. You and your queen."

I had had about enough of this. "Can we pass, or must we stand here and be insulted?"

He frowned at that and said, "I'd keep that fancy armor hidden. There are those who would take it from you."

I smiled at him, forcing him to stare into my alien eyes. "It is good armor, but surely men aren't eager to die for a suit of armor they would never fit into."

He returned the smile and said, "I would love to see one of your Varellian women. You're pretty enough to eat yourself."

I said, voice low, "Your two friends over there can tell you I'm a wizard. And this wizard has grown very tired of you." I flexed a hand for dramatic emphasis, and he backed away. Truth was, an earth-witch wasn't big on instant magic, but they didn't know that. With my power tied to the spring, I sparkled like a sorcerer. It was a good time of year to bluff.

The gate opened, and he called after us, "May you run afoul of a black healer."

I answered back over my shoulder, "And may the next wizard you torment blow your head off."

Forest stretched on either side of the road. The birds and beasts didn't know they had crossed a border. In truth, it looked much like the wild lands where we had spent the winter, except for the road.

Farmland opened on either side of the road, fighting back the trees; the smell of fresh-plowed earth was strong and good. The soil was a rich black. I felt an urge to crumble the dirt in my hands and feel its growing power, but I resisted. Ulliam danced nervously under me.

Forest returned, hugging each side of the road. But no blade of grass, no wildflower dared to encroach upon the black road. It was late in the day when we heard a loud cracking noise, like a cannonball striking wood. The horses pranced in fright, and even Ulliam shivered under me. There was a tearing sound, as if the earth itself were being pulled apart. We rode cautiously toward the sounds.

A wide path had been freshly cleared from the forest. Trees with jagged trunks lay in heaps on their sides. Stumps lay in a second heap, earth-covered roots bare to the sky. Stooping to pull another great stump from the ground was a demon. His skin was night-black. Muscles bulged along his back and arms. His ribbed bat ears curled tight with his effort as he strained upward. The roots ripped free of the earth. He put the stump in the pile with the rest. He caught sight of us on the road, and we all stared at each other. A silver necklace glittered round his neck. The cold eye of a diamond the size of a hen's egg winked out from it. From here it glowed with magic.

Celandine looked at me. Was this our demon's help, or was the token inside the demon? I hoped it wasn't the latter. I didn't see myself slitting the gullet of a greater demon.

A man stepped out of the trees. He was thin, and a scraggly beard edged his pointed chin. He said, "Be on your way. You're distracting him."

"I am sorry, good farmer, but I have never seen a greater demon before."

A look of incredulity passed over his face. "You swear by Loth's bloody talons that you've never seen a greater demon?"

"I swear."

He smiled then, friendly. "Well, you have started out with a greater demon named Krakus. He's been ensorcelled to the farmers hereabout for over fifty years. He's cleared most of the fields along this road."

I stared at the demon, and there was something in his smooth yellow eyes that said hatred. A hatred deeper than anything I could feel.

"Good farmer, are you never afraid of him breaking free?"

"No, the enchantment on him is strong enough."

"What would happen if he ever was freed?"

The farmer looked back at the demon, the smile gone. "Why, he'd kill me and everyone else he'd worked for."

"Where do you keep the demon when he's not working? Does he go back to the pits from which he came?"

The man found the question very funny. "Why, you don't know anything about demons. An ensorcelled demon can't leave the place he's been put, just can't leave. We keep him chained at night near where he's working."

I shivered under the gaze of those sullen yellow eyes. "I hope you keep a guard on him at night, farmer."

"Oh we do, but nothing to worry about. He'll still be pulling stumps fifty years from now." The farmer walked back into the cleared area and slapped the demon lightly on the arm. "No, we couldn't lose such a good worker. Get back to work, Krakus." The demon turned without a word or a snarl and stood before a full-grown tree. With one gesture and a flash of sorcery he felled the tree, blasting it off a few feet above the ground. The farmer went to sit in the sunshine. Our interview was over.

Celandine and I rode in silence for a short time, then she asked, "Do you think that is the demon who will help us?"

"I don't know."

"You don't know. Then what are we doing here? What good is prophecy if you don't know what it means?"

"None, I suppose."

"Then what are we risking ourselves for?"

I grabbed the reins of her horse and said, "The only way to understand prophecy is to do what it says. Now stop sniveling."

She glared at me but kept her peace. Her fear kept her silent more than I did.

TWILIGHT had fallen, spreading a blue haze across the trees. An inn sat in a small clearing. In the dim light I made out a sign. It had a crude drawing of the demon we had just seen, and words proclaimed it the Black Demon Inn. Krakus had been here a long time.

I tied the horses up outside, and we entered. The place smelled stale. The windows were open, and the spring wind blew through the place, but it would take weeks for the sourness of winter to be blown away. When my eyes adjusted to the dim lighting, I saw the place was almost empty.

Only three of the small scarred tables were in use. A group of five farmers sat drinking and laughing. Two men in chain mail sat eating at another table. Their swords were out on the table beside them, sheathed. And a young man dressed all in black sat at the last table near the stairs. A young girl no more than twelve sat with him. Her eyes were downcast, and she was obviously afraid.

Celandine stiffened beside me. She had recognized the robes of a healer, a black healer. The host came over to us, smiling, "And how may I help you this night, travelers?"

"Food, stabling for the horses, and a room for the night."

"One gold ducat will get you all you desire." His leer was obvious. I looked blankly at him. He explained patiently, "All our guests have the choice of three fair ladies to keep them company for a time."

"No, thank you. My wife and I are quite fine, alone."

He shrugged. "As you wish, but if I were you I'd have my wife pull up her hood. And have her lower her eyes."

"She is fine as she is."

He shrugged again. "Just trying to help. The stables are to the left. My boy will see to them. When you return, I will have your dinners waiting."

We went out and led the horses and Ulliam to the stables. They were cramped, and a dirty boy of about ten scuttled up to take the horses. He did not try to take Ulliam, and I did not offer. While he brushed down the horses, I tended the unicorn. The boy was dirty and perhaps not quite bright, but he brushed the horses well, and the feed he gave them was good quality.

We took a small table near the wall so I could watch the room. It was then that I noticed a small demon, barely three feet high, cleaning tables. He balanced the dirty dishes above his head with impossibly long arms. He was a bright green in color and scaled rather than skin-covered. Celandine and I stared after him as he disappeared into the back.

She stared at me, and I shrugged. In the end it would be Celandine who said what the token was and where it was. My job was just to help her get it.

The little demon also brought our food. Neither of us spoke as it put down bowls of stew, thick slices of brown bread, and tankards of some liquid. He seemed accustomed to silence and raced back through the tables with his empty tray.

The stew was hot, the meat and vegetables a little stringy, but it had been a hard winter. Stores were running low everywhere, but the bread was fresh and good. One of the farmers I had noticed earlier came to stand beside us. He bumped into our table, unsteady on his feet. He smelled of beer. "Is this pretty thing your wife, Varellian?"

"Yes."

"How much for a night with her?"

I stared at him a moment, not sure I had understood. "I said she is my wife."

"I heard you. How much for the night?"

"We are new to Lolth and do not understand all the customs. Are you saying that Loltuns sell their wives for money, like whores?"

"You brought her in here, with her face showing. She looked at every man in the place, bold as a basilisk. What else would you be doing but selling?"

I understood the host's warning now, but it was too late. "We are not Loltun, and I am not selling my wife."

He scowled at that. "The other three women are busy, and I don't go near a black healer. I have need of a woman, and she is the only one available."

"You'll have to wait then."

"Loltun men do not wait for women." He grabbed at Celandine surprisingly fast and jerked her to her feet.

My sword was out before I had time to think. "Let her go, or die."

The sight of naked steel seemed to catch his attention. He let go of her, and she sank back into her seat. The man stared at the end of my sword, and finally said, "Well, if you don't want to sell, then have her keep her eyes to herself. You could get a man killed over a misunderstanding like this."

I said nothing as he shuffled back to his companions. Celandine pulled up her hood without being asked. I resheathed my sword, and we ate in silence. But there was another scene taking place.

The black healer and his girl were having a fight of sorts. He would touch her and then laugh, and she would scream. And then he would touch her again and laugh. I asked Celandine, "What is he doing?"

She swallowed. "I think he is hurting the girl and then healing her."

"To what purpose?"

"Many black healers are insane. They pervert their healing power into harm, and it contaminates them."

The girl was pretty. She had long yellow hair and light eyes that I guessed were blue, but couldn't be sure at this distance. Her body had just begun to swell to womanhood, but she was still more child than woman. A bleeding scratch appeared on her cheek. He touched it, and the cut vanished.

"How did that cut appear? He didn't touch her."

"He is a very powerful black healer. He has a gift similar to sorcery."

"As you have."

She nodded. "As I have, but I must not use it again on peril of my soul."

That was what the quest was all about. The token, whatever it was, would cleanse the healer's soul of the stain of black healing.

The girl screamed, a full-blown shriek. She stood, knocking her chair backward. Even in the dim light I could see the open sores on her arm.

Celandine started to rise, and I gripped her arm. It was automatic for her to help the sick, but not here. My grip seemed to remind her of her fear, and she sat down.

I had seen this sudden bravery many times. It came from her healing. She was afraid of so many things. But her healing made her different. I had seen her risk death to save a drowning child.

Many times she had walked among bandits to heal their sick. It was as if all her strength, all her bravery, went to healing, and there was none left for Celandine herself.

The black healer caught the girl-child. She struggled as he clutched the diseased arm. She broke away from him and stared at the now-healed arm. He laughed.

The host went up to him, and his voice carried in the sudden silence. "Sir, we are honored at your business, but your lady friend is upsetting the other guests. Would it please the most honorable healer if he would take her up to his room?" The man had bowed low but never took his eyes off the healer.

What would the host do if the healer moved to touch him? The healer laughed again. "You should be honored that I come to this piss hole of an inn. I am of the highest rank of healer. I talk to your Gods for you. I face them when you cower in fear." He was addressing the entire room now. "I hold the power that pacifies the Gods themselves. I consort with the demons of the pit. I do things that would crack your minds like brittle kindling." And he walked over to the now-quiet farmers. "But you turn away from me when I show power. Oh, heal me, please, heal me. But then leave us alone. That's how it is."

He went back to the girl, and she backed away crying. She begged him, "Please, let me go, please."

"Come, girl, it is time someone here learned what it is to embrace a black healer." She screamed as he grabbed her. He pulled her toward the stairs. Her hand gripped the banister, and he tugged her. Her fingers slipped, and he grabbed her close to his body. He carried her like that up the stairs and paused at the very top. He yelled at the host, "Which room is mine?"

The host made a half bow and said, "Turn to your right. It is the last door on that side. It is the nicest room in the inn."

"And it will be poor," the healer said and walked from sight with the struggling girl in his arms.

My fingers bit deeply into Celandine's arm. Her blue eyes glowed with anger. But I thought some of it was directed inward at her own fear. There were white healers I knew who would have challenged him regardless of the cost. They would not let such evil go unquestioned. For once I was glad that Celandine was not so zealous. She would be killed for being a white healer, and I would be killed defending her. It was not the way I wanted to die.

The first shriek sounded from upstairs. It cut through the fresh conversation and killed it. Everyone downstairs sat, waiting. A second scream came, piteous, all hope gone, choking sobs followed it.

The farmers got up and paid their bill. Only the two fighters were left. And they, like us, were travelers with no other place to go.

Celandine nodded. I motioned to the host, and he came over. There was a light dew of sweat on his face.

"Good sir, we are ready for our room."

"Was the stew to your liking?"

"The food was good, but we seem to have lost our appetites."

"He is a high priest of our people. But to strangers, who do not understand, well . . . he may seem extreme."

"On the contrary, mine host, I do understand. Even in other lands some magics drive the sense from a man."

The host looked nervously about as if someone might overhear. He said, "As you wish. Your room is to the right, the first door. It is as far away from the noise as I can put you."

"We appreciate that."

He nodded, and we stood. Celandine followed me, hooded, eyes down, more to hide her anger than to hide her face.

We mounted the stairs to the sounds of screams. The screams became words, a prayer. I didn't need to look behind me to know Celandine was stiffening. The girl was praying to Mother Blessen. She was praying to Celandine's God.

The prayer was cut short as if she had been cuffed. We stepped into the dark hallway, and both of us simply stood as if waiting. The child's voice rose again in prayer. He was beating her. But she had decided that she would probably never see daylight. So she prayed, and he hit her. Celandine let her hood slip back. She turned to me wordlessly, and I met her eyes.

I whispered, "The token?"

She nodded.

There was logic to it. The girl was inside the Black Demon Inn. The token was inside a demon just as the prophets had told us it would be. My sword sighed from its sheath, and I hefted my shield, balancing it on my arm. She smiled at me then. Fear danced in her eyes, but that curious strength that she had when healing, it was there, too.

She whispered to me, "You must cut off his head, or take out his heart. He will simply heal himself otherwise. And you must kill him as quickly as possible, for he can do us all great harm."

"Surely he has used most of his power already tonight."

"He is high in the favor of the dark Gods. He may have more than his own power to draw from."

I prayed silently. "Balinorelle, let it not be so. Guide my hand and allow me to slay this demonmonger."

Celandine waited for me, and we walked to the room. She opened the door quietly, for we didn't want to alert the men down below. I went in ahead of her, shield held close, wondering if it would help.

The girl lay on the bed partially nude. Her small breasts and entire upper body were covered with the green spreading sickness. It was something that killed thoroughly and quickly. The black healer lay next to her fondling her diseased body. Celandine closed the door behind us.

The man said, "What do you want?"

He spied Celandine behind me and leered. "Have you come to offer a gift? For a gift as fair as she, you could have much."

"I have come to ask if you will sell the girl to me."

He stared down at the dying girl and laughed. With a careless hand, he healed her, the disease absorbing into his skin, where the green sickness faded away. She was pure and unblemished once more. "I don't think I'll sell her to you, elf. But I might trade."

I shook my head. "No, black healer, no trade."

He knelt on the bed and said, "Then you can fight me for her." A thin smile curled his lips. He gestured, and I felt claws sink into my cheek. Blood trickled down my face, from under my helmet.

He laughed. "How badly do you want her?"

I wiped the dripping blood with the back of my hand and said, "Badly enough."

I advanced, holding shield and weapon up, but another claw raked me across the ribs as if my armor were not there. Stealth gained me nothing, so I rushed him. He motioned, and my sword hand was cut and bleeding.

A sorcerous claw raked over my eyes. I shrieked and fell to my knees. I gripped shield and sword in the crimson dark. Blind, I fought the pain and the panic. I had been trained to fight blindfolded: darkness was darkness. The pain was overwhelming, and I crouched and tried to think past it, tried to hear past it.

A sound, footsteps. The girl's scream. A rush of cloth that

was Celandine's dress. The heavier sloppy footfalls of the black healer.

"It seems I will enjoy two beauties tonight."

Celandine backed away from him but kept close to the bed and the girl. She called out to me, "Bevhinn!"

He moved round to the foot of the bed to come at Celandine. I had to make my first strike deadly or all was lost. I listened to his breathing and his movements. I would go for stomach and chest, not knowing if he was facing me or not. Then he spoke again. "Such a pretty pair." He was facing away from me.

I rose and struck. The blade sank into flesh. I pulled it free and struck point first through his neck. The blade grated on bone and was through to open air. I knew where everything was now. I took five strikes to cut off his head. The smell of blood was thick and violent.

Celandine said, "Bevhinn, you've killed him."

She was beside me lifting off my helmet. I felt her fingertips touch my eyes. I felt the pain again like a lance through my brain, and it was gone. I blinked.

The black healer lay sprawled on the bed. His head was a short distance from his body. Blood soaked the bedclothes to drip on the floor. The girl looked up and smiled her gratitude at me. She paled only a little at the sight of the headless body. She had probably seen worse things in her stay in Lolth. Celandine retrieved the girl's cloak and spread it over her torn dress.

I cleaned my sword on the edge of the sheets and sheathed it. I forced open the wooden shutters on the window. I strapped my shield to my back, and scrambled out to kneel on the sloping roof. The girl crawled out to me, and Celandine followed.

We slipped unseen and, hopefully, unheard to the ground. I led the way to the stables. We entered, and the boy scrambled down from the loft where he probably slept. I said, "Come here, boy."

He came, but he was afraid. I gripped him quickly and put a hand over his mouth. "Find some rope and cloth for a gag."

Celandine and the girl moved to obey. The boy's eyes were huge with fear, showing the whites of his eyes. "Boy, we will not harm you." He wasn't convinced, and I didn't blame him.

When he was tied with some good-quality rope and gagged with a questionably dirty rag, I shoved him up in his loft. Hopefully, no one would find him before morning.

We saddled the horses while the girl kept watch. So far no alarm had been raised. But sooner or later the host would raise courage enough to check the strange noises from the healer's room. We had to be away before that.

We led Ulliam and the horses out onto the road, but I motioned for them to follow me back the way we had come that day. When we felt it safe to talk, Celandine asked, "Why are we going back?"

"We cannot go on to the next inn. You and the girl might be able to disguise yourselves, but Ulliam and I are not so easily changed. We could run back to the wild lands, but the Loltuns would chase us down. We are at least five days from the Meltaanian border. Every hand will be against us by morning. We must leave Lolth tonight."

"But how?"

"We're going back to the demon, Krakus."

"The help of demons?"

"Let us hope so."

The girl rode our spare horse, and she rode well enough. We raced through the night, riding the horses hard because we wouldn't be needing them much longer.

We came at last to an area of newly cleared land. The demon's shattered stumps and trees were piled high on either side of the road.

I left Celandine and the girl-child with Ulliam and the horses. And I crept through the woods toward the two men who were guarding the demon. One was simple, a dagger thrust in the throat when he went to relieve himself. But the other stayed near the fire and kept his sword naked and near at hand. Guarding a demon seemed to make him nervous. Every time Krakus rattled his chains, the man kept staring back at the demon. I stepped up behind him and put my sword through his throat. I cleaned the blade in the tall grass and sheathed it. The demon was watching me with eyes that caught and reflected the fire.

Heavy chains bound Krakus, but the keys to those chains glinted at the dead man's belt. Celandine and the girl entered the clearing with the horses and Ulliam. The demon's eyes flicked to them and then settled back on me. I said, "I would bargain with you, Krakus."

His voice was deep and seemed to come from a long way off, as if from the bottom of a well. "What manner of bargain?"

"You teleport the three of us and the unicorn just across the Meltaan border at the city gates of Terl, and I will free you from your enslavement."

"I like this bargain, elf. Free me, and I will do as you ask."

"Not yet, demon. First we take blood oath so I know you will not desert us, or teleport us to a harmful place."

"Why would I do that to the ones who free me?"

"Because you are a demon."

It laughed, baring white fangs. "I like you. You understand the way of things."

His voice sank even deeper until it was almost painful to hear. "But what blood oath could bind a demon?"

"One to the hounds of Verm and the birds of Loth."

The smile vanished from his face, and he said, "Have you ever made blood oath with a demon?"

"No."

He laughed again. "Then let us proceed."

I cut my right hand in a diagonal slash. The blood was bright red and poured in a sheet down my palm. It stung with the sharp pain of all shallow cuts. The demon extended his left hand, and I sliced it. The blood was black and slow to ooze.

We clasped hands and suddenly I felt dizzy. I stared up into those intent yellow eyes and said, "What is happening, Krakus?"

"What always happens when you bargain with demons, warrior. I am taking blood price. But because this oath holds us both, you are getting my blood in return." He hissed, "You are demon kin now, elf. Those who have the power will see the taint and act accordingly."

It felt as if someone had thrust a red, hot poker into my hand. Fire filled my veins. I fell to my knees, gasping in the cool night air. I could not afford to scream. If we were being chased, screams would bring them. That was the last thought I had before blackness engulfed me.

I heard Celandine from a distance. "What if she dies? Then you will still be a prisoner because only she can free you."

The demon's voice came: "It is the way of demon bargains, healer. The mortal must risk more than the demon. I cannot change my nature, not even to save myself."

I woke with the sky clearing toward dawn. The cut on my

hand had been burned shut and formed a scar across my palm. It had not been Celandine's magic that had closed the wound.

She was there beside me. "How do you feel?"

"Good enough." I sat in the morning-damp grass, waiting to feel whole again. I got tired of waiting and called to my magic.

It answered but with a difference. It seemed sluggish, as if it moved through thick air to reach me. My magic felt tainted, but there was no time to worry about it. I had to free the demon.

The spring dawn was close, and the spring night still here. The world was poised between the two, so I called upon both. I drew the cool spring darkness and the soft call of an owl. I breathed in the first hint of dawn on the wind.

A rabbit stirred in its sleep, and I took its dreams and wove them into my spell. The bark of a fox and the fleeting shadow of a nighthawk mingled with the aroma of fresh-turned earth. The power stretched like a second moon, swollen with spring's bounty. I stood and cupped my hands, letting the magic fall into my palms like moonshine. I engulfed the diamond of the demon's necklace in white magic. I felt the enchantment snap. Krakus bowed his head, and I slipped the necklace free of him. The diamond still glittered like warm ice, but it would take an enchanter to reactivate the necklace. For now it was only a piece of jewelry.

He rose to his full seven feet and stretched. The chains fell away without benefit of keys. He leered down at us. "Let us go and fulfill my part of the bargain." He offered me his left hand, and I saw the matching burn scar across his great palm. I took his hand, and Ulliam shied but came to stand on the other side of me. Celandine touched his white flank, and the girl clung to her. We were an unbroken chain. The world shifted, and we were before the gates of Terl. It was already dawn there, and a farmer with his load of chickens fought his mule to keep it from running away. It did not like the smell of demons.

Krakus let go of my hand and said, "I am sure I will not be the last demon you see, earth-witch; blood calls to blood." He vanished.

Later that day we stood before the High Priestess, and she welcomed Celandine back into the fold of the white healers. The girl-child had some healing magic and was being sponsored as an apprentice healer. She was a worthy token for such a quest.

Celandine's father held a great feast, and I was invited. I had the gratitude of the most powerful petty king in Meltaan. And I had a diamond only slightly smaller than my fist. It would be a long time before I was forced to guard someone else's treasures again.

Celandine was in her element, bejeweled and dressed in white silk. She did not look my way. She was cleansed, and her soul was her own again. And I was a reminder of less pleasant times.

I watched the girl we had saved, laughing with the other young healers. I felt good at having saved her, but my eyes were drawn back again and again to the burn scar on my palm. Celandine had done nothing on this quest. Yet she was cleansed, and I was tainted. I wondered, was there a cleansing ceremony for the demon-touched?

A CLEAN SWEEP

My daughter was a very small baby when I got the invitation to join this anthology. I was getting very little sleep, and the house was a disaster. So when asked to write a superhero story, I knew the superhero I most wanted to see on my doorstep.

CAPTAIN Housework materialized on the doorstep of 11 Pear Tree Lane. His emergency beeper had awakened him, code red. Was it his nemesis, Dr. Grime, or the infamous Dust Bunny Gang, or perhaps Pond Scum, the destroyer of bathrooms?

He had to levitate to reach the doorbell. As crimefighters go, Captain Housework was on the short side. His white coveralls, silver cape, and mask—formed of a billed cap with eyeholes— were gleamingly clean. He stood on the top step shining as if carved from ivory and silver.

He looked perfect, crisp, and clean. And he liked it that way.

The door opened, and a woman dressed in a bathrobe stared down at him. "Oh, it's you. Please come in." She held the door for him, waving him in eagerly.

He stared up at her, a grim smile on his face. "And what dastardly villain is plaguing your home, dear lady?"

She blinked at him. "Dastardly villain?" She gave a small laugh. "Oh, no, it's nothing like that. My husband made the call. Did he say we had a supervillain in the house?"

Captain Housework drew himself up to his full three feet and said, "It was a code red, madam. That means a supervillain has been spotted."

The woman laughed again. "Oh, dear, no. I've got a party of twelve people coming at six o'clock and my maid canceled."

"You called the superhero hotline because your maid canceled." His voice had a harsh edge to it that the woman didn't seem to notice.

"Well, my friend Betty had you over when her kids threw that wild party. You did miracles with her house."

"I remember the incident. I made it clear that it was an exception to the rules that I aided her."

"But you've just got to help me, Captain Housework." The woman went to her knees, gripping his arms. "Please, it's too late to turn to anyone else." Tears glittered in her eyes.

Captain Housework crossed his arms across his thin chest, his mouth set in a firm line. "Madam, I am a superhero, not a maid. I do not think you realize how terrible my foes can be. Have you ever had a wave of black mildew engulf your husband and eat him to the bone before your eyes?"

She blinked at him. "Well, no, but surely that doesn't happen all that often. In the meantime, couldn't you help me, just this once?"

It was true that his archenemies had been lying low for a while. Work had been slow. He stared into her tearstained face and nodded. "All right, but only this once."

She hugged him, crumpling the bill of his mask. He pushed away from her, straightening his costume. "That will not be necessary. I will get to work at once, if that is all right with you?"

"Oh, that's wonderful. I'll just go get dressed." She raced up the stairs, trailing some floral perfume behind her.

Captain Housework sniffed. He preferred the cleaner scents of household air fresheners. Pine was his favorite.

He sighed and walked into the living room. For a moment his heart beat faster; surely such destruction could only be the work of the Dust Bunny Gang. Sofa cushions were scattered across the floor. A vase had fallen on its side, spilling water.

Dying flowers made a sodden mess on the gray carpet. The fireplace was choked with ash and the partially burned carcass of a doll. Toys covered nearly every inch of the floor. Children. The only natural disaster that could rival Dr. Grime. Perhaps children weren't as deadly, but they were just as messy.

This was the fifth time in a month that he had been called in and found no archvillain but only bad housework. His name was being traded around like that of a good maid. He, Captain Housework, had been reduced to drudgery.

He, who had fought the great dust invasion of '53, would have no problem with this mundane mess. His superhuman speed would make short work of it all. But that wasn't the point. People did not call the Purple Avenger to change a tire. They called him to save their lives.

Once they had called Captain Housework for the same thing. Dr. Grime had nearly engulfed St. Louis in a giant rain of grease. All cars, trains, and planes had come to a slippery halt. Pedestrians caught in the first greasy rain had melted into puddles of sizzling goo. They had called for Captain Housework then, and been glad to have him. But that had been ten years ago.

Dr. Grime had retired. The Dust Bunny Gang had split up over contractual differences. There just weren't that many supervillains who specialized in true dirty work.

It wasn't really the mundane cleaning that bothered him. It was the repeat business. People had been calling him back; again and again to clean up after them. He'd get a house spotless, perfect, and they'd mess it up again.

It was a never-ending drudgery. Even with superpowers over dust and dirt, he was tired of it. They were taking advantage of him. But without any supervillains to fight, a superhero had to fill some need. It was in his contract that he had to be useful to mankind, just as a supervillain had to harm mankind. If all the villains needing his special powers to thwart them had retired, he had to answer the call of need. Captain Housework sighed and waved a white-gloved hand. The sofa cushions danced back in place, fluffing themselves before snuggling down. "I am a glorified maid," he said softly to the empty room.

The kitchen was the worst. Dishes were stacked nearly to the top of the windows, thick with grease and moldy food. He conjured a super-scouring wind and cleaned them with the force of a hurricane without cracking a dish.

When every room was spotless, he appeared before the woman who had summoned him. "The house is clean, madam."

"Oh, gee, thanks." She held out money.

Captain Housework stared at the offending hand. "I am a superhero, not a servant. I don't need your money." His voice was very tight, each word bitten off.

"No offense. I'm grateful."

"Be grateful and don't call me again."

"But I want you to come back after the party and clean up," she said.

"You what?"

"The maid can't come tonight at all. I thought you'd clean up after the party. The superhero hotline said you would."

"They said I would?"

She nodded. "The operator on the hotline said you would be happy to be of service. She said something about superheroes needing to be of service to mankind."

Captain Housework stared at the woman for a few heartbeats. He saw it all then, his future stretching out before him. An eternity of cleaning up after parties, repairing the damage of crayon-wielding tots and unhousebroken dogs. He saw it all in the blink of his sparkling eyes. It was intolerable, a hell on earth, but the woman was right. A superhero had to serve mankind. If all he was good for was maid service, then so be it.

The woman had been putting on red nail polish. She reached back to tighten the lid, but was unwilling to grip it with her wet nails. The bottle went spinning. Bright red liquid poured out onto the white carpet, trickled down the newly polished vanity.

"Oops," the woman said. "You'll get that, won't you? I've got to finish getting ready; the guests will be here any minute." She stood, waving her nails to dry them. She left him staring at the spreading red stain on the carpet he had just shampooed.

His tiny hands balled into fists. He stood trembling with rage, unable to utter a word. An eternity of this—it was intolerable! But what else could he do? Talk Dr. Grime out of retirement? No, the villain had made millions off his memoirs.

Memoirs of the Down and Dirty had been a bestseller. Captain Housework stared at the slowly hardening stain, and a great calmness washed over him. He had an idea.

The police found fourteen skeletons at 11 Pear Tree Lane. The bones were neatly arranged, sparkling with polish, lacquered to a perfect finish. The house had never been so clean.

THE CURSE-MAKER

I would set myself goals of magazines, or editors, to sell to. Dragon Magazine was one of those goals. They published only one fiction piece an issue, so it was a tight market. I made it with this story. It's the second appearance on paper of Sidra and her semifaithful magical sword, Leech. You'll get to meet most of her small band of mercenaries in this story. They are her family, and she theirs. I still have a soft spot for Sidra and her gang, and Leech was always a lot of fun to write.

MILON Songsmith was dying. Brown hair clung to his face in limp, sweat-soaked strands. His skin was gray-tinged, like dirty snow. Breath was a ragged choking sound, his body trembling with the effort to draw air into his lungs.

Sidra Ironfist stood looking down at her friend. Her strong, callused hands gripped the hilts of her swords until her hands ached. Sidra's solid gray eyes stared down at her friend and willed him to live. She ran a hand through long yellow hair and turned to the wizard leaning against the wall.

Gannon the Sorcerer was tall, as tall as Sidra. His hair was yellow, his eyes the fresh blue of spring skies. But his face was set in cynical lines, as if he had seen too much of the world, and it all disappointed him. Today his eyes held anger and sorrow.

"I will not let him die like this," Sidra said.

"It is a death curse, Sidra. You cannot stop it. The bard is a better friend to me than any man alive, and I am just as helpless," Gannon said.

"Can nothing stop it?" Her eyes searched his face, demanded he give her some hope.

"It is the most powerful death curse I have ever seen. It would take days for another curse-maker to remove the spell. Milon has only hours."

Sidra turned away from the sorcerer and his compassionate eyes. She would not let Milon die. He was her bard. They had ridden together for eight years. Even with a bard's safe conduct, accidents could happen. If you rode into battle, unarmed, you took your chances. But this—this was a coward's way of killing. By all laws, Milon should have been safe in the tavern. Harming a bard, save in self-defense, was punishable by death.

Someone had hated him enough to risk that. But who? And why?

Sidra Ironfist knelt by the bed. She reached out to touch Milon's forehead with one scarred finger. She could feel the heat before she touched his skin. The magical fever was eating him alive.

She whispered to him, though he could not hear her, "I will not let you die." She turned to the sorcerer. "What of the curse-maker who placed the curse?"

Gannon frowned. "What of him?"

"Could he remove the curse?"

"Well, yes, but why would he?"

Sidra smiled, tight-lipped. "I think we could find ways to persuade him."

Gannon nodded. "We might at that, but how to find him in such a short time?"

There was a knock on the door. Sidra pulled her long sword from its sheath and called, "Come in."

A woman hesitated at the doorway. Her hair was streaked with gray, and she wore the robes of a white healer. "I was told you had an injured man." She caught sight of the bard and stepped into the room past Sidra's bare steel. "That is not a wound."

Sidra sheathed her sword. "Tell her, Gannon."

He explained briefly. Outrage showed on the healer's face, then anger, a white burning anger that Sidra found comforting and frightening all at the same time. "By all the civilized laws, bards are sacred. A death curse on one such as this is an insult to all we hold dear." The healer asked, "Who has done this?"

"Unknown," Gannon said, "but we will find out."

Sidra said, "Yes, we will find out." There was something—in her voice, in the steel gray of her eyes—that was frightening.

The healer stepped away from the tall warrior woman. "You look like calm death, warrior."

"Can you keep him alive until we return?"

"I will keep him alive, but be swift. There will come a point from which no one can bring him back."

Sidra nodded. "Keep him alive, healer. He's important to me."

"That I knew when I saw your face, warrior."

Sidra looked away from the healer's wise face. She was uncomfortable that anyone could read her so easily. "Come, Gannon." She was through the door and on the stairs before Gannon had time to move. He jogged to catch up with her. "Where do we begin?"

"Malhari."

Malhari was a big, beefy man. The muscle of his mercenary days had run to softness but not to fat. He was still a formidable man. His black hair was close cropped, framing a nearly perfect roundness of face. His right arm ended abruptly a span above the wrist. A metal-studded leather sheath hid his stump. It had given the tavern its name: The One-Armed Man. His dark eyes caught them as they came down the stairs; no words were needed. He called one of the bar-lads over to pour drinks and motioned them into his office—small, neat, and orderly, the way Malhari had run campaigns years ago.

He eased his big frame into a chair and motioned them to sit. They remained standing. "What has happened to your bard, Sidra?"

"A death curse. He has only hours to live."

Malhari's eyes went wide. His fingers curved over the metal studs as another man might drum his fingers. "Why come to me?"

"Where in Selewin do you go for a death curse?"

"I go nowhere for such things. Curse-makers are unlucky, Sidra. You know that."

She sat down across from him, hands spread on her legs. Gannon remained standing like a guard at her back. Sidra said, "You did not pay for that splendid house in the hills from this small inn. You are the person in Selewin to come to for information, for a price. Tell me what I need to know, Malhari. Do it for friendship or money; I don't care which."

"If I am what you say I am, and if I had your information, how much would it be worth to you?"

Sidra's eyes narrowed, as if from pain. "Not friendship, then, but money."

"You cannot spend friendship on a cold winter's night."

"I think you would be surprised what you can do with friendship, Malhari." She did not wait for the puzzled look on his face to pass but threw a leather pouch on the desk. "Gold, Malhari, twenty-five pieces."

"And," he said.

Sidra hesitated.

"You would quibble over the life of your friend?"

Sidra pounded her fist into his desk twice—violent, painful, but it helped the anger. It kept her from drawing steel and slitting his throat. Her voice came low and soft, the whisper of steel through silk. "That is three times your usual pay."

"This is a seller's market, Sidra. Supply and demand."

"Our friendship is no more, Malhari."

"I know."

"If Milon dies because of this delay, I will kill you."

"You will try," he said.

Sidra leaned toward him, and suddenly Malhari was staring at six inches of steel. The knife caressed his throat with no pain or blood, yet. He did not try to move, though he had several secreted blades of his own. He knew better than to try.

Sidra's words came careful and neat, soft and angry. "You have grown soft, Malhari. In the old days, I could not have taken you without your at least clearing a blade of your own. I will kill you if I want to."

He said nothing but felt the blade dig into his throat as he swallowed. "You have paid a fair price. The one you seek is Bardolf Lordson. I saw one of Bardolf's lackeys talk to your bard tonight. Bardolf is powerful enough to have done the spell."

Gannon cursed. "When we worked for Duke Haydon, I detected magic on Bardolf. I thought that it was not quite enough to warrant training as an herb-witch. But a curse-maker! It suits him."

Sidra nodded. Bardolf had thought to bed a warrior. Sidra had broken his arm for the insult. Neither she nor Bardolf mentioned the incident to Duke Haydon.

"He is Duke Haydon's favorite son, bastard or not. We cannot kill him after he has cured Milon. I will not risk everything we have worked for in one act of vengeance. If Milon dies, things are different. But our true purpose is to save the bard, not to get revenge."

Gannon said, "Agreed. We save the minstrel. If the curse-maker just happens to perish," he smiled, "well, that is an added bonus."

Sidra smiled. "Even a duke's son can have an accident."

She bent close to Malhari's face. "Tell me where he is."

"You wish more information from me, Sidra? I am a businessman."

"You are a fool," Gannon said.

The blade tip bit into Malhari's neck. Blood trickled down his throat. Sidra said nothing.

The innkeeper's breath caught in his throat. "For you, Sidra. Bardolf has a house on Silk Street." He stared into her eyes and saw death. "Take the money, Sidra. I give you this information freely."

She smiled then. "No, Malhari. If it was a gift, then the bonds of friendship would constrain me. This way it is only money, and I owe you nothing."

He tried not to swallow around the point of the knife. "I don't want you to sell this information to anyone else," Sidra said.

Malhari was having trouble talking. "I give you my word, I will not."

"Your word means nothing. Gannon, if you please."

"With great pleasure." The sorcerer smiled. There was something of fearful anticipation in that smile.

Sidra stepped back from the man, quick and careful.

"Please, Sidra, I would not tell. I swear to you."

Gannon made a broad sweeping gesture, hands upraised to the ceiling, and brought his hands down in a fast clap, pointed at the man.

Where Malhari had sat there was a large black tomcat missing one front paw. It yowled once and fell silent. Sidra had never seen horror on a cat's face, but she saw it now.

Gannon said, "It is a permanent shapechange, Malhari, unless I remove it." He knelt, eye level with the cat. "It is almost a curse, but not quite."

The big cat just stared at them, yellow eyes dazed.

Sidra said, "Come, we haven't much time."

Precious minutes had passed before they stood in an alley that spilled into Silk Street. They were in a wealthy part of town. It was well known that Bardolf was the duke's favorite son, and the grand house showed it. The wealthy could afford magical guardians, things that normal steel could not touch. Sidra's long sword was such ordinary steel. The short sword was not.

Sidra unsnapped the locks on the hilt, and the short sword sprang to her hand, rising of its own accord. The sword said, "Ah, free." Without moving, it gave the impression of catlike stretching.

"I may have work for you tonight," Sidra told it.

The sword hissed, "Name me."

"You who were Blood-Letter when the world was new. You who were Wound-Maker in the hands of a king. You who were Soul-Piercer and took the life of a hero. You who were Blood-Hunger and ate your way through an army. I name thee blade mine, I name thee Leech." For every name the sword had taken, the legend had ended with the blood blade slaying its wielder.

The sword chortled, "I am Leech, Leech. I am the blood-sucker." The sword's voice dropped to a whisper. "Feed me."

Sidra pressed the naked steel against her bare forearm.

The sword felt like any steel against her flesh. Gannon assured her that, once activated, Leech gave off an aura of evil. "Feed gently, Leech, for we have much work to do."

There was always the chance that Leech would take too much and kill her. It had happened to others, great heroes. But the sword bit once into her arm. Blood poured in a sharp painful wash down her skin. The blade said, "Sacrifice made, contract assured."

Sidra ignored the wound. It would heal in a moment or two to join the dozens of shallow white scars that crisscrossed her hands and arms. She did not bother to clean the blade. All blood was absorbed cleanly. It truly did feed.

Gannon stepped close, and the sword struck at him.

Sidra held it two-handed, saying, "Behave."

"You don't frighten me, little knife," the sorcerer said.

"Not afraid," the sword whined. "No fun." The sword turned in her hands as if looking for something. "Where is bard? Bard fears Leech. Baard," the sword called, drawing the word out in a singsong, "Baard."

"Silence, Leech." Sometimes the blood blade seemed aware of everything that went on. It would spring from its sheath ready for action. At other times it acted as if it had been asleep until called. Sidra wondered what, if anything, the blood blade dreamed of. She doubted she would enjoy the answer, and she knew Leech would lie about it anyway. Blood blades were notorious liars.

She told the sword only that the bard was away. If the sword knew that Milon's life was at stake, it would demand a larger blood price.

Sidra sheathed Leech but left its locks undone in case she needed it quickly. The blade did not fight being sheathed; it was strangely content tonight. It hummed one of Milon's own tunes—Leech's favorite—"Lord Isham and the Goose Girl." There were two versions: one for the taverns and one for the prince's halls. Leech, of course, preferred the bawdy version.

She persuaded the blade to stop humming and scouted the

house. She was a flicker of shadow, gone before you could look directly at it.

She returned to Gannon. "Two doors: this one and another that leads into a small yard. Both doors are posted with warning signs. They're both warded."

It was the law in Selewin that you had to post signs for wardings. There had been too many innocent people killed.

"All windows are barred, no traps that I could see."

She asked Gannon, "What kind of warding is on the front door?"

He concentrated a moment, staring at the door, and then said, "Fire, powerful enough to kill whatever touches it."

Sidra gave a low hiss. "I thought death wards had to be marked as such?"

"By law they do."

"Can you get us past it?"

"Yes, but stay well back while I'm testing it."

Sidra knew what would happen if he failed to negate the warding. He would die, and he didn't want to risk her life as well. But Gannon had risked himself before, as had they all.

Sidra nodded, and Gannon walked alone into the street. He pressed his hands wide and moved them toward the door. Leech began to hum a drum roll. "Brrrrrm, brrrrm."

"Hush."

The sword did not stop but only hissed an accompaniment as the sorcerer touched the door. Gannon's back bowed outward, and the sword hissed a crescendo. Sidra slapped the sword's sheath, and it made a muffled sound and fell silent.

Gannon was walking toward them, cape pulled close about him. The door looked just the same to Sidra. A sorcerous ward was always invisible until you tripped it, unless you had eyes that could see magic.

The sorcerer stepped into the alley, and Sidra said, "Let me see your hands."

He hesitated only a moment, then drew them from inside his cloak. The palms were scorched and hung heavy with huge watery blisters.

Sidra drew a hissing breath. "Gannon, can you go on like that?"

He shrugged and grimaced. "There will be many sorceries I cannot do with injured hands. I can still levitate and teleport, but not much else."

"Our luck is low tonight." She touched his shoulder. "It is up to you, Gannon. I cannot ask you to go on."

"No one asked me to come."

She nodded. It was his choice, and she would not tell him to stay behind.

The door looked ordinary enough except for the sign next to it that read, "Warning. WARDINGS in place. Please ring bell." A brass bell hung from a bracket by the door, its cord swinging uneasily in the night wind.

Sidra knelt beside the door and touched the rough wood. No fire, no warding—Gannon had done his job. The lock was cheap and easily picked. All that money on a sorcerous ward, then skimping on the lock itself. Bardolf wasn't spending his money wisely.

She reached for Leech, and it leapt to her hand. Shield held close, she pushed open the door. They had just stepped into the inky blackness when Gannon said, "Someone teleports nearby."

There was no time for stealth. If they hoped to trace the teleport, they had to find the point of departure quickly. Gannon said, "This way." Against all caution, she let the wizard lead in a mad flight up the broad stairs. Two dim lanterns threw pools of shadow and light on the steps. She glimpsed her own reflection in half a dozen gilt-edged mirrors. Glass and gold were both rare and costly. Bardolf was well off indeed.

Light spilled from a room at the end of a long hallway. Dark rooms with closed doors led up to that one shining door. Sidra pushed past Gannon so she could enter the room first.

It was a bedroom. Silks and pillows were strewn over the carpet like a child's toys, used and carelessly forgotten. A huge candelabra hung from the ceiling, and it sparkled like pure gold. A sobbing woman knelt on the carpet. Her raven-black hair was thrown over her face, and she curled naked near a pile of clothing.

Gannon strode to the middle of the room and picked up a now-blank scroll. He sniffed it as if he were a hound on the scent of a fox and said, "I have it."

There was no time, and Sidra stood beside the sorcerer. As the woman glanced up, Sidra had a glimpse of a lovely pale face that was bruised and battered.

The world spun and Sidra caught her breath. They faced outward, back to back. Sidra crouched, sword and shield ready. Then she recognized the throne room of Duke Haydon. Bardolf had run home to his daddy. Someone shouted orders, and the room was suddenly full of the red and silver of Duke Haydon's guards. Sidra wondered if they would have time to explain before someone died.

It was the head of the guards, Jevik, who recognized them and called, "Hold!" He strode forward through his men and stood before Sidra. He sheathed his sword, and she did likewise. Leech complained about missing such a lovely sight.

Jevik only blinked. He had fought beside her and tasted the sword's humor before. "Why are you here like this, Sidra?"

"It is a long story, Jevik. But we give chase to an outlaw."

"What sort of outlaw?"

"One who would kill a bard."

"Did this bard give up his safe conduct?"

"He never had the chance. He was attacked in his room, alone."

Jevik waved the guards back and said, "And how did you trace this outlaw here?"

"Gannon traced a teleport."

"Come, we will talk to the duke," Jevik said.

The guards had formed a wary but respectful line to either side of the newcomers. Lord Haydon himself sat upon his throne. His beard was still as full and gray as before. He did not shave because it was court fashion to be smooth-faced. And he did not waste sorcery on looking younger than his years. He smiled a greeting at them and extended his hands.

"Sidra Ironfist, you who saved my castle and all that I own." She bowed and took his hands. He touched hands with Gannon and saw the sorcerer wince. The duke drew a sharp breath when he saw Gannon's hands. "Go with one of the guards and use my own healer."

Sidra did not like the idea of Gannon being separated from her. He looked at her a moment, smiled, and followed a guard from the room. He was right, of course. When a noble offers you hospitality, you do not refuse it.

"Now, Sidra, tell me what has brought you here so unexpectedly."

She told the story quietly, leaving out only the name of the curse-maker.

Haydon's eyes were a glittering icy blue when she finished. "It is against all civilized laws to harm a bard. How are we to hear of the great deeds of heroes if bards are not safe in battle?" He asked her then, "And do you have a name for this outlaw?"

"Yes, my lord. It is Bardolf the Curse-Maker."

He opened his mouth, then closed it. An angry flush crept up his neck. "These are grave accusations, Sidra. If you leave now and say no more of this, I will let it pass."

"It pains me to have to bring you such news, Duke Haydon, but it is the truth. I swear it."

He took a deep breath that shook with rage and perhaps a touch of apprehension. Sidra wondered if others had come before her and told tales of evil against Bardolf. If so, they had been bullied into silence. Sidra would not be bullied. She did not want to believe that Haydon would simply kill her out of hand, but if that was the case, she would not die easily.

At last the duke said, "You will persist in this lie against my son?"

"It is not a lie, my lord."

"Jevik, have my son sent to me now." The guardsman half-ran from the room.

Gannon was back with his newly healed hands before Bardolf was escorted in.

Bardolf strode in just ahead of Jevik. He was short, with the soft lines of a man who has never done physical labor.

His sensual pouting mouth was set in a confident smile. He was dressed all in brown silk worked with black pearls. When he saw Sidra and Gannon, his smile vanished. Jevik led him in front of the duke, then stepped back, leaving Sidra, Gannon, and Bardolf in a semicircle around the throne.

Bardolf greeted his father first and then very correctly turned to Sidra and Gannon. "Sidra Ironfist and Gannon the Sorcerer. How good to see you again." He stared up at his father, eyes unreadable. "Father, what is this all about?"

Haydon sat very still upon his throne and kept his face blank.

He was a noble and knew how to hide his emotions. He told his son of the accusations. Confusion, then anger crossed Bardolf's face. Sidra would almost have believed the act herself. Some people had a true talent for lying.

"Would you convict me of such a vile crime on the word of an information peddler?"

The Duke smiled. "No, Bardolf, not on that alone. I want you to take an oath for me."

"Of course, Father."

"Swear by the birds of Loth and the hounds of Verm that you did not harm Milon Songsmith."

"I have never taken such an evil oath!"

"It is only evil if you have something to fear. Swear, Bardolf, swear to it."

"If you insist."

"I do."

"I swear by the birds of . . . I swear." He stared up at his father, a sort of pleading look upon his face.

Haydon's noble mask slipped, showing pain in his eyes.

"Swear." His voice held a note of begging.

"I cannot, Father."

"If you are innocent, the oath means nothing. You are guilty, then."

"I cannot take the oath you ask. Perhaps another to Mother Gia."

Haydon looked down at the floor and drew a deep breath. He seemed suddenly older than he had a moment before. "Only the oath to Loth and Verm is binding enough for this. Will you swear?"

"No, Father."

The duke's face seemed to crumble. The tears that threatened in his eyes were chased away by anger. The same anger he had been willing to use against Sidra, to protect his child, now turned against his son. "Why, Bardolf? Have I not shared my wealth with you?"

"Yes, Father."

"Then why?" He stood and walked the few steps to stand before his son—the son who could still look him in the eye and lie, even now.

Bardolf said, "You gave me crumbs from your table, Father. I wanted my own table. My own money. My own lands."

"I have given you all that and more."

Bardolf shook his head. "They are mine until I anger you. Then you take them away as a punishment, as if they were sweets and I were a child."

"There are honest ways to make money!"

"Not enough money."

"Not enough, not enough!" Haydon raised a hand as if to strike him. Bardolf cringed, throwing up a hand. The duke stepped back. Sidra watched the man gain control of himself. It was a painful thing to see. When he spoke again, his voice was soft and controlled. "Do you know the penalty in Meltaan for killing a bard?"

"Yes."

"You will be executed, and your blood money will do you no good."

"Father, even if I cured the bard and gave back the money, my client would see me dead."

"Who, who will see you dead? Who ordered such a vile deed?"

"I cannot say. As your son, I beg that you do not ask me again."

Duke Haydon said, "No! No son of mine would do such a thing." A soundless tear trailed down his face; his voice remained firm, but he cried.

Sidra looked away.

Bardolf's face showed fear. "Father?"

Haydon turned to Sidra. "Do with him as you see fit. Let all here be witness. Bardolf Lordson is no son of mine." Tears flowed in silver streaks down Haydon's cheeks. Everyone in the room was pretending not to see. Bardolf knelt before the lord, touching the hem of Haydon's robe. A tear trailed down his face. "Father, please. If I cure the bard, I will be killed."

Duke Haydon jerked his robe free of the man and left the room. All but two guards left with him. Sidra had wanted to call after the duke, but what could she say? "Thank you, Duke Haydon, for being just and law-abiding"? The man had just signed the death warrant of his favorite son. "Thank you" did not even come close to covering that.

Bardolf stood slowly, rubbing his eyes. Sidra and Gannon moved to stand beside him. Bardolf tensed to run and found himself entangled in a spell. He could not move his arms or legs. Sidra said, "Nicely done, Gannon."

The sorcerer shrugged. "Healed hands do wonders for a person's magic."

Sidra stepped near him and asked, "Do you know what a blood blade is, Bardolf?"

The younger man's eyes flared wide, showing white. She could see the pulse in his neck jump.

Gannon hissed near his face, "Answer the question."

"Yes," he whispered.

Sidra said, "What is it?"

"An evil sword that can suck a man's soul." All the color had drained from his face.

She leaned against the cool marble throne and asked, "Have you heard the song 'Blade Quest'?"

Bardolf whispered, "Yes."

"I think Milon captured the essence of a blood blade in that song: dark, hungry, evil." Leech chuckled.

Sidra drew the sword. It gleamed in the torchlight. She said, "Leech, I want you to meet Bardolf the Curse-Maker."

The sword hissed, "Fresh blood, yumm."

Sweat beaded on Bardolf's face, but his words were brave. "You can't feed me to that thing."

"I think I can." She bent close to him, the naked blade quivering near his neck. She held it two-handed, not trusting it. She spoke low and close to his frightened eyes.

"The duke, your father, has decreed that I can do anything I want to you. Up to and including taking your soul."

"No, please."

"Gannon." Gannon unlaced Bardolf's sleeve and began to roll it upward. The skin was pale.

Leech crooned, "Blood, fresh blood, new blood."

The man struggled until sweat dripped down his face, but he could not move. Only his head was free to thrash from side to side.

"Please, please don't let it touch me."

"Tell us who hired you, agree to cure the bard, and you will live."

"I won't live. He'll kill me. Or have me killed."

"But he is not here, and I am. I'll kill you now."

Bardolf shook his head and closed his eyes. "Please, he'll kill me."

Leech hovered over the flesh and said, "Blood." Bardolf opened his eyes and watched the blade come closer to his arm. "No!" The point bit into his flesh and he screamed. Blood spurted out from a cut artery. Leech chortled in a rain of blood. Bardolf cried, "Lord Isham! Lord Isham hired me!"

Sidra didn't remove the sword but watched it lapping his blood.

"Get it away! Get it away!"

"Why would Lord Isham want Milon Songsmith dead?"

Bardolf swallowed, closing his eyes against the sight of the sword in his arm. He looked as if he might faint. When he finally spoke, his voice was as pale as his skin. "The song that Milon wrote about him. Lord Isham took insult."

Sidra asked, " 'Lord Isham and the Goose Girl'?"

"Yes. Now, please, get that thing away from me."

Sidra drew Leech back from the wound, but it did not want to come. She fought the sword two-handed as it struggled and cursed. "Not enough, not enough. Fresh blood, not enough."

The sword was quivering, fighting against her, and she could not sheath it. Gannon said, "Sidra." He bared his arm.

She said, "No."

Leech stopped shrieking and began to wheedle, "Just a little more, a taste, fresh taste."

It was a very unhealthy habit to disappoint a blood blade.

Sidra held the blade carefully and said, "Gannon, I would not ask this."

"You did not ask. Do it. I have often been curious."

She laid the blade tip against his arm, and it bit deep into muscle. The wizard winced but stared as the blade wiggled in the wound like a nursing calf.

Sidra pulled Leech free of the wound, and the sword said, "Ah, good, yumm." Gannon ignored the sword and stared curiously at his wound as the edges knit together. Soon there was nothing but a whitish scar.

She sheathed the short sword and turned to Bardolf. "Are you willing to cure the bard now?"

Bardolf nodded weakly. "Anything you want. Just keep that sword away from me."

Leech chuckled.

Gannon stood on one side of him and Sidra on the other. Then Gannon released the spell hold, and Bardolf nearly fell. With Gannon steadying him against the dizziness, they teleported to the inn.

The three appeared in front of Milon's bed. His skin was gray, his eyes sunken and black-smudged. If he was breathing at all, Sidra could not tell it. The healer gasped.

Sidra's heart felt like lead in her chest. "Are we too late?"

The healer shook her head. "There is time."

Sidra pushed Bardolf forward against the bed. "Cure him or the blood blade will taste your soul."

Bardolf half-fell to his knees beside the bed. He laid a hand on Milon's forehead and over his heart. The curse-maker's face went blank. It was the tranquility Sidra was accustomed to seeing on a healer's face. She found it strange for a curse-doer.

Milon took a deep, shuddering breath, then his chest rose and fell. Bardolf stood up, looking relieved. Gannon forced him to stand back from the bed.

The healer touched the bard's forehead. "The fever has broken; he sleeps. With a few days' rest, he will be well."

Sidra asked Gannon, "Can you take that one to the jail?"

"I think I can manage." Gannon placed a hand on Bardolf's forehead and spoke one strange syllable. The curse-maker's eyes went blank, and he followed obediently as Gannon moved to the door. He turned back and asked, "What of our feline friend?"

"Do as you think best."

Gannon smiled, a broad cheerful smile. "I will attend to it with pleasure." He left with Bardolf following behind.

Sidra knelt by the bed and smoothed the sweat-darkened hair from Milon's forehead. The healer moved a short distance away, giving them privacy. Sidra whispered to the bard, "I did not let you die."

Leech was singing softly in its sheath. The words came up faint and hollow. "Lord Isham went a-riding, a-riding, a-riding. On his great bay stallion he went riding over his land. First he met a milkmaid, a milkmaid . . ."

Sidra asked, "Leech, have you ever tasted the blood of a province lord?"

The sword stopped in midsong and whispered, "Never, but I hear they're quite tasty."

"We will be visiting Lord Isham."

Leech asked, "When?"

"Very soon." Sidra fought the urge to smile. One should never smile when contemplating another's death. The sword giggled, and Sidra found herself laughing with it. She saw the healer make the sign against evil. Sidra sighed. Evil had many faces. Some were just more obvious than others. She brushed her lips on Milon's forehead and whispered, "Very soon." She made it sound like a promise.

GEESE

This is the only story that I ever wrote through pure inspiration. My first apartment in the St. Louis area was on the edge of a lake. It had Canada geese on it. I took the trash out one night with the sunset spread across the sky and the geese settling down for the night. I stood there in the coming darkness, watching the geese, and the first line of the story came into my head. By the time I got back inside to the computer, the first paragraph was in my head. All I had to do was sit down and type fast enough to write the story. It was amazing, this rush of ideas, character, a whole story from beginning to end. I have never had this happen again. I've had moments of inspiration, but never so complete.

THE geese lay in the long shadows of afternoon, gray lumps, with rustling feathers and flapping wings. I dozed, long neck tucked backward, black bill buried in my feathers. I watched the other geese through black button eyes. Soon I closed my eyes and gave myself to the peace of the flock.

Perhaps I had been a goose for too long. Perhaps it was time to become human again, but the desire was hazy. I was no longer sure why I wanted to be human. I could not quite remember the reason I had hidden myself among the geese.

I realized I was losing my human identity, but it had borne so much pain. This was better. There was food, the freedom of wings, the open sky, and the comfort of the flock. I did not remember humanity as being so simple, so peaceful, so restful. I had lost the desire to be human, and that should have frightened me. That it did not was a bad sign.

Beside me, head nearly lost in the feathers of his back, was Gyldan. That was not his real name, but a human name I had given him. One of the last things to leave was this need to name things. It was a very human trait.

In my own mind I still called myself Alatir. As long as you had a name, you were still human.

Gyldan was a young gander, but he had been with me for two seasons. He was a handsome bird; jet black, cloud gray, buff white, all markings distinct and artificial in their perfectness.

He had chosen me as his mate, but I offered only companionship. I was still human enough not to wish to bear goslings.

He had stayed with me, though there were other females who would have taken him. We had spent long summers on empty lakes, claiming our territory but never going to nest. If I did that, I would never be human again. The thought came that I wanted to be human, someday, but not today.

The children came then, peasant children with their dark hair and eyes. They came from a prosperous household, for they fed us scraps of vegetables and bread. They had almost tamed us, almost.

The oldest was a girl of about fourteen, her black hair in two thick braids around a slender face. The next oldest was a boy of perhaps eleven. The rest were all sizes, with laughing brown eyes and gentle hands.

I had flown over their father's mill many times. I had watched them help their mother in the garden and play tag in front of their house.

They came earlier by human standards, for the days were growing autumn short. By geese standards, the sun was in the same place.

The bread was day-old, crisp, and good. I remembered other

bread, formed in curves and sculpted for feast days. Gyldan did not press me to share my bits of bread. He sensed my mood and knew my temper was short. There was a sound of horses riding along the road. All of us craned our necks to hear, to see danger. The oldest girl noticed it and asked us, "What's wrong?" as if we could speak.

We thundered skyward as the horses rode out beside the lake. The children were still stunned by our beating wings, afraid. The girl recovered and screamed, "Run, hide!"

The children scattered like wild things. The girl was cut off by one prancing horse, and the oldest boy would not leave her.

I circled back, Gyldan beside me. I settled at a safe distance and listened. It took magic for me to hear them, and I found the knowledge to stretch my senses came easily.

The men wore the livery of the Baron Madawc, a white bull on a background of silver, a sword through its heart. I knew Lord Madawc well. Human memories tore through my mind. Blood running between my mother's dead eyes. My father's chest ripped open, so much blood. I had been but newly made a master of sorcery when Madawc slaughtered my family and took over our lands. Five years ago, I had been a child, though a powerful one. Lord Madawc had mocked me when I challenged him to a duel. He had let me live and put a geas on me, a geas to kill him, thinking that it would surely mean my death. Having a geas-ridden child seek the death of a powerful sorcerer amused him.

So I had hidden myself in a form that the geas would not touch. My human mind roared through my animal body. I remembered. I remembered.

One soldier had placed the girl across his saddlebow. "Our lord will be pleased with this." He slapped her buttocks. She was crying.

The boy said, "Let go of my sister." Another soldier swooped down on him and carried him, struggling, to the front of his saddle. He said, "There are those at court that like a bit of little boy. You can come along if you like."

I could not let this happen, and I could not stop it as a bird. I hid myself in some reeds. Gyldan felt the magic begin. He hissed but did not leave me.

Human form was cold. I found myself crying. Crying, for the family I had forgotten. I huddled in the reeds, in the mud. My skin was pale; my black hair, waist-long. I know my eyes were blue, the pale color of spring skies.

I could pass for a lord's bastard daughter just as easily as a true aristocrat. Peasant blood was peasant blood, to some.

Gyldan touched my shivering skin with his firm beak. He croaked softly at me, and I touched his feathered head. "If I live, I will be back to say a proper good-bye, I promise."

I walked up the sloping bank toward the soldiers. He followed me on his thick, webbed feet, but he stopped before I reached the men. He launched skyward in a thrust of feathers and fear.

The soldiers saw only a naked woman walking toward them. I had grown older and was no longer a girl, but a woman. I doubted Madawc would recognize me. But because of his own magic, I was compelled to find him and slay him, if I could. Fear tightened my stomach, yet there was no time to be afraid. I had to help the children now.

"Let the children go."

"Oh yes, my lady . . ." They laughed.

I gestured, a bare pass of wrist and hand. The children were set upon the ground, and the soldiers said one to another, "Chil-

dren—who needs children? We will take a woman to our lord."
Freeing the children was their own idea now.

The children were frightened and huddled near me. I whispered to them, "Go home; do not be afraid. I may come there seeking shelter later."

The girl dropped a clumsy curtsey and said, "You are most welcome, my lady. Be careful."

I nodded, and one of the soldiers gave me his cloak as a damp autumn drizzle began to fall. It was his idea to let me ride in front of him, covered, a special gift for Lord Madawc. He was their captain, and the only one I had to control. I had been lucky that none of these soldiers was a spell caster. It would never have gone so smoothly with magic to fight.

It was miles to the castle, and by the time we arrived, the captain believed it was his idea. No magic was required to maintain my safety.

The castle gate was brilliant with torchlight. Our group was one of dozens. Many had brought children, both male and female. One little boy was perhaps six, frightfully young. He clung, crying, to the soldier that held him. The soldier looked decidedly uncomfortable. I marked him for later use, though if I needed help, it would probably be too late. Too late meant dead. I took a deep calming breath. If I panicked, I would be useless.

Somehow I would kill Madawc. Even if it meant my own death.

We were escorted through the main hall, where there was a party going on. I heard one of the soldiers murmur, "Pigs, all of them."

The captain whispered, "Don't let Madawc hear such talk. He'll skin you alive for entertainment."

Another said, "I'm leaving this foul place when my contract is up." There was a lot of head nodding.

Five years without my father to stand guard against him had not made Madawc popular.

The place smelled of spilled wine, vomit, and sex. Drunken voices, both male and female, called out bawdy suggestions. There was a young man of about fifteen, chained to the center of the room. A line of silk-clad ladies were taking turns with him.

I turned away, and the captain jerked me roughly forward. Fear knotted in my belly, and for the first time I felt naked under the cloak. I had magic, but so did Madawc, and he had beaten me before.

The little boy was given over to an older man. The soldier looked near tears himself as he pried the boy's fingers from him. The old noble offered the child sweetmeats and held him softly. He would gain the child's confidence first. I recognized Lord Trahern. He had been thrown out of my father's court for being a child-lover.

The captain led me by the arm through the crowd. Hands pulled at the cape, saying, "A beauty, did you taste her before you brought her here?"

He ignored them and went to the front table. Madawc had not changed, except to grow thicker around the middle. His black hair was dark as any peasant's, but his eyes were the cool blue of autumn skies.

Anger flashed through me warm and whole. Hatred. Memories. My mother's cries for help. Her screams, "Run, Alatir, run!" But there had been no place to run. I needed no geas to want him dead.

The captain went down on one knee and pulled me down as

well. We waited, kneeling, faces hidden from the man. Would Madawc recognize me? I was afraid and didn't try to hide it. I was just another victim, a bit of meat. I was supposed to be afraid. Finally, Madawc said, "Yes, what is it?"

"A special treat for you, Lord Madawc." He pulled my head back, so my face showed.

Madawc said, "Ah, blue eyes. Did you find another one of my own bastards for me?"

"I believe so, my lord."

He smiled and traced my face with his hand. "Lovely. You have done well, Captain. I am pleased." He held out a ruby and gold ring. The captain bowed and took it. I was left kneeling.

Madawc pulled aside the cloak. It fell to the floor. I hunched forward, using my long hair as a screen. Fear thudded in my throat. He laughed. "Naked, all pleasures bare, as I like my women. And modest, I like that as well." He touched my breast, and I jerked away with a small gasp. I would not let him touch me. I would destroy myself first. No, the geas would not allow that. I had to try to kill him. But I could not perform death-magic here and now. He was not drunk; he would break my concentration long before I completed a spell. I could damage him but not kill him. I needed to get away from him; I needed time.

It came to me then what I needed to do. I had been too long away from the nobility; I had forgotten how silly even the best of them could be. Even Madawc, tainted as he was, would not refuse challenge, especially from a woman he had defeated before.

I draped the cloak around my shoulders and said, "I am Alatir Geasbreaker, as you named me. Daughter of Garrand and Allsun." I stood, cloaked in deepest blue and the mane of black hair. I was ivory skin and eyes of sapphire. I felt the magic of true challenge flow through me, born of anger, righteousness, and five years of magic almost untapped. Fear was gone in a rush of magic.

Madawc knocked his chair backward to scrape along the marble floor. "What trick is this?"

"No trick, Madawc of Roaghnailt. I am Alatir Geasbreaker, and I challenge you to battle."

If it had been another who was trained in sword as well as magic, it would have been a foolish challenge. I knew nothing of weapons, but neither did Madawc. He was of the belief that magic was always enough. Now we would see.

A hush ran through the throng. They turned eyes to their honored lord. He could not refuse, for to do so, even in front of this silken rabble, would be to lose all honor. A lord without honor did not get invited to the king's courts. A lord without honor became the butt of songs by bards known for their comedic talents and biting wit.

I was remembering what it meant to be human and a Meltaanian noble.

"I accept challenge, of course, but you cannot be Alatir, daughter of Garrand. I put a geas on you that would have forced you to kill me years ago."

"It was your spell. Test it; see if it still holds me."

I felt a tentative wash of magic, a mere butterfly's wing of power. "You bear my spell, but how have you hidden from it?"

"Shapeshifting, Madawc. Even as a child, shapeshifting was my best spell, and animal cannot answer geas."

"What brought you back?"

"You called me. You might say, I am what you made me: someone who hates you, someone who has to kill you, at risk of her own life if necessary. I am under geas to see you stretched dead before me."

His jaw tightened; the shock and fear were gone. "I defeated you once, easily. I will do so again. This time I will not leave you alive."

"This time," I said, "you will not have the chance."

Meltaanians love spectacle more than anything. In short order, torches were set in a circle outside the castle grounds. You never let sorcerers fight within walls. The walls had a tendency to tumble down. Even that thought did not frighten me. The magic of challenge still held me safe. Fear was a muted thing, for now.

One of the ladies had found me a dress to wear. It was blue silk and matched my eyes. My hair was braided down my back and threaded with silver ribbons. Silver was echoed at bodice, sleeve, and dress front. It was a very simple dress by Meltaanian standards, but the people needed to be impressed, needed to remember what was about to happen.

Madawc faced me in black, run through with silver threads. He glittered like ice in the sun when he moved. He spoke to me as we stood, waiting. "You are Alatir."

"Did you doubt it?"

"I thought you long dead."

"You thought wrongly."

He gave a half bow, a strange self-mocking smile on his face. "I think, dear lady, that you are some lovely phantom come to haunt me."

"I am flesh and blood and magic."

Magic grew in the circle of torches. Magic ran along my skin and tugged at my hair, like an unseen wind. I called sorcery to me but did not want to commit its shape to any one spell. I wanted to know the measure of the man I fought. In my terror, he had been twelve feet tall, an endless fountain of magic. Now he was a man, and I was no longer a child.

Fire exploded around me, orange death. The air was choking, close, heat. The fire died, and I stood safe behind a shield. Lightning flared from his hands. The bolts struck my shield and shattered in an eye-blinding display of light.

I faded inside my shield, willing myself into another shape. I was small, thin, hidden in the grass. A green adder hidden in the uncertain torchlight.

I could feel the vibration as he moved over the earth, but I could hear his puzzled voice asking, "Where is she?"

I felt his magic wash over me, searching, but I was a snake and had no real business with magic. He did not come too near the empty folds of the silk dress, but I slipped out a sleeve hole and began moving cautiously, thin and hidden, toward him.

I was a small snake and could not bite through his boots. As he passed me, put his back to me, I grew. I was an older snake, thick as a man's wrist. There were gasps from the audience. He turned, puzzled, and I struck. He screamed as my fangs tore his flesh, poison pumping home. His struggles flung me away to lie half stunned in the grass.

I began to shapeshift, slowly. He was yelling, "Get me a healer, now!"

A soldier, the one who had brought in the littlest boy, said, "You cannot be healed until the fight is over, Lord Madawc. That is the rule."

"But I've been poisoned!"

The mercenaries whom he had bullied and made into whore-mongers formed a wall of steel. "You will not leave the circle until the fight is done. Isn't that right, Captain?"

The captain, who had brought me in, didn't have a problem with Madawc, but he licked his lips and agreed. He knew better than to go against all his men. "You must wait for healing, Lord Madawc."

"I will see you all flogged for this, no, hanged!"

It was the wrong thing to say. The soldiers' faces went grim, dispassionate. They waited for someone to die.

I stood naked and human once more. All I had to do was stay alive until the poison took effect, and that wouldn't be long.

Madawc turned on me with a snarl. "I'll take you with me, bitch!"

He formed a soul-beast, made of magic, hatred, and fear. It was a great wolf that glowed red in the night.

I had never made a soul-beast before. It took great strength, and if it was destroyed, the spell caster died with it. I formed mine of power, vengeance, the memory of five years of unused magic, the quiet stillness of water, and the freedom of skies. It flowed blue and burst into being a moment before the wolf leapt. Mine was a thing of feathers and claws, no known beast.

I felt the power as never before. I rode the winds of it. It lifted me in a dance of death and joy. I was fanged claws and whirling feathers of gold and sapphire. I bit the wolf and raked his sides with claws. I bled under his teeth and staggered under the weight of his body.

The wolf began to fade. As it lost substance, I gained its magic. I drew its power like a hole in Madawc's soul; I drained him until I fell to my knees, power drunk, stunned.

The soul-beasts were gone. It was effort to turn my head and see Madawc on the grass. His body convulsed, and bloody foam ran from his lips. The green adder is a deadly thing.

I was stronger than five years ago, but all those years had

been without training. Madawc might have killed me without the aid of poison. Then again, he might not.

The geas was gone, and I felt pure and empty of it. I had expected triumph; instead I felt relief, and a great empty sadness.

A voice declared the match over and Alatir the winner. There were hands, a cloak thrown over my nakedness, the warmth of healing magic, and a warm draught of tea.

Dawn light found me rested, healed, and in the bedchamber that had once belonged to Madawc. By Meltaanian law it was all mine now, both my father's lands which had been stolen and Madawc's. Madawc had never bothered to appoint an heir from his many bastards. No royalty would marry him.

There was a knock on the door, and the captain entered with the mercenary who had brought the little boy in. They both knelt, and the captain said, "My lady, what would you like for us to do? We have weeks left on our contract, and our contract is now yours, if you want it."

I asked, "Have you a guard outside my door?"

The younger man spoke. "Yes, my lady, some of the dead lord's friends are less than pleased at the duel's outcome."

I smiled at that. "Is Lord Trahern still within these walls?"

"No, my lady."

I ignored the captain and asked the other man, "What is your name?"

"I am Kendrick Swordmated."

"You are now Captain Kendrick."

The other captain sputtered, but I interrupted him. "I want you gone from here and never come back. Take the four men who rode with you on search yesterday."

There must have been something in my eyes that told him not to argue. He gave a stiff bow and left the room.

"Now, Captain, how long ago did Trahern leave?"

"Only moments, my lady."

"Then take what men you think you need and find him. Relieve him of the peasant boy he got last night. The boy is to be healed, then taken back to his home. A gift of gold will be given to his family."

He smiled. "Yes, my lady."

"And free all the others. They are my people now, and no one mistreats my people. No one."

He bowed, grinning. "All will be done as you ask, Alatir Lord-Slayer."

"Lord-Slayer?" I questioned.

"Yes, my lady, from last night."

"Go then, Kendrick." I stopped him just before he left. "I must attend some business and will be away perhaps until tomorrow. But I will return and expect everything to be done as I asked."

"I will inform the castle staff of your absence and will do as you ask." He bowed and left the room.

I stood at the open window and let the autumn wind shiver over my skin. I changed into a familiar form and took to the sky on gray wings.

I settled on the lake's dark waters and looked for Gyldan. I could not remain with the flock now. I remembered too much, but I had promised him a good-bye.

He called to me from shore, his voice different than any others. I paddled over to him and hopped up on the grass. Regardless of what shape I wore, I loved him. We caressed, touching necks and bills. How could I leave him behind? And how could I take him with me?

He stepped back from me, and I saw magic shimmer over

him like silver rain. The flock awoke with cries of alarm and took to the safety of the sky. I watched him change, slowly, but his magic was strong and sure.

He lay, a naked man, pale, white hair like moonlight. Eyes sparkled black so they showed no pupil. He blinked up at me with wide uncertain eyes. His voice was deep and song-filled, full of rushing wind and the freedom of wings. "I saw how you changed."

I was human beside him, crying.

He ran hands down the length of his new body. "I could not follow you as a bird, but as a man . . ."

I knelt and kissed his forehead. "You are not a man."

He gripped my hand. "I am your mate. I will follow you, whatever form you take."

We held each other as the sun rose and knew each other as a woman knows a man. Afterward he lay panting beside me with innocent eyes. How much he had to learn. I could take the memory of my magic, of his magic, away. I could leave him as I found him. I ran a fingertip down the sweat-soaked length of his body. He shivered. "Your name is Gyldan, and I am Alatir."

He tried the names on his human tongue, "Gyldan, Alatir. Are they nice names?"

"Yes, I think so." I stood. "Come, we can take shelter at the mill for today. They will give us clothing and food."

He nodded, and I helped him stand on his uncertain legs. I led him by the hand along the path that the children took to feed the geese. We shivered in the dim autumn sunlight. It was colder without feathers.

HOUSE OF WIZARDS

This is another story about domestic skills being more important than magic. I have no talent for organizing a household. None. Over the years I've come to realize that being able to cook, clean, and make order from chaos is a skill of the highest order. It is a different way of looking at the world, almost a polar opposite to the absent-minded artist thing I've got going. I wouldn't trade who and what I am, but sometimes I get glimpses into that other way of thinking, of being, and I think, wouldn't it be nice. But I am definitely one of the wizards making a mess, and more work for Rudelle.

R UDELLE was a practical woman. The fact that she had married a wizard did not change that, though marrying Trevelyn Herb-mage was the most impractical thing she had ever done.

Her husband was tall, as were most Astranthians. His eyes were the color of a Red-Breast's eggs. His hair was the yellow of early summer corn silk.

Rudelle knew she herself was not a great beauty. Her hair fell thick and wavy to her waist, was only the color of autumn-browned leaves. She wore it in a long braid, piled like a crown atop her head. Her eyes were plain brown, like polished oak. She was not tall, though she did possess ample curves, of which many men were fond. She was a good cook and tidy, laughed often and well, but had a sharp tongue. Her brothers learned early that she was not to be trifled with.

She had no idea why the tall, blond stranger had asked for her hand. And she found it a sense of wonder that his eyes shone with love when he looked upon her.

She knew she would be the only non-magic in the house full of wizards. Trevelyn was the eldest and would inherit the family estate. He tended the family magic shop already, freeing his parents so they could further their magical research.

So Rudelle and her husband would live with his parents, two sisters, and a brother. All were spell casters.

Rudelle would cook and clean and help tend the shop. She would raise fat children and fend for herself in a house of magic.

Her brothers had thought her mad to travel across the sea to Astrantha. Calthu was a land where magic was rare and often persecuted. What did she, a Calthuian farmer's daughter, know about Astrantha—land of a thousand magics? Nothing.

But from the moment their boat docked Rudelle had loved the city of Almirth, capital city of Astrantha. It was noise, the frantic calls of multicolored parrots being unloaded from a boat, the high neighing of unicorn-horses with their spiraling horns, the soft mumblings of spells as sorcerers lifted cargo boxes with word and gesture, and the hum of any busy port.

Trevelyn said, "Look up, there."

She followed where he pointed but at first saw nothing against the summer blue sky. Then something, something silver, flashed in the sun. The silver point whirled and raced itself and was joined by a flashing bit of gold. A third point of light, like a ruby winking in the sun, joined the mad flight.

"What is it?" she asked.

"Dragons," he replied, "playing tag."

Rudelle stood and stared until the point of light became a rainbow of scattered stars, a dozen colored fireflies, high in the vault of the day.

Trevelyn touched her shoulder gently. She turned, startled, and winced. Her neck was stiff from looking up.

"My family is expecting us."

"Oh, I'm sorry."

He hugged her. "Don't be sorry. I love the way you enjoy such ordinary things."

She blushed. "I am a country bumpkin."

"No, never. Most of these people would be lost without their magic. They couldn't cook, or do business, or even marry without magic. They would be just as amazed at ordinary things in your world."

Rudelle shook her head. "If you say so, husband."

He kissed her forehead. "I say so."

As they walked arm in arm through the bustling crowd, he warned her of his parents. "They liked the idea of having children, but raising us didn't interest them much. Their primary interest is the study of magic, not family."

She frowned.

He squeezed her hand and smiled. "That is one reason I did not wish to marry another wizard. I wanted a wife, and I wanted to be a real father."

She smiled, then, and felt warm and whole in the shadow of his eyes.

The house was on a quiet street with large, fenced yards and tall, stately houses. There was a woman walking very fast from the house. Her shoes *clump-clumped* on the stone walkway. She nearly ran into them in her haste to get through the gate. She gasped, made a vague curtsey, and said, "I resign my position. You can't cook in a kitchen that explodes," and she was gone, half-running down the quiet street.

Rudelle looked at her husband.

"That was the maid," he said, as if that explained everything.

Rudelle was about to ask for a more detailed explanation when the world swam for a dizzying moment and they were no longer in the yard.

Rudelle grasped his arm in a panicked grasp. "Trevelyn, what's happening?"

"It's all right, Rudelle. Mother teleported us to her study. No harm done."

Rudelle wasn't sure she agreed. Her stomach was twisting, and she was forced to breathe deeply of the stale unpleasant air. Rudelle hoped she would not embarrass herself by throwing up all over her new mother-in-law.

A tall, blond woman stood in a room. She could have been Trevelyn's younger sister, but Rudelle had been warned that sorcerers lived a very long time and aged accordingly. She was still grateful that Trevelyn was a mere herb-witch and herb-healer, and thus would age normally.

The woman was beautiful, like a princess. But her yellow-gold hair was straggling from a loose braid, and her blue gown, which matched her eyes perfectly, was stained with ink in a large smear from bodice to midknee.

The woman smiled; it was Trevelyn's smile. "Welcome, wife of my eldest son." She closed her eyes a moment and yelled, "Gaynor, your son is home! Where is that man?"

Her voice seemed to echo in an unnatural way. Rudelle glanced at Trevelyn.

He said, "The only way to communicate from Mother's study is by magic."

Rudelle turned in a circle, searching for the door. There were only rough-hewn stone walls. "There's no door."

"No. In case one of Mother's spells goes awry, the house above us is protected."

Rudelle stood in the middle of the room, trying to keep her face blank. A thick, gray coating of dust touched everything. Spider webs stretched across the room like garlands strung for a party. Broken bits of crockery lay on the floor. Ancient bits of food had dried to their surface.

His mother vanished to find his father. Trevelyn whispered to her, "Mother never allows a maid to touch this room."

"Why not?"

"It is her work room."

"She works in this?"

He grinned. "She never allows anyone to clean this room."

"We shall have to see about that. It's filthy."

His mother reappeared accompanied by a slightly older replica of Trevelyn.

Trevelyn said, "May I introduce my mother, Breandan Spell-weaver, and my father, Gaynor the Researcher. And to you, my parents, may I introduce my wife, Rudelle the Quick-fingered."

Breandan asked, "May one ask how you came to have such a name?"

"I am quick with needle and thread."

"Oh, I suppose if you have no sorcery that sewing is a useful talent."

His father interrupted, "You are not a sorcerer, for you do not shine." He squinted at her. "She does not shine at all, Breandan."

"She is a healer, Gaynor. Healers do not shine until they perform their magic."

He nodded. "Yes, a healer. We've never had one of those in the family."

Trevelyn stopped them. "Rudelle is not a healer."

"Then what is she?" his mother asked.

"A woman and my wife."

Neither parent understood, then his mother said, over slowly, "You . . . mean . . . she . . . has . . . no . . . magic?"

"Correct."

She flopped down into a dust-covered chair. "You married a non-magic, a non-person? She can't even vote."

"She can vote because she is married to me."

"But if she wasn't your wife, she would be a non-person. A peasant."

"Mother, please remember, she is my wife, and I love her."

His father added, "Son, why, why did you do this?"

Trevelyn took Rudelle's hand and drew her aside. "This could take some time, my beloved. Why don't you go out in the garden for a time?"

"No, I will stand beside you."

"It will be an argument. An argument with my parents means magic. I would rather have you settled in a few days before being turned into a frog."

Rudelle's eyes widened. "They could really do that?"

"My parents? Without a word or a gesture. Most sorcerers have to at least say a spell, to help their concentration, but not my parents."

Rudelle swallowed. "I'll remember that, and go wait in the garden."

She paused before a blank wall and asked, "How do I get there?"

He kissed her then, hard and full on the lips. "Enjoy the garden. Mother, if you please, teleport her gently into our garden."

His mother looked unhappy but waved her hand and the world vanished for a moment.

Rudelle appeared in the garden. Two teleports so close together were too much for her stomach. She vomited into the grass. At least she hadn't thrown up in front of anyone, but she decided then and there that she did not care for teleportation.

The garden was a contrast to the house. Neat, trimmed fruit trees formed a small orchard in the west. An herb garden formed an intricate green-leafed knot around a small garden. Flower beds were isolated and planted to be viewed from every side: carnations in pink and scarlet, delphiniums in shades of royal blue, and brown speckles over all, the pure white of crystal stars on their dainty nodding stems.

A vegetable patch opened behind a screen of hedges. Never had Rudelle seen such perfect red tomatoes, crooknecks so large and glossy yellow that they did not seem real. Bees hummed among the bean blossoms. The bean plants were rainbows of bean pods; purple, spotted and streaked, bright yellow and pale pink. Two short rows and every color Rudelle had ever heard of, and some she had not. No one grew them like this, for the eye's beauty more than the harvest.

Then Rudelle came to the rose garden. She stopped and simply stared. There was nothing else to be done. The reds were an eye-searing scarlet, pinks from the palest dawn's blush to deep coral, yellows the color of goldfinches and buttercups, and whites like crystal shining in the sun. Then she came to one of pale lavender. Another was orange like the rare fruit itself. The scent on the afternoon breeze was almost intoxicating. Then the sound of humming came to her ears. For a moment she thought the roses were singing, then she spied a young girl kneeling among the bushes.

Long yellow hair blew free in the wind. The white and silver of a party gown was bunched underneath her knees. She was working with a small hand trowel in the soil underneath a yellow rose.

Rudelle cleared her throat quietly. The humming stopped abruptly, and the girl turned, flinging her hair from her eyes. There was a smudge of fresh dirt on one cheek. Her eyes were the startled blue of an autumn sky.

They stared at each other a moment, then Rudelle said, "I am Trevelyn's new wife, Rudelle."

The girl smiled. "I am Ilis, his youngest sister." Ilis stood, bunching the silk of her dress in muddy hands.

Rudelle asked, "Do you always garden in a party dress?"

The girl smiled down at the ruined cloth. "Well, sorcery can fix it instantly, so it's not ruined. It is the last clean dress I have. Mother and Father have both been terribly busy with their research as of late."

"Trevelyn tells me you're an earth-witch."

"Yes."

"And you made this garden."

"Helped it." Ilis stroked a rose bud, and it opened instantly, bursting with color and scattering scent both rich and welcoming.

"That rose, it opened when you touched it."

"Of course, it did. I am an earth-witch, and this is my special bit of ground." Ilis looked at her new sister-in-law critically for a moment. Then she laughed, "You aren't magic, are you?"

"No."

"Oh, Mother must have had a fit."

"Something like that, yes."

"Where are you from?"

"Calthu."

"Oh, no. No magic. You've never seen it, have you?"

"Not really."

The girl laughed and grabbed Rudelle's hand. "Come. I'll show you some real magic."

Rudelle had to laugh. A feeling of such warmth, health, wholeness came through the girl's touch.

She let her pull her along the grass paths until they came to the center of the rose garden. There they stopped, still hand in hand.

There was a white painted arbor with a bench underneath. A rose climbed and fell and curved over the wood until it was like a small house. The roses were the size of cabbages, white like frost, the lip of each petal kissed with the palest pink, and outlined and ribbed with silver that sparkled metallic in the sun.

The girl walked forward, leaving Rudelle to gawk. Ilis touched the bending flower, larger than her own face. The flower nodded in response, moving all on its own. It rubbed against her cheek, like a cat.

"It moved."

"This," the girl said, "is real earth-magic. Not just every earth-witch can animate a growing thing. It took me three years to get flower color and size, and only the last month has she lived for me."

"She?"

"Yes. Blinny." Ilis held out her hand. "Come. She'll like you."

Rudelle approached slowly, noticing now how the flower heads wavered independent of the wind. The ruffling of petals was a soft, sibilant sound. A half-opened rose nodded over her and touched pink-tinged lips to her face.

"Oh," Rudelle said.

A lightning bolt struck near Rudelle. She screamed and Ilis dragged her to the ground.

Ilis tried to hide Rudelle underneath her, as a sound of explosions and lightning cracks got closer.

Rudelle struggled to raise her head and asked, "What is happening?"

"Elva and Ailin are having a quarrel."

"What . . ."

There was a roaring whine overhead; Ilis dragged Rudelle to her feet and screamed, "Run!"

They ran, Ilis leading them toward dubious safety, as fire rained down from the sky. They huddled at the base of a small oak tree. Now Rudelle could see the combatants.

A young woman of about seventeen was shooting balls of greenish flame toward a boy of about ten. The green flame splattered harmlessly against nothing that Rudelle could see, as if there were an invisible shield around the child. The boy was flushed and sweating; the girl calm and unstained. She waved aside his attacks with a careless hand. Then, laughing, she vanished.

Ilis let out a sigh and slumped against the tree trunk.

"Where did the woman go?" Rudelle asked.

"Elva? She teleported. She'll stay gone until Ailin cools down."

"You can't teleport, though?"

"No."

"How do you hide from your brother when he's angry?"

"I stay out of his way as best I can."

The little boy was furious. His pale face was flushed, and his hands balled into fists at his side. Rudelle could see him trembling with rage.

There was no sound in the garden but the boy's labored breathing. Then the climbing rose moved; a mere whisper of silken petals, but it was enough. Ailin pointed one small fist at the bush and began to chant.

Ilis cried, "No, Ailin, no, please!"

Rudelle was uncertain what was happening, then fire like a furnace blast swallowed the climbing rose. Half the bush melted like hot wax.

Ilis screamed, wordlessly, and hid her face in her hands.

Rudelle was numbed at the careless cruelty of it. She wondered, briefly, if she had drawn attention to herself, if the boy would have melted her. Then she stood and strode toward the child.

Ilis called, "Rudelle, don't!"

Ailin turned, still angry.

Ilis called, "Ailin, this is Trevelyn's new wife, your sister-in-law. She doesn't mean any harm. Don't hurt her." Ilis got to her feet, uncertain what to do.

Rudelle wasn't certain either, but one thing she knew, no ten-year-old boy was going to bully her. And no one had the right to destroy such harmless beauty.

Ailin said, "I can blast you, just like I did that stupid rose."

Rudelle kept moving.

"I can change you into a toad. I bet Trevelyn wouldn't like you so much then."

Rudelle ignored the threats and kept coming. She was furious and let the anger show on her face.

Uncertainty showed in his eyes. "I'll do it! I'll change you!"

His hands raised, and the first word of an invocation trickled from his mouth. Rudelle hit him hard, closed fist, against the jaw. He slid to the ground, boneless as a sack of wheat.

Ilis crept closer, a look of wonder on her face. "Is he dead?"

"No, just unconscious."

Ilis knelt beside the fallen sorcerer and looked up at Rudelle, her eyes shining.

"But didn't you know he could have killed you?"

Rudelle shook her head. "I am the middle child of seven, all boys except for me. I am not about to start letting little boys bully me, magic powers or not. Once you let them think they have the upper hand, they do. And he doesn't have it with me."

Elva reappeared. Ilis introduced them. Elva said, "He'll kill you when he wakes up. No one insults Ailin like that."

"You speak of him as if he were a grown man; he is not. He is a little boy, and little boys respect and need discipline."

"Ailin is a sorcerer."

"And a little boy."

Elva shrugged. "Have it your way, farmer's daughter."

Trevelyn walked through the destruction, calling for Rudelle. He hugged her when he found her. "I was worried when I saw the signs of battle."

Ilis said, "Did you see what Rudelle did?"

"No."

Ilis told him, the deed growing a bit with the telling.

Elva spoke to Trevelyn as if Rudelle were not there. "She won't live out the week."

Elva vanished.

He hugged Rudelle tighter and said, "I'll carry Ailin inside and put something on his face to keep the swelling down."

"I'm sorry that I hit him."

"I'm not," Trevelyn said.

She asked, "Ilis, can your rose be saved?"

The girl walked close to the wounded vine, tears glistening in her eyes. "Yes, but she hurts." The girl sat on the ground, and the surviving blossoms shivered and cringed above her head.

Trevelyn motioned for Rudelle to come with him and leave Ilis to her magic.

Rudelle asked, "How are your parents?"

"Down in the caverns under the house. They have research to do and spells to prepare. They've neglected the magic shop. It'll take me weeks to catch up."

"They don't like me very much."

"No, but I love you, and that will be enough for them, eventually."

Rudelle nodded, but was unconvinced.

Dinner preparations went forth in the only truly clean room in the house, the kitchen. The maid had kept up in there. Trevelyn watched through the open doorway. Ilis worked beside Rudelle. The girl wore a clean brown dress and clean undergarments. Rudelle had even shown her how to mend rips without magic.

Ailin was nursing a wondrous bruise, but the boy was peeling potatoes, something his mother could never have gotten him to do. Of course, his mother wouldn't have been basting a turkey either.

Ilis watched everything Rudelle did with a kind of wonder. Ailin watched her with a wary and unusual emotion, respect.

Elva came to stand beside Trevelyn. "What have you brought into this house, brother?"

He smiled. "Peace, cooked meals, love, discipline." He shrugged, "Rudelle."

"How did you know?"

"I went to a prophet and paid gold."

Elva laughed. "It looks like you're going to get your money's worth."

He nodded. "Rudelle will see to it."

An explosion shuddered through the house. "What was that?" Rudelle asked.

Ilis answered, "Mother or Father, they are working spells."

"Well, my cake is going to fall if they keep doing that. Go downstairs and tell them to please not rock the house until after dinner."

Ilis looked like she'd lost her mind.

Elva saved her. "I'll do it. Should I tell them you said so?"

"Please do, and tell them that if they can refrain from blowing up the house, we will have layer cake, turkey with walnut stuffing, candied orange breads, potato cakes, and fresh greens, courtesy of Ilis's magic."

Elva grinned. "You fixed all their favorites."

Rudelle grinned back. "Did I?"

Ailin said, "Candied orange breads? Really? But it isn't a holy day."

Elva gave a small bow in Rudelle's direction. "I will tell my parents to stop rocking the house. If you can scold them like children, I can be brave enough to bear the message. Though I will have a sorcerous shield ready when I tell them."

Rudelle said, "Thank you, Elva."

Elva laughed and hugged her brother. "That new wife of yours may live out the week." Then Elva vanished.

"People certainly leave rooms quickly here," Rudelle said.

Ailin asked, "May I have a candied orange bread?"

"Just one, or you'll ruin your dinner."

The boy nodded.

Rudelle handed him the treat and said, "You've done a wonderful job on those potatoes. You've been a big help, and you didn't waste a spell on it."

He grinned, mouth full of orange bread, and mumbled, "I don't need magic to peel any old potatoes."

"Of course you don't."

Ilis asked, "Rudelle, the water's boiling, now what?"

"We cut up the potatoes and put them in."

"Oh."

Trevelyn listened to the rise and fall of voices, smelled the rich fragrance of cooking food, and smiled.

HERE BE DRAGONS

This is the only science fiction story I've ever completed. Hardware-oriented science doesn't interest the writer in me. It's the softer sciences that fascinate me on paper. Of course, just because it's soft science doesn't make it a soft story. One editor rejected this story by writing that it made her feel unclean. Cool.

SOME people are just born evil. No twisted childhood trauma, no abusive father, or alcoholic mother, just plain God-awful mean. Dr. Jasmine Cooper, dream therapist and empath, believed that, knew that. She had spent too many years looking inside the minds of murderers not to believe it.

Bernard C. had been born evil. He was sixty, tall and thin, a little stoop-shouldered with age. Thick white hair fell in soft waves around a strong face. At sixty, he still showed the charm that had allowed him to seduce and slaughter sixteen women.

He wasn't your typical mass murderer. First, he was about fifteen years too old; second, until he started murdering people he had seemed quite sane. No abuse of animals, no child beating, no rages, nothing. Perhaps it was that very nothing that was the clue. Bernard had been the perfect husband until his wife died when he was fifty. He had raised two children, the perfect father.

Everything he did was perfect, so squeaky normal that it screamed when you read it. Too perfect, too ordinary, like an actor that had his role down—to perfection.

Jasmine had studied the pictures; the basement slaughter room with its old-fashioned autopsy table. Bernard had been a mortician before he retired. Jasmine had found morticians to be some of the most stable and sane people she had ever met. You had to be pretty well grounded to work with the dead, day after day. As a mortician, Bernard had been the best, until he retired.

He brought sixteen women down his basement steps, ranging in age from forty-five to sixty-nine. He tapped them on the head, not too hard, strapped them to his table, and started the embalming process while they were still alive. Technically, most of them just bled to death. Bernard drained out their blood and pumped in embalming fluid, simple. They bled to death.

But Jasmine knew it was not simple, that they hadn't just bled to death, that they had strained against the tape over their mouths, struggled against the straps at wrist and ankle until they rubbed the skin away and bled faster. As you grow older the skin tears more easily, thin and fine as parchment.

And Jasmine was in charge of Bernard's rehabilitation. Dreaming. Images swimming, colored clouds floating across the mind. Brief glimpses of places, people, sharp glittering bits of emotion. The dreamer moved in his sleep, almost awake, dreams surfacing, spilling over his conscious mind. Bright memories of make-believe following his thoughts like hounds on a scent. He would remember. Jasmine would see that he never forgot.

Bernard C. woke screaming. It was the best that Jasmine could do. She had tried to make him remorseful, sympathetic to his victims, but Bernard was a sociopath; he didn't really believe in other people. They were just amusing things, not real, not like he was real. He had embalmed sixteen women alive because he had wanted to do it. It was pleasant—amusing.

She could not make him feel things he had no capacity to feel. His emotions were a great roaring silence. But he could feel fear for himself. He could feel his own pain. So every night when he slept, Jasmine hurt him. She strapped him to his own table and had his victims bleed him dry. She buried him alive; she closed him in the dark until air burned in his chest and he suffocated. She terrorized him night after night, until Bernard did feel one emotion. Hate. He hated Dr. Cooper, not the burning hatred of a "normal" person but the cold hate of a sociopath. Cold hate never dies, never wavers. Bernard's fondest wish was to strap Dr. Cooper to a table.

Jasmine knew this, felt it. The therapy was working. And if Bernard C. ever got Dr. Cooper alone, he'd do worse than kill her. He wasn't alone. If you asked most of the men in Clarkson Maximum Security Prison what they most desired in the whole world it was to have Dr. Cooper at their mercy.

The Clarkson Prison had the highest rate of successful rehabilitation for violent criminals in the country, perhaps in the world. Some had found in their dreams the taste of other people's tears, sympathy for others, at last. Other dreams held the taste of blood, the pulse of their own hearts dying.

Distance is no protection against psychic ability. Dr. Cooper knew what their dreams tasted of; she could find them wherever they would go. Only death would free them from her, and some of them weren't sure about that.

Dr. Jasmine Cooper, empath/dream therapist, most hated and feared person in a building full of monsters, was at her desk doing paperwork when the phone rang. She ignored it, knowing the machine would pick up. It did. Her voice first and then, after the beep, a man's voice, "Hello, Jasmine, this is Dr. Edward Bromley, again." Silence, then, "Well, we have a problem at the school that requires your special touch. This is the fifth message I've left, Jasmine. Call me or a child's going to die."

She picked up at the last moment. "Dr. Bromley." Her voice was utterly neutral, a trick she'd picked up from some of her patients.

"Ah, yes. Jasmine. I'm glad you picked up. Can we have a visual to go along with the voice?"

She stared at the small credit-card-thin screen just above the phone. The screen was a blank silver-gray. "No," she said. "What do you want, Dr. Bromley?"

He sighed. "Jasmine, or should I call you Dr. Cooper?"

"That would be fine. What do you want?"

"I would really like to see your face when I tell you."

"Why?"

"Damn it, Jasmine . . . Dr. Cooper. Do you know how hard it was for me to come to you with this?"

"No," she lied. His anxiety oozed over the lines, trembling with distance and electricity and a touch of fear. Something was very wrong.

"Tell me what you want, Bromley. What needs my special touch?" Her voice held a bite, sarcasm leaking through her professionalism. She could feel her face crumbling. She didn't dare let Bromley see her like this. She could feel the hate blazing through her eyes, trembling down her hands. He'd see it too. Even he wasn't that blind.

"There's a problem at the school." He hesitated, only his breathing still hissing through the line.

"What sort of problem?"

"Bad dreams, no, nightmares. Freaking, bloody, awful nightmares. We've had one attempted suicide."

"Student or teacher?"

"Student, but he was an advanced student. He had training, but the dreams just ate him alive. He slit his wrists because he didn't ever want to fall asleep again."

Jasmine smiled. "You've been doing this long enough, Bromley. You've got a powerful untrained dreamer in the school. Police yourself."

"We tried, Jas."

"No," she said, "no one calls me that anymore." The old nickname crept along her skin, raising the hairs on her arms.

"Jasmine, then. Do you remember Nicky?"

"He was a dreamer a few years older than I was."

"Yes. He's dead."

She stared at the phone receiver wondering what Bromley's face looked like right now, this minute. A trickle of sweat oozed down her forehead; she wiped it with the back of her hand. "What happened?"

"He tried to take care of the nightmares. We think he linked up with our rogue dreamer and a blood vessel in his brain burst. An embolism."

Jasmine swallowed hard, hoped Bromley couldn't hear it. "It happens." Her voice was level, so bland she knew the strain showed.

"Not to fully trained dreamers. Nicky was almost as good as you were. People with that kind of talent don't burst their brains, not without help."

"It is impossible to truly kill someone during a dream session. A bad heart, well it happens. Nicky didn't die in dream. He just died. Coincidence."

"You don't believe that any more than I do."

"Read any textbook on psychic phenomena, Bromley. You wrote the standard: no one can kill another person by dreaming them to death."

"We both know that isn't true."

"There is no record of it ever happening."

"Because I destroyed the record, Jasmine. You owe me."

There it was, bland and clear, and no ignoring it. "Are you recording this?"

"No."

"Don't be."

"You think I'd get you to admit something on tape and then blackmail you with it?"

"Obligate me, maybe."

"I'm not recording this, Jasmine. Talk to me, please."

Maybe it was the *please* that did it, or perhaps the rushing sense of fear. "So you've got another dreamer that can kill during dream. Someone at least as powerful as I was."

"God, Jasmine, don't ever say it like that again. If someone should overhear . . ."

"You said talk, I'm talking. Do you know who it is?"

"We think so. A student who just arrived two months ago. A ten-year-old girl named Lisbeth Pearson."

"Why do you think it's her?"

"We've only got one other dreamer in school right now. Malcolm hasn't got the control. Lisbeth's sucking him into everyone's nightmares. We're hiding all the sharp objects from Malcolm."

"How old is he?"

"Fourteen."

"Ten and fourteen, you're still a baby-raper, Bromley."

"The school did OK by you, Dr. Cooper. You're the most respected dream therapist in this country. I saw on the news, you've set up two sister programs in different states. Did you get an invitation to do the same in, what was it, France?"

"England."

"Without this school, you wouldn't be where you are."

Jasmine almost laughed, but it wasn't funny, it was pathetic. He was right. She was keeper of the monsters, thanks to Bromley and others like him. And she hated them all.

He had asked her something, but she hadn't heard.

"Excuse me, Dr. Bromley, can you repeat that, please?"

"When can you get here?"

Her stomach tightened, palms sweating. "I swore I'd never go back, Bromley."

"I remember, Dr. Cooper, but this is an emergency. If you don't come here and defuse the situation, I'll have no choice."

"There are always choices, Bromley."

"Not here, not now, Jasmine. I write up my report and they'll execute Lisbeth Pearson as a dangerous, uncontrollable psychic. Unless you can tame her, Lisbeth won't see her eleventh birthday."

Using the child's name twice in a row—manipulation, a tug at the heartstrings. It worked like it was supposed to.

"I'll come. It will take me a few hours to divide my patients between my fellow therapists, then I'll be there."

"Thank you, Dr. Cooper."

"Send all the material you have on the child. I'll give you my fax number. I'll study it all on the trip and be ready to work when I arrive."

"It'll be to you as soon as we hang up."

"One more thing. How do you know it's the child?"

"I told you we don't have any other students that could do it."

Jasmine smiled, a bitter twist of lips. "What about a teacher, a trained dreamer that's gone off the deep end?"

"We screen our workers, Jasmine."

"I remember."

"Dr. Roberts was a fluke. It couldn't happen again. We see to that."

"If you've got everything under such bloody good control, then what do you need me for?"

"Jasmine . . ."

"No, I don't want to hear any more. I'll be there as soon as I can." She hung up the phone. Sweat was beading on her forehead despite the air-conditioned quiet of the room.

Dr. Roberts had taken a butcher knife to two students, and Jasmine would always carry the scar where she had thrown up an arm to keep the doctor from slashing her face. A guard had shot Roberts then, and she had fallen forward on her knees, still whispering, "Evil, you are all evil."

Jasmine could control her dreams, but Roberts still accused her, questioned her at night before she could stop it. "You're evil, aren't you, Jasmine? You know you are."

"Yes, Dr. Roberts, I know I am." But Jasmine knew that everyone was evil, down deep when you scrape the skin away. Inside their heads everyone hunted, everyone killed, everyone was a monster.

The thought that Dr. Roberts couldn't deal with was not the children's evil, but her own. That morning when she woke she saw a monster looking back at her from the mirror. She had set out to kill the monster and gotten killed for it.

Jasmine knew the truth. You couldn't kill The Monster. It was always there just behind your eyes. You could kill *a monster*, though. Jasmine was a great believer in the death penalty. It was the ultimate therapy. It cured everything. The first stirrings of fear crawled in her belly, low and real. It would get worse. Jasmine knew that it would get worse.

Dr. Cooper cradled her face on her arms, cheek pressed into the coolness of her desktop, and cried. *The school*, that was all it was ever called, it had no other name. A lot of secret government projects had no names.

Thirty years ago, almost Jasmine's lifetime, psychic phenomena became a proven scientific fact. In fact, there were so many psychics that scientists started making jokes about pod people. It didn't stay funny for long. Most of the new breed were children. They had powers that were dependable and as testable as such phenomena ever would be. There were lots of theories as to why, suddenly, we had empaths and telepaths and dreamers coming out of the woodwork. The evolutionists said it was proof of their ideas; mankind was evolving. Others thought it was junk food, chemicals and preservatives in the American diet. The majority of talent did occur in industrialized nations. Maybe it was the pollution. Inoculations. The beginning of the Apocalypse. No one knew. Jasmine doubted anyone ever would.

But a few of the children had been dangerous, their powers so far beyond the dreams of normality that their families couldn't cope. In most cases the families were afraid of their children. Glad to give them up to someplace that would care for them.

Jasmine's family gave her up when she was five. Her mother cried and kissed her. Her older sister and brother hugged her dutifully. Her father said, "Be a good girl, Jas."

The smell of pipe tobacco could still bring back the memory of her tall, dark-haired father. A twinge of memory like a badly healed scar.

What she remembered most of her mother was the cool

sense of fear. That red lipsticked mouth kissing her, laughing, and wiping the lipstick smear off Jasmine's cheek with a Kleenex. Laughing, golden hair, and the sick smell of fear. No perfume in the world could hide the stench from an empath.

But then maybe Mommy didn't know, maybe she didn't understand, maybe she had done her best. Maybe.

LISBETH Pearson was small for ten, with coppery red hair, almost dark enough to be auburn, but not quite. The hair fell in thick waves to her shoulders. Her face was that peaches-and-cream skin that some redheads have; no freckles, just creamy skin. Her eyes were a pale brown, almost amber. She wore a dress that seemed too young for her, with lace-topped white socks and patent leather shoes.

She looked like she was dressed for Halloween, or like someone else had dressed her. She was playing alone with a dollhouse on the other side of a one-way mirror. Jasmine found that very funny. She remembered being on the other side of the glass. She had always known who was watching and what they were feeling. Always.

Lisbeth looked up and stared directly at the mirror, and smiled. Jasmine smiled and nodded back.

"Can she see us?" Dr. Bromley asked.

"No."

"You acknowledged each other, I saw it."

"Did we?"

"Don't bullshit me, Jasmine."

She turned to stare at the infamous Dr. Bromley, protector and tormentor of her childhood. He was five foot eight, but the weight he had gained made him seem smaller. His curly brown hair was fading back from a gleaming expanse of scalp. His hands, which had once looked strong, now resembled uncooked sausages. His face was blotched with red. Was he sick? She stared into his small eyes and thought, *yes, maybe.*

Beth could have told Bromley if he was dying. She had had a feel for death. Beth was dead, had been for twenty years. Tall, laughing, gray-eyed Beth. She had been able to think people to death, a wasting illness. She hadn't meant to kill people, just didn't know how to stop it. Neither did anyone else. So they killed her.

"Jasmine . . . Jasmine."

"I'm sorry, Dr. Bromley, I was thinking about something."

"Are you all right?"

"I was going to ask you the same thing."

"Why?" he asked.

"You don't look well."

He fidgeted, glanced away, and knew that it wasn't his eyes she could read. He laughed, abrupt and harsh. "No, I'm not well. It's none of your damn business what's wrong, Dr. Cooper. Let's get back to Lisbeth. You're here to save her, not me."

"Could I save you?"

"No."

"I'm sorry, Dr. Bromley." And Jasmine realized she really was sorry. She didn't want to be sorry for him, to feel anything but hatred and contempt, and fear. Not sorrow, not for Dr. Bromley.

"Tell me what you think about Lisbeth Pearson."

"I don't think anything yet. I want to talk to her alone." Jasmine smiled. "As alone as this place allows."

"We have to monitor the children. It's part of the project."

"I remember the arguments, Dr. Bromley."

* * *

LISBETH was placing tiny gilt-edged chairs around a miniature dining room table when Jasmine entered. The child ignored
her and continued to rearrange the furniture. She seemed completely absorbed in the task, but Jasmine felt the child's interest,
her power, glide over her skin like a cold breeze.

"My name is Jasmine."

Lisbeth looked up at that, one small hand cradling a flower
arrangement. "I've never met anyone named Jasmine before."

"And I've never met anyone named Lisbeth before."

The child grinned, perfect lips, eyes sparkling. "No, you've
never met anyone like me."

Jasmine looked into those brown-amber eyes, shining with
humor, and felt the threat. The words were subtle; the power
that emanated from the child was not.

The power climbed over Jasmine's skin, raising the hair on
her body, like insects crawling, or a faint buzz of electric current.
You could breathe in Lisbeth's power, choke on it.

The child smiled, even white teeth flashing, but her eyes didn't
sparkle anymore. Games were over; Lisbeth didn't have to pretend
to be "normal," so she didn't try. Jasmine stared into her eyes and
found—nothing. Inside her head was a great roaring silence.

Jasmine had never met a sociopath at such a tender age. She
knew that they were born broken, but to feel it, to feel that
emptiness stretching inside this lovely little girl, to feel the
void . . . was the most frightening thing she had ever felt.

The child laughed, sweet and joyful. "You're afraid of me,
just like all the others."

Fear meant control. It meant Jasmine was controllable, so
Lisbeth lowered her defenses; she allowed Jasmine to glimpse
what was there. Or what wasn't.

Jasmine's power eased through the girl, along her mind, and found other things missing. She was an empath; no empath could be a sociopath and bring harm to people, because they would feel that pain as their own. Unless they couldn't feel anyone's pain but their own.

Lisbeth was blind to positive emotions; she could only absorb the negative. As far as she was concerned, she alone felt joy, happiness, love. Everyone else was full of hate, fear, shame, or nothing. It was an empath's version of hell. And the child had never known anything else.

The curling auburn hair had little pink barrettes that picked up the small pink design in the dress. Perfectly matched. Perfect. If she hadn't been a psychic, Lisbeth Pearson would have been the perfect daughter, the perfect student, the perfect worker, or wife, or mother, until the day that she broke. The day that The Monster came out.

But The Monster was too close to the surface in Lisbeth; there was almost nothing else left.

The child had gone back to her dollhouse, ignoring Jasmine. She no longer considered her a threat.

Dr. Jasmine Cooper turned abruptly on her heel and walked out; the sound of her high heels was loud and echoing. She leaned against the door trying to breathe. She was shivering uncontrollably, fear soaking like frost into her bones. Jasmine tried to gain control of herself and knew that Lisbeth felt her falling to pieces. Knew that a closed door was no barrier at all.

An echo of the child's joy filtered through Jasmine's nerves like distant, mocking laughter.

*   *   *

JASMINE entered Bromley's office all cool professionalism. No seams showed; she had swallowed the fear whole. Years of practice.

Dr. Bromley was sitting behind his paper-strewn desk when Jasmine entered. His eyes looked tired, wary. "Well?"

"Just being in the room with her raises the hairs on my arms. You don't have to be an empath to know that."

"She's evil," he said.

"If you've already made up your mind, Dr. Bromley, why did you bring me here?"

He stared at her, without saying anything.

"You want me to save her."

He nodded once up, once down.

"Do you know what she is?"

He rubbed his fingertips over his eyes. "She's a sociopath. She's an empath that can only feel negative emotions."

Jasmine didn't try to keep the surprise off her face. "If you know, why is she still alive?"

"Because, Dr. Cooper, I'm tired of killing children. So many of them come through with talents we can't begin to understand. They can do things that make Lisbeth look safe. But most of the time we just don't understand them enough to help them. We destroy them because we don't know what else to do. But Lisbeth is like you were, in some ways; I hoped you could help her, understand her. Keep her alive."

"And if I can't help her? If I think she's too dangerous?"

He shrugged. "I fill out a form, submit it to my superiors, and in a month she'll be dead."

"Just like that," Jasmine said.

"Just like that," he said.

She stared at the doctor, tried to feel what he felt. Sorrow, an

almost unending sorrow. The school had eaten him alive, just as
it had the children. There was nothing left of him but sadness,
fear, and a dogged sense of duty. A fragile wish for hope, for
meaning. He was looking for peace.

"I can't give you absolution, Bromley."

He flinched. "Is that what I want?"

Jasmine nodded. "You're wondering if you played God, or
were just a murderer."

He gave a weak laugh. "You are merciless."

"I had good teachers."

He nodded. "All right, no absolution for me. Can you save
this child?"

Jasmine knew she should say, "Kill her." Lisbeth Pearson was
too dangerous for words. But she looked into Bromley's tired,
sick eyes, and said, "Maybe."

JASMINE was walking to her room, down the familiar empty
corridors. No matter how many children were in the school,
there were never people in the hallways. Always there was the
feeling of abandonment, emptiness. She walked the halls alone,
tracked by the blinking red lights of cameras.

A woman came from around the corner; long yellow hair
swept nearly to her knees. She had the height for the hair, slender
and graceful. The face was dominated by pale blue eyes. Jasmine
stopped and waited for the woman to come to her. A feeling of
horrible déjà vu swept over her. An almost claustrophobic sense
of time spinning backward. "Vanessa?" It came out a question,
though it wasn't meant to be.

The woman smiled, and held out her hands. "Jasmine, it is
you." Vanessa hugged her tight, and Jasmine fought the urge to

pull away. She relaxed into the arms of her best friend from childhood, and one of the most powerful telepaths the school had ever had.

When she could, Jasmine pulled back, and said, "Are you visiting?"

Vanessa turned away. She hid her eyes, and her mind was as tight and closed as a locked door. She stepped back from Jasmine. "No, I'm an instructor." Her voice made it bright, cheerful.

"An instructor. For how long?"

"Since high school."

"You went away to college, just like I did. We rode to the airport together." Jasmine felt panic like a cold weight at the pit of her gut.

Vanessa paced back and forth, then whirled, smiling. "I didn't finish college. They needed me here to help with all the little telepaths."

Jasmine worked very hard at keeping her own mind locked tight. No empath's control can match a telepath, but she tried. Her face was absolutely blank, pleasantly so, practice, years of practice. "Do you enjoy . . . teaching?"

"Oh, yes, I really feel like I make a difference—you?"

Jasmine nodded.

"You've done really well. My best friend, the famous doctor." Vanessa laughed and hugged her again.

Best friend—they hadn't seen or talked to each other in ten years. Jasmine found herself crying, hugging the tall stranger who used to be her friend, and crying.

"Hey," Vanessa said, "Hey, what's the matter?"

She pulled away and shook her head. What could she say that wouldn't hurt Vanessa? *You betrayed our dreams. You gave up and came back here to hide. We swore an oath that we would never come here to hide, better death than this tomb.* Jasmine wanted to scream it all out. To find out why Vanessa had failed, the ultimate failure, she had come back here. Once you came back, you never left. No one ever left a second time. The words echoed in her head, and the walls seemed to be closing around her, narrow. Jasmine hadn't noticed how narrow the halls were. The roof was close enough to touch. The school was crowding her, crowding.

"Jasmine, what's wrong?"

She drew a deep, shaking breath. "Panic attack."

"Do you still get those?"

"First one in ..." *Breathe deep and even, breathe.* "Twelve years."

"Open your mind to me. Jasmine, I can help. Remember." Jasmine backed away until she hit the wall. She pressed against it. Vanessa took a step forward, reaching.

"No!"

"Let me help you."

Her breathing was beginning to slow, pulse going down. The corridor was still hot and too close, but it was going to be all right. It was going to be all right. "I'll be all right, Vanessa."

"I can help you with whatever is wrong. Telepaths are great counselors."

Jasmine stared into her eyes. "You wouldn't like what I was thinking."

Vanessa froze, hands still outstretched, smile sliding away from her face. It was one of those moments when you don't need empathy. When truth stretches between two people. Truth could be violent, could strip you of dignity and hope just as quickly as a gun.

It was one of those moments when you can look in someone else's eyes and see your own reflection so sharp and true that it slices like glass.

Vanessa turned away first and began to walk down the hall, then to run. Her footsteps thundered against the narrow walls.

Jasmine stared up into the watching monitor, red light blinking. She spoke to it. "The monitor in my room better be disabled before I get there, Bromley. If it's not, I'm going to tear it out of the wall." She took a deep shaking breath. "You should have told me Vanessa was here. What else haven't you told me?"

There was no answer from the whirring monitor. She hadn't expected one. If Bromley had answered, she wouldn't have believed him anyway.

THE room was like all the other rooms. It was rectangular with pale blue walls. A single bed was against the right-hand wall, white sheets, brown blanket. When Jasmine was a child, she had longed for colored sheets. The kind with animals and clowns on them. In her house were bright-colored sheets, and none of the rooms were painted blue.

There was a white bureau with mirror against the left wall, and a closet in the far wall. That was all. Small or not, the rooms always seemed empty.

There was a monitor up in one corner. The red recording light was off, no whirring, no moving to scan the room. Bromley had turned it off; supposedly that meant that Jasmine was alone, unobserved.

Jasmine pressed her palms on top of the perfectly clean bureau top. She leaned forward until she was almost touching her own reflection. The old litany came back, "This is not the whole world. You will get out. You will make it on the outside. You can do it. This isn't forever." How many nights had she told her reflection that? How many years?

This wasn't the whole world. She had gotten out. She had made it on the outside. She could do it. It hadn't been forever. And now she was back. To save another little girl. The thought came, *But does she deserve saving?*

Jasmine answered aloud, "I save monsters all the time." Fear had settled in the pit of her stomach, hard and thick. This place pressed so many of her buttons, so much shit to wade through here. And the child, that frightening, beautiful child. Why was so much evil pleasant, pretty on the outside, like poisoned candy? Most mass murderers were the nicest people.

Lisbeth Pearson was already in bed. It was an hour past dark. She would be out there in the dream network, hunting. For the first time someone would be hunting Lisbeth. Did the child suspect? No. There was one other trait of the serial killer that Lisbeth shared: arrogance. The predator never expects to be hunted.

Jasmine had never been hunted either. It would be a night of firsts.

That night Jasmine dreamed. Her own dreams first. Nothing pleasant; fears about the school, Lisbeth, Bromley, childhood nightmares, she brushed them away. Then the sensation that her skull evaporated and her mind eased outward like mist. She floated through one dream at a time. She could touch more than one mind at a time, bringing other people into the same dream, but they had to share a single dream. Multiple minds, but not multiple fantasies. No one was sure why that particular restriction. It was just the way it worked.

Jasmine swam through the colors of other people's dreams, searching. A boy played catch with his dead father, sorrow, things left unsaid; a woman held a stranger in her arms, naked, unafraid, private, lust flowed warm and felt like anger; Bromley dreamed of flowers surrounding a coffin, rage, hate. Jasmine moved on before she could see who was inside the coffin. She could have wandered all night from dream to dream like a butterfly in a field of fantastic flowers, but something burned through her mind, screamed along her nerves: terror.

Jasmine followed it like a beacon. The silent rush of fear called her as surely as a scream for help. She appeared in the dream with an almost physical jolt. She had rushed, hadn't taken her time; the reality of the nightmare was concrete, touchable, breathable, visible, real. A boy stood with his back to her. He was tall, slender, hair neatly buzzed next to his scalp, skin the color of dark coffee. He was struggling to lock the door to a dingy room. Windows leaked gray daylight through dirty glass. Wallpaper fell in strips from yellowed walls. The place reeked of damp, rot, urine.

The bolt slid home and he turned, leaning against the door, relieved. His eyes flew wide. "Who are you?" His voice hadn't caught up to his tall, leggy body; it sounded like a child's voice.

"I'm Jasmine. I've come to help."

"You're that new dream teacher."

Jasmine started to explain that she was not a teacher, was not a part of the school, but standing there soaking up Malcolm's terror, she let it go. "Yes."

The smell was growing worse, a choking outhouse stench that was filling the room, coming from under the door. Malcolm backed away from the door, until he bumped into Jasmine. He jumped and she gripped his shoulders. He didn't pull away. His breathing was coming in short gasps. The whole dream focused on that door. Jasmine could feel the pull of it. Fear. Fear forced down their throat until more than anything in the whole world you didn't want that door to open. You didn't want *IT* to come through and get you. And you knew that that was exactly what was going to happen, and there was nothing you could do about it. The helplessness of nightmare, but Jasmine could do something about it. Nightmares were her specialty.

The girl's focus was strong and pure. Jasmine could not look away from the door. The sound of heavy footsteps scraped outside; the smell of rotting corpses, sweet and putrid, filled the room.

Jasmine concentrated, willing the walls to dissolve, the dream to end. Nothing happened. She took a deep breath and choked on the stinking air.

Malcolm's voice was thin with fear. "Do something!"

She tried. Manipulating dreams was just a matter of will and concentration. Jasmine knew this wasn't real; if you knew that, you could change it. But she had never been inside the dream of someone who matched her powers so exactly.

"I can't break the dream."

Malcolm made a small sound low in his throat. He sagged against her. "Oh, God," he said, "oh, God."

Jasmine swallowed the first rush of real fear, not Lisbeth's creation but her very own fear. She was as trapped as the boy. Trapped in the mind of a sociopathic child.

Then things began to melt from the walls. Hands, arms reached outward; rotted flesh falling away from white bone, rags of clothes. Things long dead crawled out of the rotting walls and began to drag themselves closer.

One man had half his face blown away; his tongue rolled between bone and raw meat, a large fat worm twisted round the corpse's tongue.

Malcolm screamed, one high shriek after another, as four of the things shambled toward them.

The faces were recognizable; a man, woman, two teenage children. They had been black; now they were the colors of old death.

Jasmine grabbed Malcolm's hand; his fingernails dug into her palm. His screams became words. "My father, my father! Noooo!"

Of course, the dead things were Malcolm's family. They were horrible, paralyzingly so to the boy, because this nightmare was designed with him in mind, not Jasmine. The dead things were slow; little pieces of them fell away as they walked, slow.

Jasmine dragged Malcolm toward the door. He fought her, the dead things turned toward them, but Jasmine was at the door with the boy screaming, tugging at her hand, trying to get free, to run, but there was nowhere to run.

Jasmine couldn't break the dream, but maybe she could manipulate it. She unlocked the door and flung it open. The dream lurched; the dead things wavered. There was nothing on the other side of the door. *Sloppy, Lisbeth*, Jasmine thought. There was a sensation of vertigo, then Jasmine filling the emptiness with a stairway, leading down.

She dragged Malcolm onto the stairs and shut and locked the door behind them, with a thought. Malcolm was running now, still gripping her hand as if afraid she would vanish and abandon him. They clattered down the stairs; suddenly there were walls on either side. The stairs led downward, but now there were walls to hold them, rotting yellow walls.

Hands grew out of the wall, pale arms, they fluttered, hands wringing. A hand grabbed Jasmine's wrist. The flesh was too soft, doughy, rubbery, but strong.

Malcolm screamed as hands grabbed his shirt.

Jasmine needed to be free of the hand; she thought of a sword. It levitated over the hand, and sliced downward in a glittering arc. The arm flopped, spraying warm blood into her face. The hand still clung to her wrist, but she pulled Malcolm free of the bloated hands, and they ran.

Jasmine sprayed the walls with blood from the sword as it sliced the hands in front of them like a thrasher, cutting wheat. The stairs were littered with pale hands that twitched and bled.

The stairs spilled onto a landing, and the walls closed in, dead end. Jasmine had been concentrating too much on the sword and the hands to maintain the stairs. The smell of rotting corpses began to fill the air.

"Malcolm, is this the same dream every time?"

"No."

"Is there anything that is the same every time?"

"My family, she always kills my family." Both of his hands dug into her arm. His fear was nearly choking her. Her fear was nearly a cold heat on her skin. The bloated hand had fallen off in the running. She and Malcolm stood alone on the landing, as the stench became stronger. The dead things were coming.

Malcolm's family, turned into rotting corpses that would tear the boy apart, maybe eat parts of him alive while he watched.

Yes, that would be what Jasmine would do, if she really wanted to terrify. To horrify. If she really hated someone.

That was it: hatred. Jasmine called out, "Lisbeth, I know why you hate Malcolm. I know."

The first rotted corpse began to pull itself from the wall. "You're jealous of his family. Malcolm's family loves him. They love him, Lisbeth. Malcolm's father loves him. His mother loves him. His sister loves him. His brother loves him."

The corpses had pulled free of the wall and were reaching for them, but the smell was fading. "You're family hates you, Lisbeth. Your mother is afraid of you, Lisbeth. I read your file. Your father tried to kill you, and you punished him for it. Didn't you? Didn't you!"

The dead things began to melt. There was the sensation of something large sliding through the nightmare, like a whale swimming next to you in the dark. Lisbeth's power.

"No one loves you. They hate you, Lisbeth. Everyone hates you. Even your own family."

Silence, not of the ear, but sensation of feeling, silence more profound than soundlessness.

The dream broke and Jasmine was spilled back to wakefulness. She sat up in bed, heart hammering in her chest. That was it. Lisbeth had never been loved, not by anyone, ever. Even sociopaths need the illusion of acceptance from someone. Lisbeth needed to be loved.

THAT morning Jasmine went to Malcolm. They met for the first time in the flesh. She promised him that Lisbeth would never hurt him again. One way or another Jasmine meant to keep that promise.

LISBETH was playing with a nearly life-size doll when Jasmine walked through the door. She knew that Bromley was on the other side of the one-way glass. She no longer cared.

"Nice doll," Jasmine said.

"My mommy sent it to me."

"Why?"

Lisbeth frowned up at her. "Why what?"

"Why did your mommy send the doll to you?"

"What do you mean?" Lisbeth asked. The lovely, golden-haired doll lay very still in the child's lap.

"Why did your mother send you a doll? Why would she send

you anything? Most parents never contact their children once they come to the school."

Lisbeth gave a lovely smile, eyes shining. "Because she loves me," she said, very matter-of-fact, very sweet, and as soon as she said it, Lisbeth knew it had been a mistake.

Jasmine laughed, then the laughter died. She stared down at the child, met her brown eyes, and did not look away. "No one loves you, Lisbeth; you and I both know that."

"I hate you," Lisbeth said, voice quiet and precise.

"I know," Jasmine said. "Why did you kill Nicky?"

"Didn't."

"Why, Lisbeth?"

"Why what?" the child said, voice sulky.

"Why did you kill Nicky?"

"I could have killed you last night."

"Then why didn't you?"

"Get out! Get out!" She stood, screaming. Lisbeth began to beat the doll against the floor. Bits of plastic began to shatter onto the floor. One blue eye lay winking to itself, naked against the floor.

"Why did you kill Nicky?"

"Because he wouldn't let me do what I wanted to do. Just like you won't let me!"

"No," Jasmine said, quietly, "I won't."

JASMINE waited the following night, waited until the children had been asleep for a couple of hours. Malcolm wasn't sleeping tonight. Vanessa was sitting up with him, keeping him awake, at Jasmine's request. He would be safe tonight, she could see to that.

Tomorrow night was another problem. Jasmine had made her decision; either Lisbeth was "tamed" tonight, or the child would die. There was one more possibility: that Lisbeth would kill her.

The thought flowed over her skin like a cool breeze, tickling the hairs on her arms, sliding down her spine like an ice cube. Fear; it was an old companion. Dr. Cooper wouldn't know what to do if she wasn't afraid of her patients.

Jasmine flowed from dream to dream; bright glimpses of color, motion, thoughts, feelings. She pushed forward like a swimmer, concentrating on getting to the other shore. Then it came, terror, it screamed along Jasmine's nerves, opened her mind, called to her.

She didn't enter the dream this time, she pushed at it from the outside, shoved the fear aside. Lisbeth's anger flared over her, but there was nothing for the girl to use to trap Jasmine. Outside of dreams, you were safe. "No, you can't. You're afraid of me, like all the others."

Jasmine smiled. "You made the mistake they all make. Just because I'm afraid of you doesn't mean you shouldn't be afraid of me."

Lisbeth began to gather her forces. Jasmine could feel it, like a thunderstorm building in the distance. She might break the dream, or at least change it. "How would you like to visit one of my patients?"

The girl hesitated, power swirling around her. "Patients?"

Jasmine explained what she did; by the time she finished Lisbeth was smiling, that same angelic twist of perfect lips. Lovely and meaningless as a lifelike doll.

"Would you like to see one of their dreams?"

"Do you mean it?" Lisbeth asked.

"Yes."

Lisbeth licked her lips, breath easing out. It was almost a lust reaction, anticipatory, and far too old for the child. But then in many ways Lisbeth was no longer a child; she had haunted people's dreams too long for that. "I'd like that."

"All right." Jasmine paused as if thinking. "We'll visit William. You'll like William, and I know he'll get a kick out of you."

Lisbeth giggled, the first real little-girl sound Jasmine had heard her make.

"I can hold on to you and take you to his dream, if you stop fighting me."

Lisbeth frowned at that. "What does that mean?"

"Just relax and let me do the work. Be the passenger for once instead of the driver."

"You promise to take me to this William. Promise I'll get to see a real killer's dream."

"Promise," Jasmine said.

Lisbeth nodded, and lowered her protection. Jasmine felt Lisbeth's consciousness slide against hers, almost a faint bump as the child released all control. An adult empath would never have lowered everything, but Lisbeth didn't have the experience in dealing with people who were her equals. Until now she had had no equal. Ten was still very young.

William was asleep, and he dreamed, as he often did, of past glory. He was lying on a twin bed with a little girl. She was wearing blue shorts and a red tank top with cartoon figures on it. Jasmine remembered the clothes from photographs. This was six-year-old Caitlin, and it was William's version of a wet dream.

Lisbeth sighed. "Oh, this is great."

The child was crying, saying, "I want to go home now, please."

"Not yet," William said, voice soothing, as his hand rubbed

the tiny bare leg. "Not yet, soon. If you do everything I say, I'll take you home."

"You said there were kittens here. Where are the kittens?"

"I'll show them to you."

"I don't want you to touch me. Don't!" The child's fear stabbed outward like her words. A sharp gut-jerking cry.

Lisbeth hovered as close as Jasmine would allow, soaking up the terror. Feeding off the child's small body. The cries for help, the pleading; Caitlin would ask about the kittens William had promised to show her just seconds before he placed one hand around her slender baby neck and squeezed. He would crush her windpipe. He was a very strong man.

Her small, nude body lay beside the man, dead. Her head was thrown to one side; eyes mercifully closed. She looked like a broken doll, skin perfect and flawless.

Jasmine brought herself and Lisbeth into the dream. The broken little girl vanished, and William was suddenly fully clothed again.

He stared up at her, fear plain on his face, his fear crawling along Jasmine's body. She enjoyed his fear, enjoyed making him suffer.

Lisbeth said, "He's afraid of you."

"I know."

"I been good," William said. "I done everything you told me to. Why should I be punished? What'd I do wrong?"

"Oh," said Lisbeth, "he's so afraid." She walked closer to the bed, and he shrank back from her, eyes shifting from Jasmine to this new little girl.

"I'm not here to punish you, William. I want you to help me."

"Anything, anything you want, Dr. Cooper. You just name it."

Lisbeth reached for him, and he jerked away as if she had burned him.

"Did you enjoy William's dream, Lisbeth?"

"Oh, yes, it was great."

"Would you like to see another?"

Lisbeth turned, eyes shining, genuinely excited. "Oh, please, yes."

Jasmine nodded. "She's yours, William."

"Wh-what!" he gasped.

"It's the girl that needs punishing, not you. I'm giving her to you."

"You can't scare me," Lisbeth said.

"Is she real?" he asked.

"Very."

"You think threatening me with him will scare me. It won't. I can make him disappear."

"I control this dream, Lisbeth."

William grabbed her wrist. She turned, completely confident that she would destroy him. Jasmine held William's mind and protected it.

The first trickle of fear rose out of Lisbeth. Fear for herself. She struggled to get her hand free. "You won't let him hurt me. You're not bad. Only bad girls let people get hurt." The fear was still in check, because she believed what she said. Jasmine was a teacher, a doctor, an adult, and would not really hurt a child.

"I'm not a good girl, Lisbeth, never have been."

William dragged her against his chest. "NO!" Lisbeth yelled it, anger still stronger than fear. "You can't scare me. You can't make me behave. I'm not like the other children."

"No," Jasmine said, "you are not, and neither was I." Jasmine vanished from the dream, leaving Lisbeth to the man's tender mercies. She did not want to see it happen, but she was drawn to feel it. Fear at last, full-blown and wonderful. Lisbeth terrified. Lisbeth feeling the only thing she could feel, her own pain. Dr. Jasmine Cooper hovered on the edge of the dream and fed off the fear, the lust, the horror. She drank the sweet breath of evil, and it filled her up. Jasmine, like the child, not only was attracted to darkness but fed off it.

She broke the dream before William was finished but long after Lisbeth had begun to cry. Jasmine woke and went down the dark hallways to Lisbeth's room. She opened the door to find the child gasping and sweat-soaked. She cringed when she saw Jasmine.

"You're like me, aren't you? You're like me."

"Yes, Lisbeth, I'm like you." Jasmine sat down on the edge of the bed.

"I don't want to be punished anymore."

"Then you've learned your first lesson. I'll show you how to stay alive, Lisbeth. They won't kill you now, not if you let me teach you." Jasmine leaned close to the child, whispering so the monitor wouldn't hear her, "I'll show you how to feed off them, so that they don't know. You can do what you like with them within limits. You can torture and get paid for it."

Lisbeth's breathing had slowed to almost normal. "You are just like me."

Jasmine nodded and reached a hand out to the child. Lisbeth came to her, small arms hugging her. They sat together in the dark, holding each other. Lisbeth couldn't love, not really. But every child needs love, whether they can give it or not.

"You won't leave me?" Lisbeth asked in a small voice.

"I won't leave you. You can come visit me during holidays."

"You're still afraid of me, aren't you?"

"Yes."

"But now I'm afraid of you."

"Yes."

The child leaned her back against Jasmine, small hands holding the woman's arms around her. Every child needs to be held.

She rested her chin on top of Lisbeth's head, and rocked her gently, comforting herself as much as the child. *From one monster to another*, Jasmine thought, *I'll show you how to stay alive. I'll show you how to drink tears and spill blood. We'll carve them up and feed off their fear, and no one will know but us.*

Jasmine glanced up at the room's monitor. *Are you there, Bromley?* she thought, *are you there?* Maybe he knew, maybe he had always known. *Why did you keep me alive, Bromley? Why?*

She hugged Lisbeth, and felt the first hot trails of tears on her own cheeks. Jasmine whispered into the child's hair, "Monsters beware, here be dragons."

WINTERKILL

This story, like the Sidra and Leech stories and "A Token for Celandine," is set in the world of Nightseer. *The main character is an assassin, and like Edward in the Anita books, Jessa found that killing ordinary humans was too easy. She kills only wizards. This story shows some of her origins, and that you really can't go home again.*

JESSAMINE Swordwitch stood among the ruins of Threllkill village. The forest had moved in to reclaim the small clearing. Twenty houses it had been at its largest, a tiny inconsequential place, but it had been home.

One of her mother's roses had gone wild. It climbed over the broken chimney, pale pink flowers clustered against the sun. The air was thick with its scent, cloying sweet. The black-limbed cherry still stood against the shattered pile that had once been the garden wall.

Jessamine felt her mother's magic pulse through the wild growth. An earth-witch's touches stayed with the plot of land. Mother would not have minded that an orange-flowered trumpet vine strangled her garden or that wild grass grew where she had tended her strawberries.

The thought that her mother's body could still be there, hidden in the green growth, came suddenly. She caught her breath, eyes darting for a glimpse of white bone amidst the wilding strawberries. But there was nothing left of her mother save the roses and the cherry tree. Scavengers had long since picked apart the bones. Twelve years was a long time this close to the forest.

"What happened here, Jessa?"

She jumped, startled, and turned. Gregoor leaned against a soft green mound that had once been a part of the kitchen. "I'm sorry, my thoughts were elsewhere."

He snorted. "I could see that." He gestured, arms wide. "What destroyed this place?"

"Old age, an act of the gods."

He frowned and crossed arms tight over his chest. "Are you going to tell me the story behind this place or not? You drag me out to the wilderness. Tell me nothing. You accept a job without consulting me and then tell me I don't have to come along." He pushed a hand through his short brown hair. "Jessa, we've been swordmates for a year. Don't I deserve some type of explanation?"

She smiled at that and walked over to stand against the leaf-covered wall, beside him. Her hazel eyes looked at a place somewhere over his head, while her strong, small hands stroked his hair. "In Zairde there are no peasants, only the poor. We were poor, but I didn't know that as a child. We had food, shelter, toys, love. I did not think we were poor, but we were not rich. My mother was the village earth-witch. She never used her magic for personal gain or to harm, unless attacked. Even then she was squeamish of the kill. She wouldn't understand my entombing people in living rock."

"You've only done so twice, and both times it saved our lives."

She smiled down at him. "Yes, there is that. But I stand here with my mother's magic still strong in the earth and I shield myself."

"Why?"

"I'm afraid, Gregoor." The summer wind stirred her dark hair. "I promised my mother I would never use my power for evil. I have broken that promise many times."

"You're afraid her disapproving ghost will haunt you."

"Yes."

"Jessa." He hugged her to him. "Please tell me what happened here."

"One day an old sorcerer and his son came to spend the night. I had never seen a truly old sorcerer, for they can live a thousand years. But this one was old. His son was young and strong and handsome; the village girls watched him out the corners of their eyes. During the night the old sorcerer died." Jessamine's hands stopped moving. She stood absolutely still. "The son accused us of poisoning his father. He destroyed our village with fire and lightning, storm and earthquake. My father and my brothers were all killed. When it was over, only my mother and I crawled away."

Jessa took a deep, shaky breath. "My mother, as the village earth-witch, took our grievance to the Zairdian courts. They did nothing. Two days after they declared the sorcerer's son innocent of wrongdoing, an assassin killed my mother." She looked down at him, meeting his eyes.

His brown eyes were wide, astonished, pain-filled. "Jessa."

She placed fingertips over his lips. "It was a very long time ago, Gregoor. A very long time ago."

He gripped her hand. "What happened to the sorcerer who destroyed this village?"

"He died." She smiled down at him. It was a smile he had seen before—a slow, tight spreading of lips that filled her eyes with a dark light. He called it her killing smile. "He was the first wizard I ever killed."

"And that is why we specialize in assassinating wizards?"

"That is why I do. I do not know why you do it."

He stood eye to eye, no taller, no shorter than she. "I do it because you do it."

"Ah," she said and gave him what no one else had received from her in twelve years—a smile full of love.

"You took this job so you could come home, then?"

"I took this job because the sorcerer I slew had a mother, as I had a mother. It seems she has gone mad. The entire province wants her dead. The sorceress is Cytherea of Cheladon."

"You have sent us to kill Cytherea the Mad, Jessa . . ."

She stopped him with a gesture. "She seeks her son's killer, Gregoor, and has killed hundreds seeking me. I think it is time she found me."

THEY came to the first town at dusk. A gibbet had been erected in front of the town gates. Three corpses dangled from it, moving gently in the summer wind. They had been hung up by their wrists, and there was no mark of ordinary violence upon them. No hangman's knot, no knife, no axe had killed the three.

Gregoor hissed, "Mother Peace preserve us. I have never seen anything like that."

Jessa could only nod. The corpses, one man and two women, had been drained of life, magic of the blackest sort. The flesh was a leathered brown, like dried apples. Their eyes had shriveled in their heads. They were brown skeletons. The women's hair floated around their faces that were cracked with horror, mouths agape in one last silent scream.

Jessa shook her head: that was nonsense. The dead did not retain the last look of horror. The jaws had simply broken and gaped open, nothing more.

"Come, Gregoor, let us get inside."

He was still gazing at the dead. "This is Cytherea's work?"

"Yes."

"And you have set us the task of killing her?"

"It would seem so."

Gregoor pushed his horse against hers and grabbed her arm. "Jessa, I am not a coward, but this . . . Cytherea drained their lives like you or I would squeeze an orange dry."

Jessa stared at him until he loosened her arm. "We have killed sorceresses before."

"None that could do this."

Jessa nodded. "She took their lives when she took their magic, Gregoor."

He caught his breath. "I am only an herb-witch. I can't tell. Did she steal their souls?"

Jessa shivered. Though she shielded her magic, protected herself, she could still feel the answer. She understood now why she had thought the corpses were screaming silently. "No. Their souls are still there, trapped in their bodies."

"Verm take that pale bitch."

Jessa nodded. "That is the plan, Gregoor, that is the plan."

They were challenged at the town gates. A woman called down, "What do you want here, soldiers?"

Jessa answered. "A room for the night, food if you have it to spare, and stabling for the horses."

"Don't you know that you ride into a town that is cursed?"

Jessa kept the surprise from her face. "Cursed? What do you mean?"

The woman gave a rude snort of bitter laughter. "Did you not see the gibbet and its burden?"

"I saw three corpses."

"They are the mark of our curse. You would do better to ride on, soldiers."

Jessa licked her lips and eased back to speak with Gregoor. "I don't feel a curse, except on the corpses, but I am shielding myself."

He looked surprised. "You've been wasting energy shielding yourself, for how long?"

"Since we entered the edge of Cytherea's blight."

"Blight. What are you talking about?"

It was her turn to be surprised. "Look around you. Look at the plants."

The summer trees hung with limp black leaves. The grass was winter dead at the side of the road, crumbling and brown. It was utterly silent.

"Where are the little birds, the brownkins? There are always brownkins."

"Not here, not anymore." Jessa wanted to ask him how he had not noticed, but she knew the answer. He was an herb-witch, a maker of potions; his magic was a thing of incantations and ritual. Her magic was tied to the earth and what sprang from it. This desolation wounded her in a very private way. This was blasphemy. And Gregoor had seen nothing in the summer twilight.

"If you will distract the guard, I will spy out the curse, and see if it is safe to enter."

He nodded. "They might not be happy to see more spell casters after Cytherea."

"Yes, I would rather not be advertised as an earth-witch."

He rode over to the gate. "What has happened to your land?"

Jessa turned inward and did not hear the rest. She listened to the rhythm of her own body, blood flowing, heart pumping, breathing, pulsing. She came to the silence deep in her own body where everything was still. Jessa released her shield and swayed in her saddle. It took all she had not to cry out. The land wailed around her. Death. The land was wounded, dying. It was not just the witches on their scaffold that Cytherea had drained, but the earth itself. She had taken some of the life-force of the summer land. It would not recover. The town was doomed. It could not survive where no crops would grow. There were no brownkins because the birds had fled this place; everything that could had fled this place. Everything but the people. And they would leave soon enough. When autumn came and there were no crops, they would leave.

The destruction was so complete that it masked everything else. Jessa was forced to turn the horse so she could look at the town, concentrate on it, and see if it was indeed cursed. Her eyes passed the corpses and three sparks of life fluttered in the corpses, bright and clean. The souls wavered and struggled. Jessa turned away and stared at the walled town.

She stretched her magic outward, no longer flinching from the earth-death around her. The town was just a town. There was no curse. A curse would be redundant after what Cytherea had done to the land.

Jessa rode up beside Gregoor. She whispered, "There is no curse on the town. We can enter safely."

The guardswoman called down, "What was your lady friend doing so long?"

Jessa answered, "I was praying."

The woman was silent a moment. "Prayers are a good thing. Enter, strangers, and be welcome to what is left of Titos."

There was one small tavern in the town, and they were the only strangers. The windows were shuttered, though the summer night was mild. An elderly woman muttered in her sleep, dreaming before an unnecessary fire. Jessa wondered if they thought fire and light would keep out the evil, like a child crying in the night. The place stank of stale beer and the sweat of fear. The tavernkeeper himself came to take their orders. He was a large beefy man, but his eyes were red-rimmed as if from tears.

The tavern sign had said simply, "Esteban's Tavern." Jessa took a chance. "You are Esteban?"

He looked at her, eyes not quite focused, as if he were only half-listening. "Yes, I am he. Do you wish to eat?"

"Yes. But more than food we would like information."

She had his attention now. His dark eyes stared at her, full of anger, and a fine and burning hatred, like the sun burning through glass. "What kind of information?"

Gregoor brushed her hand, a warning not to press this man. But Jessa felt a magic in the room, untapped but there. It was not coming from the tavernkeeper. "A gibbet stands outside your town gates. How did it come to be there?"

Large hands knotted the rag he had stuck in his belt. His voice was a dark whisper. "Get out."

"Excuse me, tavernkeep, I meant no offense, but such a sight is uncommon."

"Get . . . out." He looked up at her as he spoke and there was death in his eyes, death born of grief.

Jessa knew about such grief and how it ate you from the inside out until there was nothing left until you died or satisfied your vengeance. She spoke, low and clear, "Where is your wife, tavernkeep?"

He threw back his head and screamed, then flung their table to the side and advanced on Jessa. She kept out of his reach, a knife in her hand, but she did not want to harm him. The magic she had felt flared and crept along her skin: sorcery.

The old woman by the fire was standing now, leaning on her walking stick. One hand was clawlike in the air before her. "Enough of this." Power rode her voice, a lash of obedience. The big man stood unsure, arms drooping at his sides, tears sliding down his cheeks.

Jessa sheathed her knife, unable to do anything else. Very few people could have forced an obedience spell upon Jessa.

The old woman turned angry eyes on her. "Did you have to hurt him?"

"You would not show yourself."

"Well, I am here now, girl. What do you want? And I warn you, if it is not something worthy of the pain you have caused, you will be punished for your rudeness."

Jessa bowed, never taking her eyes from the woman. She felt Gregoor close at her side and caught the glint of steel in his hand. So the obedience spell had affected only Jessa and the man. That was something to remember. "I seek the death of Cytherea the Mad."

The woman stared at Jessa for the space of heartbeats. Jessa knew she was being weighed and measured, tested. The old woman laughed then, an unexpectedly young sound, but the body remained old. "An assassin. Two assassins."

Jessa and Gregoor shifted uncomfortably, for there was nothing that should have given them away. "We are not . . ."

The old woman said, "Do not lie, whoever you are. I have the gift of trueseeing."

Jessa swallowed. It was a rare talent, and one that was proof against all lies, magical or mundane. "We did not enter this town under false pretenses. If you are a truthseer, then you know I mean what I say. I am here to kill Cytherea."

The woman's face was solemn as she studied them. "You believe what you say, that much is true. But saying you will kill her and doing so are not the same thing."

"That is true. We seek information to aid us in our task."

Esteban said, "Can you kill her?"

Jessa looked at him. His eyes were grief-filled wounds. "Yes. I am Wizardsbane, and this will not be the first, or even the tenth, wizard I have slain."

The old woman said, "And you, who follow her like a shadow, who are you?"

Gregoor sheathed his blade. "I am Gregoor Steelsinger, also known as Deathbringer."

"Such auspicious names, young ones. But can you live up to them?"

Jessa said, "We are willing to risk our lives to prove worthy of our names. Are you willing to help us destroy the madwoman who has raped your village?"

"I will tell you what I can, Jessamine Wizardsbane, but it is precious little. I am Teodora Truthseer."

Esteban brought food out to them, then sat to listen. Jessa would have protested, but Teodora said, "His wife and daughter hang on the gibbet outside our town. Surely he deserves a seat at this table."

Jessa nodded.

"The first we knew of trouble was a snowstorm from a clear summer sky. It was a storm driven by an ice elemental, cold as the netherhells. Cytherea came out of that storm, an ice demon at her side. She told us her terms for saving our town." Teodora paused and took a drink. "I fought Cytherea when she arrived at our gates. I challenged her to win safety for my town." Teodora smiled and looked at her age-gnarled hands. "I lost. But I did not lose through sorcery. There I could have matched her. She wore a ring on her left hand, an enchanted ring. I walked out the town gates a woman of thirty and was carried back in a woman of sixty."

Jessa and Gregoor exchanged glances. "What sort of ring could age a woman like that?" Gregoor asked.

"Cytherea did not age me, so much as curse me with old age. She wears a ring of curses."

Gregoor gave a low whistle. "That is an expensive item."

Jessa said, "Is that how she bound . . ."

Teodora interrupted her. "Esteban, could you please refill my glass?"

The man looked suspicious, but got up to do as the sorceress asked.

Teodora spoke low to them. "You were asking if the ring is how Cytherea bound the souls to the bodies."

"Yes."

"Esteban does not know his wife and daughter are still in torment. I think it would be unwise to mention it in front of him."

Gregoor asked, "Is it what she used?"

"Yes."

Esteban set the mug down and Teodora said, "Thank you, Esteban."

Jessa asked, "How did she take the earth-witches' magic and the land's magic as well?"

Teodora stared at her full mug, brown-spotted hands tight gripped. "She wears a necklace, a square-cut emerald set in gold. It is a unique enchantment. It is attuned to earth-magic and steals only that."

"So this necklace contains all the earth-magic she has stolen?"

Teodora nodded.

"You are a truthseer. Is there a way to release the magics or to destroy the enchantments?"

"The ring of curses is not unlimited in power. It has so many curses in it just like a human curse-maker. If the ring is used up, empty before being re-enchanted, then all the curses the ring caused this time will be undone."

"You would be young again?"

"Yes." Teodora studied the food on her plate and talked without looking at anyone. "The necklace is different. It has perhaps an unlimited ability to absorb power. The only way to release the magic is to destroy it."

Gregoor asked, "And how do we do that?"

"You might give it back to the earth from which it came."

"The exact earth," Jessa asked, "or metaphysically speaking, so any earth would do?"

"Any earth will do."

Jessa smiled.

Gregoor said, "You've thought of a plan, haven't you?"

"I've thought of a possibility."

Teodora asked, "How can we help?"

"Gregoor will need some herbs to make a potion. And I was wondering if your town can boast a curse-maker."

Esteban and Teodora exchanged glances. "Why, yes, but he is old and not powerful enough to curse Cytherea."

"I don't want him to curse Cytherea, I want him to curse me."

TWO days later they rode out of Titos, a new potion at their belts and a curse for each of them.

Gregoor grunted and twisted in his saddle, trying to scratch the middle of his back.

"It will only be worse if you claw at it."

He looked at Jessa through red, inflamed eyes, nearly swollen shut. "You said pick a curse, so I did. How was I to know the Verm-cursed rash would get this bad?"

Jessa sighed. "I suggested a curse that would have been serious enough, but would not have hampered your fighting skills."

He clawed at his hand. "You wanted me rendered impotent. No, thank you."

She almost laughed. "I am childless until my curse is removed."

"But that's different. You were taking a potion to prevent children anyway. I have a use for my manhood."

Jessa smiled, but she felt a heaviness in her stomach, an empty heaviness. She felt the loss. "If this rash grows any worse, you will be all but useless by the time we face Cytherea."

He rode up beside her. "I am sorry, Jessa. I did not understand. If I had known, I might even have let him unman me." He shivered in the sunlight, skin twitching. "I would not have you be killed because I was distracted by this infernal itching." He clawed at his arms, raising welts.

"You're going to bleed if you keep scratching. Don't you have an ointment to help yourself?"

"Yes, but I was hoping to save it until we were nearer our destination."

"I think we are close enough. Use the ointment before you flay yourself alive."

Gregoor rummaged in his saddlebags and came up with a sealed pot. "This will take some time."

"We have time. I have a spell to do myself."

He nodded and dismounted. The grass was shoulder high to him and brushed the horse's bellies. Wild bellis flowers filled the air with their delicate scent. A swift, quarreling flock of brownkins flew overhead. Jessa breathed in the summer bounty. Her magic pulsed and swelled with the ripening grass, the swift flight of birds, the tiny hidden creatures. Everything was magic for the taking, for an earth-witch.

Gregoor came to stand at her stirrup. His face was coated with an oily lotion. "You sparkle like pale flame."

She grinned at him, stretching arms skyward. "I feel like I should burst into flame, swollen with power."

He frowned.

Jessa laughed. "There's no danger of that, Gregoor. Don't frown so; it will make you itch." She touched his shoulder.

He jumped as if burned. "Your power poured over my arm. It was . . . unexpected."

"Surely making your herb potions fills you with magic?"

He shook his head. "Nothing like that. I'm an herb-witch, Jessa. Our magic is a quieter thing. You could pass for a sorceress, now."

"It's always like that in spring and summer, but winter," she shivered, "winter is a poor time for earth-witches."

"Then what will you do behind Cytherea's spell line?"

"I have absorbed enough power to do a few spells, if I am careful."

"Then what?"

"Then I won't be able to pretend I am a sorceress anymore. Cytherea will know me for an earth-witch, and our plan had better work."

Gregoor looked up at her, the swelling and redness already leaving his eyes.

"You look much better. How do you feel?"

"The best I've felt in three days of travel. I'll be able to watch your back."

"I never thought you wouldn't."

Gregoor remounted and they pushed through a stand of pine trees. Bushtails chattered and scolded overhead, showering them with pine needles. Jessa felt the first cool tendril of power, someone else's power. She slammed down her shields, cutting herself off from the land, but protecting herself from what lay ahead.

The horses pawed nervously at the top of the ridge. Up through the trees, mist was oozing. Sunlight cut through the mist, sparkling on a line of ice-covered trees. The summer leaves were crumbled, blackened, ice-coated. Frost and snow lay in glittering drifts at the foot of the ridge.

Jessa glanced up at the waving greenery overhead. Yellow snake lilies nodded on the forest floor. "Definitely the work of elementals and demons."

"Do you think we can bargain with the demon?"

"Our plan depends on it."

"What if it doesn't agree?"

She smiled at him. "Then, Gregoor, we will see if the god Magnus truly does cry tears of blood."

"I did not plan on meeting Him so soon."

"Nor I. Let's get out the winter gear."

Sweat trickled down Jessa's spine. The fur hood was oppressive. Gregoor waited beside her, sweat-carved runnels melting the ointment on his face.

Cool mist swirled around the horses' legs, but the summer sun beat down on them. Winter was a slash of brilliant diamond ice. Snow lay inches deep. The green belt of summer had been sliced cleanly and completely.

Jessa urged her horse forward. The hooves crunched in the snow's edge. The chill breath of winter cooled the sweat on her face instantly. Her breath fogged and began to crystallize on the fur trim of her hood. Something large moved in the trees. Jessa signaled Gregoor to wait.

She could see nothing and yet she knew something had moved. The winter-ruined trees were utterly still. Snow stretched smooth and untouched. But . . . there was a spot near a large straight elm tree that Jessa could not look at. No matter how hard she tried to stare at it, her vision kept slipping by it. *Don't look at me*, it seemed to say, *I am not here*, but of course that meant something was there. The question was, what?

She signaled Gregoor to come up beside her, slowly.

They had ridden only a few strides when the air wavered and a demon was leaning against the elm. Both sets of arms were crossed over his chest. He was about ten feet tall, only a little less white than the snow. His scales shimmered like mother-of-pearl. Two slender horns grew from his head. His tail twitched in the snow. Jessa was reminded of a cat about to pounce.

The demon's bat-ribbed ears curled and uncurled. "I am the guardian of this spell line. If you cross even one step farther, you will be trapped until the spell is complete."

"When will that be?" Jessa asked.

He blinked large purple eyes. "When Cytherea the Mad wills it, and not before." A forked tongue licked his lips, exposing teeth like ice daggers. "So turn back while you may. You have been warned."

"Thank you for the warning. If we ride farther, what will happen to us?"

He shrugged one pair of shoulders. "Cytherea will decide."

"What will you do if we ride farther in?"

"I," he said, placing a claw on his chest, "nothing, yet. You will have to huddle in the town while Cytherea does her business."

"How long will that take?"

The demon looked up at the ice trees. He smiled, flashing fangs. "Not long, I think."

Jessa said, "Then we will cross and wait if we must."

"Come across, then." The demon made a sweeping bow, motioning with his many arms.

They rode forward, skirting out of the demon's reach, though distance alone would not save them if the demon chose to be nasty.

The demon called, "Herb-witch."

Jessa looked back at Gregoor. He was staring at the ground, very determinedly.

"Look at me, herb-witch, look at me," the demon hissed.

"Stop it," Jessa said. "He does not have the magic to resist you."

"And you do?" He turned his gaze upon her, perfect violet, like the eyes of the blind. Jessa would not meet his gaze. The demon laughed.

"You said you would not harm us if we passed."

"I lied."

She looked at him without meeting his eyes. "Will you stand in our way?"

"Not now. But when Cytherea is done with her little . . . chore, then she will let me choose my reward." The demon was suddenly standing before them. Jessa's horse screamed and reared, hoofs lashing the air.

The demon grinned as Jessa fought to control the animal. "Perhaps I will ask for you, sorceress."

Jessa glared at him. "Will you beg for a treat like a well-trained dog?"

The demon's ears curled into tight rolls, his claws flexing the air. "I am no dog, woman. I am ice demon and I will show you what that means."

"You will harm me before Cytherea sees me? Is that wise?"

The demon roared, clawing at the trees, raking ice and wood into splinters. The horses went wild. When Jessa and Gregoor slowed the trembling animals, Jessa found a splinter of ice in her cheek. She pulled it out and found it bloody. She would have thrown it on the ground, but the demon was watching her, eyes intent, a strange eagerness in his scaled face. She held the bloody crystal, unsure what to do with it.

Gregoor whispered, "Jessa, try not to make it more angry than you have to."

"Cytherea is your enemy, not us. She has bound you into her service. What if we could free you?"

The demon stared at her. "How?"

"If she is dead, then you are free."

He snorted. "You cannot kill her with sorcery."

"We will not kill her with sorcery."

"Why tell me, when now I can warn her?"

"You want your freedom. We want her death."

"What do you want of me, sorceress?"

"An oath that you will not help Cytherea against us."

The demon flashed fangs. "Of course, I promise, I will not hurt either of you."

"No, demon, an oath to Verm and Loth."

His ears furled in surprise. "A vow to the dark ones will sever Cytherea's control over me. Will allow me to stand and watch." He grinned. "One of the few things that will. You are not just a sorceress, are you?"

"No," she said.

"And what do you vow, mortal?"

"We vow to free you."

"I simply watch while you kill Cytherea. Then I am free."

Jessa nodded.

"The exchange is fair, and because of that I cannot take it."

Gregoor started to protest, but Jessa silenced him. "I understand, demon; you must come out the better in the bargain."

He nodded. "You have dealt with demons before."

"Perhaps." She caught Gregoor's shocked look and ignored it.

"What do you offer to sweeten the bargain?" the demon asked.

She held up the bloody splinter. "Blood."

The demon licked his lips. "And from the man?"

Gregoor said, "No."

Jessa frowned at him. "Will you bargain with just my blood?"

"If I cannot harm either of you, then I must have blood from both of you, or we fight here and now."

"Gregoor, just a few drops . . ."

"Look at its face."

The demon's face was lined with hunger; he seemed almost

to have grown thinner. He shimmered with a horrible eagerness. "I see him," Jessa said softly.

"Then how can you offer him our blood? I am an herb-witch, and I could kill with a single drop of it. What could a demon do with blood?"

"I will taste your soul," the demon whispered.

Gregoor said, "I will not give that thing my blood."

"Then we will fight it here and now. It is your choice, Gregoor. I understand your uneasiness and I will abide by your decision."

He shifted in his saddle, hand stroking his sword hilt.

"Fight me, wizard. I will have your blood one way or another."

"No," Gregoor suddenly said. "I will give what is asked."

Jessa held out the bloody shard. The demon reached for it, and she covered it with her hand. "Swear, demon. Swear by Verm and Loth."

"Let the wizard draw blood first."

Gregoor took off his gloves and drew his dagger. He nicked one finger, letting three drops of blood fall into the snow. "There is your blood." He wiped his dagger clean and applied pressure to the small wound.

Jessa said, "Make oath, demon."

"I swear by the birds of Loth and the hounds of Verm that I will not harm you by direct actions."

The demon grimaced, claws clicking like ice breaking, but he repeated it word perfect. Jessa handed over the ice shard with its cold blood. The demon took it delicately in his claws and licked it, daintily as a cat with cream. He licked it clean, but the ice did not melt. He chewed up the ice, crunching it with his teeth.

Then the demon knelt in the snow, all glittering in a shaft of light. He rolled his eyes at Gregoor and scooped up the bloody snow. Sucking sounds filled the forest, obscene and joyous. The snow did not melt at his touch, and he swallowed. He grinned and stood, stretching arms wide. "I will see you in your dreams." He vanished.

Gregoor said, "What does that mean?"

"We will relive this in our nightmares, with certain changes."

"Jessa, what have we done?"

"We have bargained with a demon. Did you think to come out of it untouched?"

He stared down at his gloved hands. "I don't know what I thought." He drew a deep shuddering breath and looked at her. "Let's go kill this bitch and get out of here."

Jessa smiled, her eyes full of a strange dark light. "Let us go hunting. May Magnus guide our strokes and strengthen our spells."

The village of Bardou lay in a small hollow, trusting to be hidden rather than protected by a stout wall. Perhaps a dozen houses huddled in the snow. There was activity near one end, people moving. A scream carried through the cold air. Two figures were left isolated in the snow as the rest backed away into the houses. A tall figure in red, fur-cloaked, stood alone before the two who had been cast out.

Gregoor said, "It would be better to wait until she is in the middle of her spell. We could catch her by surprise."

Jessa shook her head. "Enough have died in my place already. I cannot let these two die while I watch." She met Gregoor's eyes. The killing light had faded from her face, replaced by something he could not decipher. "By saving these people our plan falls apart."

"I know, but this is your choice, Jessa. I will abide by your decision."

Jessa smiled. "Perhaps I have been playing the mercenary too long." She kicked her horse into a gallop and Gregoor followed. The red-cloaked figure was chanting strange twisted words that slid along Jessa's mind and left a stain. Jessa called, "Hold, Cytherea, mother of Soldon."

The woman looked up, startled. Jessa glimpsed a pale face. As she rode closer, the woman stared at her with eyes the cold gray of good steel. There was no expression on Cytherea's face, only a blank waiting. Thin yellow hair blew in strands around a fox-lined hood. The reddish-brown fur made the face paler.

"You seek the earth-witch who killed your only son. Is that not true?"

There was no change in the pale eyes, but she nodded.

Gregoor had a potion open in his hand, waiting.

"Let these poor fools go; I am here."

Cytherea shook her head, slowly. Her voice was as flat and unemotional as her face. "You are a sorceress. Do not stand in my way, or I will destroy you."

Jessa rode her horse between the two huddled earth-witches and Cytherea. The first flicker of emotion passed those gray eyes: anger. Gregoor dismounted, staying off to one side.

"Do you remember the village of Threllkill?"

Cytherea frowned. "They killed my husband, and my son destroyed them for it."

"Your husband died of old age. Even sorcerers die, Cytherea."

"No," she said.

"Your son destroyed innocent people, but I survived. When I was grown, I hunted him down and I killed him."

Anger flared and turned the eyes a darker color, the color of storm clouds. "Get out of my way, little sorceress, or I will kill you as I slew the earth creatures that killed my son."

Jessa dismounted and pushed back her hood. Gregoor poured the potion upon the ground.

Suddenly, the world was cold; the cold that numbs bones and steals air from lungs. A glittering figure of ice appeared beside Cytherea; vague eyes and mouth appeared, but nothing more. The ice elemental whispered to the sorceress, "The man spilled a potion on the ground."

Cytherea blinked as if trying to focus on what was happening. "Demon, where are you? Jecktor?"

The demon appeared and bowed before her. "Kill them, Jecktor, get them from my sight."

The demon said, "I fear I cannot."

She turned on him, anger flashing sorcery like embers on the wind. "What?"

Jessa reached out to the earth where Gregoor's potion lay, pooling and still warm in the snow. She touched it with her earth-magic. There was the scent of green growing earth, strong and clean.

Cytherea turned back from the cowering demon. "What are you?"

Jessa said, "I am earth-witch."

The earth exploded upward, showering down dirt and rock. A figure stood full-grown from the ground. It was ten feet tall, roughly man-shaped, formed of rich black earth and the redness of clay. One eye was a diamond, the other an emerald. It took a heavy step forward, and the ground moved.

The ice elemental grew like an ice fire and rushed over the earth elemental, shrieking like a banshee wind.

Cytherea screamed, "Then die, earth-witch!" She pointed her left hand and its ring at Jessa. A shriveling, killing magic flashed outward. Jessa staggered from its touch, but it washed past her as if she were a rock in a stream.

Cytherea stared at her. "No!" Again she raised the ring. The ground began to smoke and pop to either side of Jessa.

Cytherea turned to Gregoor. "Die!" He stood unmoved and unharmed. "What is happening here?"

"We are both already cursed. You cannot curse someone twice," Jessa said.

The sorceress shrieked and tore her cloak away. She stood, hair streaming in the wind, the emerald necklace sparkling in the cold light. She put a hand over the emerald and began to chant.

Encased in ice, the ice elemental moved forward, its movements stiff. Ice froze the earth, until the earth-giant moved in agony. The ice wind shrieked in triumph.

Jessa felt the power growing. She felt the pull of the enchantment. It called to her magic; it beckoned, a poisoned seduction. Her magic answered it, flaring and shredding on the winter wind. It drew off the magic she had absorbed. Jessa drew her sword and started forward, but she could not move against the necklace. It was sucking her dry.

A throwing knife blossomed in Cytherea's side. She shrieked and staggered.

Jessa saw Gregoor coming forward, another knife in his hand. She fell slowly to her knees in the snow.

Gregoor screamed, "Jessa!"

Cytherea had regained her control. She gestured and sorcery flared in her hands. Blue flame enveloped Gregoor.

There was a crackling thunder and the earth elemental burst free of the ice. Then it was suddenly running, shaking the ground as it came. Cytherea was forced to turn her attention to the earth-giant.

Gregoor fell face down into the snow, unmoving.

Blue light and ice crawled over the earth elemental. Jessa felt it scream through the frozen ground. She began to crawl toward Cytherea, naked sword dragging over the snow.

Cytherea was bathed in blue flame; she crackled and seemed to glow. Jessa was almost close enough to touch her skirts. Stray bits of power crawled along Jessa's skin, burning with cold fire. She staggered to her feet, sword held two-handed for an upward thrust.

The ice elemental hissed, "Behind you, mistress."

It was too late. The steel bit into Cytherea's back; the blue fire shredded and vanished. Jessa shoved the blade upward, seeking her heart. Cytherea shrieked, but she would not die. She put a hand on the emerald necklace and Jessa felt the power begin to grow.

Jessa screamed, "Die, damn you, die!"

The earth elemental leaned over them, one massive hand reaching. Cytherea yelled, "No, the necklace is mine! You can't have it!" The earth elemental stood, the broken chain dangling from his massive fingers. Earth-magic poured out of the broken enchantment, free at last. Magic that swelled and flowed and carried Jessa with it until she thought she would explode with the power. It rushed over and through her, a magically visible green fire.

Jessa drew her sword free. Bloody, but still alive, Cytherea turned and began another spell. Jessa's blade crawled with emerald fire. The silver-green blade sliced outward. The sorceress's head spun off into the snow. The body toppled into the crimson-washed snow.

Jessa dropped to the ground, unsure of how to cope with so

much power. Gregoor was huddled against the earth, staring wide-eyed. Green grass showed in the snow. Summer warmth beat down. Earth-magic pulsed and spread from the earth elemental as it grasped the emerald necklace in one massive hand.

The ice elemental had fled. The demon bowed to Jessa. "Earth-witch, I am most impressed." As he faded from sight, he said, "Perhaps we will meet again, some winter's night."

Gregoor crawled to her. "I can't stand up. The earth pulses like a great heartbeat."

Jessa could not speak past the magic. She could feel it racing over the ravaged land, healing, awakening, reviving.

Finally, she said, "Begone, earthling, back to the depths from which you came. Thank you for aid." The elemental melted into the earth, taking the necklace with it. Cytherea's body lay in a circle of black fresh-turned earth.

Jessa crawled to the dead sorceress and looked down on her. The face was blank as any dead man's. "Peace at last, mother, peace at last."

Gregoor was scratching his face. "You did it."

"We did it, Gregoor."

He grinned, then grimaced as he tore his coat to get to new itches.

Jessa smiled. "Perhaps the village of Bardou boasts a curse-maker."

He looked at her, a hopeful light in his eyes. "Oh, that would be a blessing indeed."

"Come, they should be grateful enough to remove a couple of curses." Jessa paused, staring at a pale hand; the ring of curses was still on the left hand. It was a slim band of iron, empty now, but waiting. Jessa slipped the ring from Cytherea's finger.

"It's expensive to get something like that re-enchanted," Gregoor said.

She slipped the ring into her pouch. "But well worth it, don't you think?"

"I can think of a few uses for it."

Jessa reached out and touched him and green fire flowed from her across his skin. He gasped, then forced a grin.

"Extraordinary," he whispered.

They helped each other to stand and began to limp toward the village.

There was a strong scent of roses on the air, almost choking in its sweetness. Jessa turned.

There in the earth was a fresh rosebush, blossoms flared to the new sun. The roses were yellow, the color of Cytherea's hair.

Jessa called softly, "Mother." A breeze began to blow gently against them. The earth-fire began to melt into the ground. Jessa found herself crying. She walked alone to the roses, on unsteady legs. The flowers moved, stretching toward her hands, without aid of wind. One small blossom rubbed against her hand.

Gregoor asked, "What is it?"

"I think I am being forgiven."

"Forgiven for what?"

Jessa did not answer; for some things there were no words. And some things were not meant to be shared.

STEALING SOULS

This is the first story I ever sold. It's the one I sent to Marion Zimmer Bradley after she rejected "A Token for Celandine." This story is also the one I edited after going through my one and only writing workshop. The writers who taught it were Emma Bull, Will Shetterly, and Stephan Gould. All working, selling writers, which is what you should look for in a workshop. They didn't teach me how to be a better writer, but they did teach me how to be a better editor of my own work. I also met the beginnings of my writing group, The Alternate Historians, there. Only two of the original members are still left, me and Deborah Millitello. But we've existed as a group for over ten years now. The seven of us have over forty books, and untold short stories, published. All but one of us had never sold a thing before joining the group. Not a bad track record. This story is the first appearance of Sidra and Leech, who would later appear in "The Curse-Maker."

STEALING souls was hard; stealing them back was harder. Sebastiane had spent fifteen years learning just how hard.

The Red Goat Tavern was full of people. They swirled, laughing, round Sebastiane's table but did not touch her. For she was the mercenary Sidra Ironfist. And she had passed through many lands as Sidra until she had more stories told about her under that name than her own. She towered over most of the people in the room. The two swords at her waist, one long and one short, looked well cared for and much used. Scars decorated her arms and hands like spider tracings. Her cool gray eyes had a way of staring through a person, as if nothing was hidden.

She had been Sidra so long that sometimes she wondered where Sebastiane had gone. But fighting was not her true occupation. It was more an avocation that allowed her entrance to places her occupation would have closed to her. Most people did not welcome a thief. Especially a thief who had no intention of sharing her prize with the local thieves' guild. Sidra had traveled half a continent and bartered a piece of her soul to be here. She would share with no one.

But then the local thieves' guild did not traffic in souls. And that was the goal this time. There would be jewels and magic items to bring out, but like every good thief, she did not allow baubles to distract her from the main goal.

The herb-witch had said that the bones she sought would be in two earthenware pots. They would be bound with black and green braided cord and suspended from a thin branch made up of some white wood. They would be hung high up in the room where the wizard performed his magic.

The souls in question belonged to Sebastiane's older sisters. They had vanished when she was ten. No one knew what had happened to them, but there were rumors. Rumors of a wizard that had needed twin girls for a forbidden spell done only twice before in all history. A spell to bring great power to a mere herb-witch. Enough power to allow the wizard to taste other magics.

The spell was forbidden because not only did the girls have to die but their souls were imprisoned. Imprisoning souls was a very serious offense if you never intended to let them go.

Sebastiane, the child, had been an apprentice thief and had little hope of confronting such a powerful wizard. But Sidra Ironfist, mercenary and master thief, had a chance.

The little girl of long ago had vowed to Magnus of the Red Hand, god of assassins and god of vengeance. The vow had held firm for fifteen years until she sat only an hour's ride from the wizard who had murdered her sisters.

The hatred of him was gone, killed in the years of surviving.

Her sisters' faces were distant things that she couldn't always see clearly. But the vow remained. Sebastiane had come for the bones of her sisters.

The wizard's death would be an added sweetness, but she was no true warrior to go seeking blood vengeance. She was a thief at heart, which is a more patient and practical creature. Her goal was to rescue her sisters' souls from the spell. The wizard's death was secondary.

She had left Sidra's friends behind, all save one, Milon Songsmith. The minstrel leaned back in his chair, a grin on his face. He drained his fourth tankard of ale and grinned wider. He was her bard and had been so for eight years. He had made Sidra Ironfist a legend, and his own talents were in great demand.

He would follow her until she died, and then perhaps he would find another hero to follow.

Sidra had not denied him the right to come on this adventure. If she died here, then Milon would sing of it. There were worse things to leave behind than songs.

But somehow she was not the perfect vengeance seeker she had wanted to be. Her life seemed more precious now than it had fifteen years ago. She wanted to live to see her mercenary band again. Black Abe was all right for a temporary command, but he let his emotions carry him away at awkward times. Sidra had welded them into a fighting force that any king in the civilized lands would welcome. Gannon the Sorcerer, Brant the Ax, Emil Swordmaster, Jayme the Quick, and Thetis the Archer. She would have Black Abe's heart if he let one of them die without just cause.

Sidra waved the barmaid away when Milon called her over for the fifth time. "You've had enough, Songsmith."

He flashed a crooked smile. "You can never have enough ale or enough adventure." His rich tenor voice was precise, no slurring. His voice never betrayed him no matter how much he drank.

"Any more ale and there won't be any adventuring tomorrow, at least not for you. I am not going to wait all morning while you sleep it off."

He looked pained. "I would not do that to you."

"You've done it before," Sidra pointed out.

He laughed. "Well, maybe once. To bed then, my dear Sidra, before I embarrass you any further."

Morning found them the first ones up. They were served cold meat and cheese by a hollow-eyed barmaid. She clasped a shawl around her nightdress, obviously intending to go back to sleep after they had gone. But she brought out some fresh, though cold, bread and dried fruit. And she did not grumble while she did it.

They walked out into a world locked in the fragile darkness just before dawn. The air seemed to shimmer as the dark purple sky faded to blue and the stars were snuffed out like candles in a wind.

Milon drew his cloak about him and said, "It is a chilly morning."

She did not answer but went for the horses. The stable boy stood patiently holding the reins. Sidra had paid extra for such treatment, but it was worth it to be off before curious eyes could see.

Sidra led the way and Milon clucked to his horse. He and the horse were accustomed to following Sidra without knowing where they were going, or why. The forest trail they followed turned stubbornly away from their destination. Not even a deer path led to where they wanted to go. Then, abruptly, the trees ended. It was a clearing at least fifty feet across. The ground was gray as if covered in ash. Nothing grew in it. Grass and wildflowers chased round the edges but did not enter. In the middle of the ash circle was a tower. It rose arrow straight toward the brightening sky. The first rays of sun glimmered along it as if it were made of black mirrors.

The tower was all of one shining ebony piece. There were no marks of stone or mortar; it seemed to have been drawn from the earth whole and complete. Nothing broke its black perfection. There was no door or window.

But Sebastiane the thief knew that there was always a way in. It was only a matter of finding it. She led the way onto the ash ground and Milon followed. The horses were left loosely tied to the trees some distance away. If neither one of them came back, the horses could eventually break loose and find new homes.

The ground crunched underfoot as if it were formed of ground rock. And yet it couldn't be stone; stone did not crumble to ash. Milon whispered to her, "Demon work." She nodded, for she felt it, too. Evil clung to the black tower like a smothering shroud.

Sidra stood beside the tower. She laid her shield on the ground and knelt beside it. She ran hands down the scars of her arms. The scars were far too minor to be battle wounds.

She unlocked the sword guard that held the short sword in place. Rising of its own accord, it sprang to her hand. And the sword laughed, a tinny sound without lungs to hold it.

Milon shifted and moved far away from the naked blade.

Sidra noticed it and politely moved so he would not see the entire ritual. This was one thing that her bard did not like to sing about.

The sword crooned, "Free, bare steel, feel the wind, ahhh."

Sidra said, "Our greatest task is before us, blood blade."

The sword hissed, "Name me."

"You who were Blood-Letter when the world was new. You

who were Wound-Maker in the hands of a king. You who were Soul-Piercer and took the life of a hero. You who were Blood-Hunger and ate your way through an army. I name thee blade mine, I name thee Leech."

It chortled, "Leech, Leech, I am Leech, I live on blood, I crave its crimson flow, I am Leech. So named, power given."

Sidra had risked her soul five years ago to name the sword. But it had seemed inordinately pleased from the very first at such a name as Leech.

Milon had complained that it wasn't poetic enough. But she left the poetry to the minstrel. Her job was to survive.

The blade whispered, "Feed me."

Sidra held the blade out before her, naked steel at face level. She pressed the flat of the blade between the palms of her hands. She spoke the words of invocation. "Feed gently, Leech, for we have much work to do."

There was always that moment of waiting when Sidra wondered if this time the sword would take too much and kill her. But it bobbed gently between her hands. The razor-sharp blade brought blood in a sharp, painful wash down her hands. But the cut was narrow, slicing just below the skin. The blade said, "Sacrifice made, contract assured."

Sidra ignored the wound. It would heal in a moment or two to become another scar. She did not bother to clean the blade, as all blood was absorbed cleanly. For it truly did feed.

She resheathed the blade, and it hummed tunelessly to itself, echoing up through the leather sheath. Sidra set to searching the black stone with her fingers. But she found nothing. It was like touching well-made glass without even a bubble to spoil its smoothness.

There was nothing there, but if illusion hid the door, then

Leech could find it. She bared the humming sword and said, "Find me a door, Leech."

The humming picked up a note to a more cheerful tune. She recognized the tune as the new ballad of Cullen Tunemaster. Leech seemed very fond of Cullen's tunes.

They paced the tower three times before the sword could make the door visible to her. It looked ordinary enough—just a brown wooden door with metal studding. It was man height.

"Can you see the door now, Milon?"

"I see nothing but blackness."

Sidra reached her hand out toward him, and he moved to take it. Leech fought her left-handed grip and slashed at the man. Sidra jerked the sword sharply, "Behave, Leech."

"I hunger. You did not feed me."

"You did not ask."

It pouted, "I'm asking now." By the rules she could have refused it, for it had done its task. But keeping the sword happy assured that she could wield it and live; doing both was not always easy. An unhappy blood blade was an untrustworthy blood blade. She held the blade against her left forearm and let it slice its own way into the skin. It was a mere nick of crimson. She offered her hand once more to Milon.

A drop of sweat beaded at Milon's hairline, and he took her hand tentatively, as far from the sword as possible. "I can see the door." He released her hand and backed away from the sword once more.

Sidra knelt before the door, but before she could touch the lock, she noticed that the door moved. It wasn't much of a movement, just a twitch like a horsehide when a fly settles on it. She asked the sword, "What is it?"

"It is an ancient enchantment not much used now."

"What is the quickest and quietest way to win past it? The wizard will notice us setting his door on fire."

"True, but would you rather chop through that much meat? Even I cannot kill it, only damage it. Oh, it would be a glorious outpouring of Mood. But it would not be quick." It sounded disappointed.

Sidra hated to use the day's only fireball so early on.

She hoped she would not need it later. She faced the door and pointed the sword's tip toward it. A fireball the size of her fist shot from it. It expanded in a whirling dance of heat. The wildfire exploded against the door. A high keening wail sounded. When the fire died away, the door was a blackened hull encircling the doorway. The ruined door was screaming.

The sword said, "Such work deserves a hearty meal."

Sidra did not argue but let the blade slice over her left wrist. The vein was slashed and blood welled dark and eager over the hungry blade. It stayed near, lapping at the wound until it closed.

"Follow close, Milon, but be wary. Not everything in a demon-made tower will be civilized enough to know you for a bard."

He nodded. "I have followed you into many adventures. I would not miss this one out of fear."

She said, "Then come, my brave bard, but watch your back."

She stepped over the blackened door rim of the door creature. It whimpered as she and the sword passed through it. They stood in a circular chamber made of the same black rock. But a staircase made of good gray stone curved downward in the center of the room.

"Light the lantern here, Milon, and carry it high."

The lantern's flickering yellow light soon danced in the small room.

Sidra led the way and tripped the first trap. Three darts clanged against her shield and fell to the steps. She knelt carefully, shield up and alert. The dart's tips were blackened with a thick tarry substance. She did not touch it.

She spoke for Milon's benefit. "Poisoned. Don't touch anything unless you have to. Watch where you step."

Sidra found the next trap and tripped it with the sword. A spear shot out and buried itself into the stone of the far wall. It would have taken her through the chest. And still the stone stairs wound deeper into the earth. There was nothing for a long time save the lantern's golden shadows and their footsteps echoing on the stairs. Then the stairs ended at a small landing in front of a door. But there was one last trap. And Sidra was not at all sure she could trip it without being harmed.

She studied it for a time, directing Milon to point the lantern here and there. There were six separate pressure points on the stairs that she had found. They were set in a pattern that would make it difficult if not impossible to walk the last five steps. They could jump, but Sidra didn't trust the landing either. And they were too far away for her to find traps on it yet.

She could not pass the stairs, but the sword could. If it would do it. Moving without human aid was something Leech did not prefer to do. Only twice before had she asked it to and each time the blood price had been high.

"Leech, I want you to set off the traps on the stairs and then come gently back to my hand."

"Payment," it whispered.

"Blood, as always."

"Fresh blood," it asked.

She offered the blade her naked arm, but it remained unmoving against her skin. "What do you want, Leech?"

"Fresh blood."

"I'm offering it to you."

"Fresher blood, new blood."

Milon said, "Oh, no, no."

Sidra said, "I agree. You are my weapon. You taste my blood, no one else's."

"When we kill, I taste blood."

"I will not sacrifice Milon to feed you."

She could almost feel it thinking, weighing its options. "A taste, a fresh taste, just a nick, just a bite."

Milon said, "No, absolutely not. That steel monster is not going to taste my blood."

Sidra sighed and said, "Then I will attempt to remove the traps."

He gripped her arm. "You said you couldn't do it."

"I said that I didn't see how I could do it without getting killed."

"It's the same thing."

"No, it isn't."

"I can't let you be killed."

She just looked at him, waiting for him to make up his mind.

He shuddered and held out his arm. She unlaced the sleeve and pushed it back to bare the pale skin. The sword chuckled. "Just a taste, just a bite, just a nibble." She held the sword firmly two-handed, for she didn't trust it, and placed it against Milon's arm. The sword bit deep and quick like a serpent's strike. Milon cried out, and opened his eyes to stare in horror as the blade lapped up his blood. The wound quickly closed and the sword sighed, "New blood, fresh, good, yum."

Sidra felt that the last was added for Milon's benefit. Milon took it very seriously. He yanked down his sleeve and said, "Yum or not, that is the last of my blood you ever get, you bloodsucking toothpick."

The sword laughed.

Sidra pulled Milon back up the stairs and then released the blade. It settled onto the first pressure point. A rain of poisoned darts filled the hall like black snow.

Leech floated back to her, obediently. "I have cleared the way, O master." Sidra ignored the sarcasm and led Milon to the landing. It was not trapped. But the door was.

The poisoned darts were soon removed. And the well-oiled lock clicked under her pick. The door opened into a short straight hallway. Doors dotted the walls in geometric lines to right and left. Torches were set at regular intervals along the walls. In the still air there was the sound of chanting.

Milon started to blow out the lantern, but Sidra stopped him. She spoke close to his ear so the sound wouldn't carry. "We may need light if we have to leave quickly."

The sword started to hum in time to the chanting and she hushed it.

Sidra stared at the floor and said, "Place your feet exactly where I place mine."

He nodded to show he had understood and then concentrated on following her over a five-foot-wide area of floor. She let out a breath of air as if she had been holding it. He relaxed as well, stepping back just a half step. The floor fell out from under him and he was tumbling backward helplessly. Sidra caught his arm, but his weight pulled them both downward. He was left dangling over a pit, and she on her stomach, holding him by one arm. The torches glimmered off silvered spikes set into the floor of the pit.

She hissed, "I told you to walk where I walked."

"Let us argue this later. Pull me up." She did, rubbing her shoulder. "You're lucky you didn't dislocate my arm."

He shrugged an apology and picked up the fallen lantern.

The chanting seemed to be coming from the last door on the right-hand side. They were only three doors away from it when Sidra stopped the bard with a hand movement and knelt to study the floor. She shook her head, sending light bursts from her helmet to the walls. She said, "When I say jump, leap forward as fast as you can."

"Why?"

She stared at him a moment and then looked upward.

He would have missed it, but with her gaze to direct him, he saw the portcullis spikes ready to come crashing down. He swallowed and said, "When do we jump?"

She stood beside him and said, "Now." They stepped forward and flung themselves across the stones. Sidra rolled easily, coming to her feet before the spikes had bitten into the floor. They were trapped.

There was a swimming in the air near the torches in one corner. Sidra pointed Leech at it and concentrated. Illusions bled near fire. A demon stood at the end of the hallway.

He was perhaps eight feet tall, fairly short for an ice demon. His scales were the color of new frost and winked in the light like diamond glints on snow. His teeth were ivory daggers. His four arms were crossed over his chest and his tail rustled over the floor. He grinned and said, "Welcome."

His bat-ribbed ears rolled into tubes and then unrolled. "I would speak with you before we fight."

Sidra found herself staring into its smooth blue eyes, no pupil, just empty blue like a frozen lake. Peaceful.

Milon gripped her arm and pulled her back. "Sidra."

She shook her head roughly and faced the demon in a fighting crouch, shield close, sword ready.

He said, "Perhaps you are right. Enough talk, let us fight." He strode forward and said, "And you, bard, I know the rules; by touching her, you gave up your safe conduct."

"I do not regret what I did, ice demon. You cannot harm me if you are dead."

It chuckled, then, low in its chest.

Sidra whispered to the sword, "I want you to burn for me and aid me in slaying this ice demon."

It said, "Price will be high."

She had expected nothing less. "When is the last time you tasted demon blood?"

The sword paused and said, "Demon blood."

"If we kill it, then all its blood is yours to consume."

It gave a nervous expectant giggle. "All that demon blood, all of it. You won't remove me until I have drunk my fill?"

"I won't remove you."

It snickered. "Payment is more than generous. I will do as you ask."

The ice demon strode forward, still laughing to itself. Its claws clicked together with a sound like breaking ice. Sidra kept Leech half hidden behind her shield as if she meant to only cower before the demon. Leech burst into flame with its blade like a wick in the center of the good orange fire.

The first threads of cold oozed round her shield and she knew, magic weapon or not, the first blow must be a good one. Milon simply stared up at the creature with his back pressed against the fallen portcullis. The demon stood almost directly in front of Sidra, and she kept her head down as if she could not bear the sight of him. He spoke to the bard. "Your protector is not doing much protecting, but be patient. When I have finished with her, you will have my undivided attention."

Sidra forced Leech up while the demon was looking at Milon. The sword took him through the chest, burning brightly as the demon blood gushed over it. The blade bit through a clawed hand and sent fingers spinning. The demon screamed.

A casual swipe of the tail knocked her to the ground, and a claw raked along the shield. The nails left grooves in the metal. A hand caught her helmet and sent her head ringing back against the floor. Leech moved of its own accord, bringing her hand with it. The blade shot through the demon's throat, and blood poured out acrid and stinking. Sidra struggled to her knees, gagging from the stench. She fought upward with the blade and shield. A claw slipped past the edge of the shield, and she felt claws sink into her thigh. Leech bit into the demon's arm, half-severing it. And it began to fade. It was running as a proper demon does when it is hurt badly enough and has the choice of leaving.

Leech screamed after the fading creature, "No, no!"

It flamed in her hand a while longer and then faded back to normal. "Cheated."

Sidra leaned against the wall, favoring her wounded leg. "It was not my doing that the demon left. I kept my part of the bargain."

The sword was dangerously silent. Sidra was almost relieved that all its magic was spent for the day. It was never reliable when it was pouting.

The last door was not locked. It opened easily to reveal the wizard in the middle of a spell. A protective code chased the edges of a pentagram, and the wizard stood in the center of it all. He was short, balding, and did not look like a demon master or an evil man. But standing outside his magic circle was no mere demon but a devil.

It was why the wizard had not aided his ice demon. It was death to abort the spell. He was trapped as if in a cage until he released the devil to its home plane. Now their only danger was the devil.

It was still only half formed, with the bottom half of its body consumed in a strange black smoke. Its upper half was vaguely manlike, with shoulders and arms. It resembled the demon they had banished, with its bat-ribbed ears and teeth, but it was covered in black skin, the color of nothing above ground. High above it all, suspended from the ceiling, were two earthenware jars on the end of a white pole.

A rope held the pole in place and the rope was tied off near the door around a peg. Sidra smiled. She raised the sword and chopped the rope. The wizard seemed to notice what she did. But he could not stop to plead with her. If he stopped, then the devil would be freed and it would kill him. Devils were very reliable' that way, or unreliable, depending on the point of view.

The pole came crashing to the ground, but the jars did not break. They were spelled against such mundane accidents. Sidra stepped toward them carefully, one eye on the devil. She sheathed Leech, for fighting devils was not a matter of swords.

She untied the two jars from the pole and passed one out to Milon. The other she balanced under her sword arm. Just before she passed out of the room with his precious power, the wizard broke and shrieked, "No."

The devil laughed. "Take your pots and go, warrior-thief. Your business is finished here."

The floor quivered. Sidra turned to Milon and said, "Run."

They ran only as far as the fallen gate. It blocked their way completely, and the floor shivered once more. "There must be a hidden lever that will raise this. Search." They felt along the walls to either side, and Milon found something that he pressed.

Slowly the gate rose upward. The walls lurched as if someone had caught the tower and twisted it.

They ran full out. There would be no more fighting, no more trap finding. It was a race to the surface.

Milon said, "The pit, what about the pit?"

"Jump it."

"Jump it?"

"Jump it or die."

He ran harder to keep up with her longer legs and he tried not to picture the spikes on the floor of the pit. It was there suddenly and they were leaping over it. Sidra went down, betrayed by her wounded leg, but was up and running with the blood pumping down her leg. The floor twisted under their feet and cracks began to form on the walls.

The stairs were treacherous. The lantern was a bouncing glow that showed widening cracks and falling rock. They came up into the tower room.

The door had healed itself shut. The tower gave a shudder as its foundations began to crumble. Sidra drew Leech from its sheath and pointed it at the door. She decided to bluff. "Open, door, or I'll burn you again." The door whimpered uncertainly and then it swung outward. They raced through the door and kept running across the ash circle and into the trees. With a final groan the tower thundered to its death. The world was full of rock and dust.

They lay gasping on the ground and grinning at each other. Milon said, "Let me look at your leg."

She lay back in the grass, allowing him to probe the stab wound. "Deep but not bad. It will heal. Now will you tell your minstrel what was so important about two earthenware jars?"

Sidra smiled and said, "I have a story for you, Milon. A story of a little girl and a vow she made to a god."

THE GIRL

WHO WAS INFATUATED

WITH DEATH

Well here we are, at the last story. This is Anita very solidly in her world, as it appears in the books. We have Jean-Claude on stage, and a distraught mother, a missing teenage girl, and a vampire who's about to get himself killed, but doesn't know it yet. This story is set before the novel Narcissus in Chains. *This is back when Anita is fighting the good fight to try not to give in every time she gets too close to her vampire boyfriend. Ah, how the mighty have fallen.*

IT was five days before Christmas, a quarter till midnight. I should have been asnooze in my bed, dreaming of sugarplums, whatever the hell they were, but I wasn't. I was sitting across my desk sipping coffee and offering a box of Kleenexes to my client, Ms. Rhonda Mackenzie. She'd been crying for nearly the entire meeting, so that she'd wiped most of her careful eye makeup away, leaving her eyes pale and unfinished, younger, like what she must have looked like when she was in high school. The dark, perfect lipstick made the eyes look emptier, more vulnerable.

"I'm not usually like this, Ms. Blake. I am a very strong woman." Her voice took on a tone that said she believed this, and it might even be true. She raised those naked brown eyes to me, and there was fierceness in them that might have made a weaker person flinch. Even I, tough-as-nails vampire-hunter that I am, had trouble meeting the rage in those eyes.

"It's all right, Ms. Mackenzie, you're not the first client that's cried. It's hard when you've lost someone."

She looked up, startled. "I haven't lost anyone, not yet."

I sat my coffee cup back down without drinking from it and stared at her. "I'm an animator, Ms. Mackenzie. I raise the dead if the reason is good enough. I assumed this amount of grief was because you'd come to ask me to raise someone close to you."

She shook her head, her deep brown curls in disarray around her face as if she'd been running her hands through what was once a perfect perm. "My daughter, Amy, is very much alive and I want her to stay that way."

Now I was just plain confused. "I raise the dead and am a legal vampire executioner, Ms. Mackenzie. How do either of those jobs help you keep your daughter alive?"

"I want you to help me find her before she commits suicide."

I just stared at her, my face professionally blank, but inwardly, I was cursing my boss. He and I had had discussions about exactly what my job description was, and suicidal daughters weren't part of that description.

"Have you gone to the police?" I asked.

"They won't do anything for twenty-four hours, but by then it will be too late."

"I have a friend who is a private detective. This sounds much more up her alley than mine, Ms. Mackenzie." I was already reaching for the phone. "I'll call her at home for you."

"No," she said, "only you can help me."

I sighed and clasped my hands across the clean top of my desk. Most of my work wasn't indoor office work, so the desk didn't really see much use. "Your daughter is alive, Ms. Mackenzie, so you don't need me to raise her. She's not a rogue vampire, so you don't need an executioner. How can I be of any help to you?"

She leaned forward, the Kleenex wadded in her hands, her eyes fierce again. "If you don't help me by morning, she will be a vampire."

"What do you mean?" I asked.

"She's determined to become one of them tonight."

"It takes three bites to become a vampire, Ms. Mackenzie, and they all have to be from the same vampire. You can't become one in a single night, and you can't become one if you're just being casual with more than one."

"She has two bites on her thighs. I accidentally walked in on her when she was getting out of the shower and I saw them."

"Are you sure they were vampire bites?" I asked.

She nodded. "I made a scene. I grabbed her, wrestled with her so I could see them clearly. They are vampire bites, just like the pictures they passed around at the last PTA meeting so we could recognize it. You know one of those people lecturing on how to know if your kids are involved with the monsters."

I nodded. I knew the kind of person she meant. Some of it was valuable information, some of it was just scare tactics, and some of it was racist, if that was the term. Prejudiced at least.

"How old is your daughter?"

"She's seventeen."

"That's only a year away from being legal, Ms. Mackenzie. Once she turns eighteen, if she wants to become a vampire, you can't stop her legally."

"You say that so calmly. Do you approve?"

I took in a deep breath and let it out, slow. "I'd be willing to talk to your daughter, try to talk her out of it. But how do you know that tonight is the night? It has to be three bites within a very short space of time or the body fights off the infection, or whatever the hell it is." Scientists were still arguing about exactly what made someone become a vampire. There were biological differences before and after, but there was also a certain level of mysticism involved, and science has always been bad at deciphering that kind of thing.

"The bites were fresh, Ms. Blake. I called the man who gave the lecture at our school, and he said to come to you."

"Who was he?"

"Jeremy Ruebens."

I frowned now. "I didn't know he'd gotten out of prison," I said.

Her eyes went wide. "Prison?"

"He didn't mention in his talk that he was jailed for conspiracy to commit murder—over a dozen counts, maybe hundreds. He was head of Humans First when they tried to wipe out all the vampires and some of the shape-shifters in St. Louis."

"He talked about that," she said. "He said he would never have condoned such violence and that it was done without his knowledge."

I smiled and knew from the feel of it that it was unpleasant. "Jeremy Ruebens once sat in the chair you're in now and told me that Humans First's goal was to destroy every vampire in the United States."

She just looked at me, and I let it go. She would believe what she wanted to believe; most people did.

"Ms. Mackenzie, whether you, or I, or Jeremy Ruebens approve or not, vampires are legal citizens with legal rights in this country. That's just the way it is."

"Amy is seventeen; if that thing brings her over underage, it's murder, and I will prosecute him for murder. If he kills my Amy, I will see him dead."

"You know for certain that it is a he?"

"The bites were very, very high up on her thigh"—she looked down at her lap—"her inner thigh."

I would have liked to have let the female vamp angle go, but I couldn't because I was finally beginning to see what Ms. Mackenzie wanted me to do, and why Jeremy Ruebens had sent her to me. "You want me to find your daughter before she's got that third bite, right?"

She nodded. "Mr. Ruebens seemed to think if anyone could find her in time, it would be you."

Since Humans First had also tried to kill me during their great cleansing of the city, Ruebens's faith in me was a little odd. Accurate probably, but odd. "How long has she been missing?"

"Since nine, a little after. She was taking a shower to get ready to go out with friends tonight. We had an awful fight, and she stormed up to her room. I grounded her until she got over this crazy idea about becoming a vampire."

"Then you went up to check on her and she was gone?" I made it a question.

"Yes." She sat back in her chair, smoothing her skirt. It looked like a nervous habit. "I called the friends she was supposed to be going out with, and they wouldn't talk to me on the phone, so I went to her best friend's house in person, and she talked to me." She smoothed the skirt down again, hands touching her knees as if the hose needed attention; everything looked in place to me. "They've got fake ID that says they're both over twenty-one. They've been going to the vampire clubs for weeks."

Ms. Mackenzie looked down at her lap, hands clasped tight. "My daughter has bone cancer. To save her life they're going to take her left leg from the knee down, next week. But this week she started having pains in her other leg just like the pains that started all this." She looked up then, and I expected tears, but her eyes were empty, not just of tears, but of everything. It was as if the horror of it all, the enormity of it, had drained her.

"I am sorry, Ms. Mackenzie, for both of you."

She shook her head. "Don't be sorry for me. She's seventeen, beautiful, intelligent, honor society, and, at the very least, she's going to lose a leg next week. She has to use a cane now. Her friends chipped in and got her this amazing Goth cane, black wood and a silver skull on top. She loves it, but you can't use a cane if you don't have any legs at all."

There was a time when I thought being a vampire was worse than death, but now, I just wasn't sure. I just didn't have enough room to cast stones. "She won't lose the leg if she's a vampire."

"But she'll lose her soul."

I didn't even try to argue that one. I wasn't sure if vampires had souls, or not, I just didn't know. I'd known good ones and bad ones, just like good and bad people, but one thing was true . . . Vampires had to feed off humans to survive; no matter what you see in the movies, animal blood will not do the job. We are their food, no getting around that. Out loud, I said, "She's seventeen, Ms. Mackenzie. I think she probably believes in her leg more than her soul."

The woman nodded, too rapidly, head bobbing. "And that's my fault."

I sighed. I so did not want to get involved in this, but I believed Ms. Mackenzie would do exactly what she said she would do. It wasn't the girl I was worried about so much as the vampire that would be bringing her over. She was underage, and that meant if he turned her, it was an automatic death sentence. Death sentences for humans usually mean life imprisonment, but for a vamp, it means death within days, weeks at the most. Some of the civil rights groups were complaining that the vampire trials were too quick to be fair. And maybe someday the Supreme Court will reverse some of the decisions, but that won't make the vampire "alive" again. Once a vamp is staked, beheaded, and the heart cut out, all the parts are burned and scattered on running water. There is no coming back from the grave if you are itty bits of ashy fish food.

"Does the friend know what the vampire looks like, maybe a name?"

She shook her head. "Barbara says that it's Amy's choice." Ms. Mackenzie shook her head. "It isn't, not until she's eighteen."

I sort of agreed with Barbara, but I wasn't a mother, so maybe my sympathies would have been elsewhere if I were. "So you don't know if the vampire is male or female."

"Male," she said, very firm, too firm.

"Amy's friend told you it was a guy vampire?"

Ms. Mackenzie shook her head, but too rapid, too jerky. "Amy would never let another girl do that to her, not . . . down there."

I was beginning not to like Ms. Mackenzie. There's something about someone who is so against all that is different that sets my teeth on edge. "If I knew for sure it was a guy, then that would narrow down the search."

"It was a male vampire, I'm sure of that." She was working too hard at this, which meant she wasn't sure at all.

I let it go; she wasn't going to budge. "I need to talk to Barbara, Amy's friend, without you or her parents present, and we need to start searching the clubs for Amy. Do you have a picture of her?"

She did, hallelujah, she'd come prepared. It was one of those standard yearbook shots. Amy had long straight hair in a rather nondescript brown color, neither dark enough to be rich, or pale enough to be anything else. She was smiling, face open, eyes sparkling; the picture of health and bright promise.

"The picture was taken last year," her mother said, as if she needed to explain why the picture looked the way it did.

"Nothing more recent?"

She drew another picture out of her purse. It was of two women in black with kohl eyeliner and full, pouting lips, one with purple lipstick and the other with black. It took me a second to recognize the girl on the right as Amy. The nondescript hair was piled on top of her head in a casual mass of loose curls that left the clean, high bone structure of her face like an unadorned painting, something to be admired. The dramatic makeup suited her coloring. Her friend was blond and it didn't match her skin tone as well. The picture seemed more poised than the other one had, as if they were playing dress-up and knew it, but they both looked older, dramatic, seductive, lovely but almost indistinguishable from a thousand other teenage Goths.

I put the two pictures beside each other and looked from one to the other. "Which picture did she go out looking like?"

"I don't know. She's got so much Goth clothing, I can't tell what's missing." She looked uncomfortable with that last remark, as if she should have known.

"You did good bringing both pictures, Ms. Mackenzie; most people wouldn't have thought of it."

She looked up at that, almost managed a smile. "She looks so different depending on what she wears."

"Most of us do," I said.

She nodded, not like she was agreeing, but as if it were polite.

"How old is Barbara, her friend?"

"Eighteen, why?"

"I'll send my friend the private investigator over to talk to her, maybe meet me at the clubs."

"Barbara won't tell us who it is that's been . . ." She couldn't bring herself to finish the sentence.

"My friend can be very persuasive, but if you think Barbara will be a problem, I might know someone who could help us out."

"She's very stubborn, just like my Amy."

I nodded and reached for the phone. I called Veronica (Ronnie) Sims, private detective and good friend, first. Ms. Mackenzie gave me Barbara's address, which I gave to Ronnie over the phone. Ronnie said she'd page me when she had any news, or when she arrived at the club district.

I dialed Zerbrowski next. He was a police detective and really had no reason to get involved, but he had two kids, and he didn't like the monsters, and he was my friend. He was actually at work, since he belonged to the Regional Preternatural Investigation Team and worked a lot of nights.

I explained the situation and that I needed a little official muscle to flex. He said it was a slow night, and he'd be there.

"Thanks, Zerbrowski."

"You owe me."

"On this one, yeah."

"Hmm," he said. "I know how you could pay me back." His voice had dropped low and mock seductive. It had been a game with us since we met.

"Be careful what you say next, Zerbrowski, or I'll tell Katie on you."

"My darling wife knows I'm a letch."

"Don't we all. Thanks again, Zerbrowski."

"I've got kids, don't mention it," he said, and he hung up.

I left Ms. Mackenzie in the capable hands of our nighttime secretary, Craig, and I went out to see if I could save her daughter's life, and the "life" of the vampire who was a close enough personal friend to have bitten Amy twice on the very upper thigh.

THE vampire district in St. Louis was one of the hottest tourist areas in the country. Some people credit the undead with the boom we've experienced in the last five years since vampires were declared living citizens with all the rights and privileges that entailed, except voting. There was a bill floating around Washington that would give them the vote, and another bill floating around that would take away their new status and make it legal to kill them on sight again, just because they were vampires. To say that the United States was not exactly united in its attitude toward the undead was an understatement.

Danse Macabre was one of the newest of the vampire-run clubs. It was the hottest dance spot in St. Louis. We'd had actors fly from the West Coast to grace the club with their presence. It had become chic to hobknob with vampires, especially the beautiful ones, and St. Louis did have more than its fair share of gorgeous corpses.

The most gorgeous corpse of them all was dancing on the main floor of his newest club. The floor was so crowded there was barely room to dance, but somehow my gaze found Jean-Claude, picked him out of the crowd.

When I first spotted him, his long pale hands were above his head, the graceful movement of those hands brought my gaze down to the whirl of his black curls as they slid over his shoulders. From the back, with all that long hair, the shirt was just scarlet, eye-catching but nothing too special; then he turned, and I caught a glimpse of the front.

The red satin scooped over his bare shoulders as if someone had cut out the shoulders with scissors; the sleeves were long, tight to his wrists. The high red collar framed his face, made his skin, his hair, his dark eyes look brighter, more alive.

The music turned him away from me, and I got to watch him dance. He was always graceful, but the pounding beat of the music demanded movements that were not graceful but powerful, provocative.

I finally realized, as he took the woman into his arms, as she plastered herself against the front of him, that he had a partner. I was instantly jealous and hated it.

I'd worn the clothes I'd had on at the office, and I was glad that it was a fashionably short black skirt with a royal-blue button-up shirt. A long black leather coat that was way too hot for the inside of the club and sensible black pumps completed the outfit—oh, and the shoulder holster with the Browning Hi-Power 9mm, which was why I was still wearing the coat. People tended to get nervous if you flashed a gun, and it would show up very nicely against the deep blue of the blouse.

To other people it must have seemed like I was trying to look cool, wearing all that leather. Nope, just trying not to scare the tourists. But nothing I was wearing compared to the sparkling, skintight dress and spike heels the woman had on; nope, I was woefully underdressed.

It had been my choice to stay away from Jean-Claude for these last few months. I'd let him mark me as his human servant to save his life and the life of the other boyfriend I wasn't seeing, Richard Zeeman, Ulfric, wolf king of the local pack. I'd done it to save them both, but it had bound me closer to them, and every sexual act made that mystical tie tighter. We could think each other's thoughts, visit each other's dreams. I'd fallen into Richard's dreams where he was in wolf form chasing human prey. I'd tasted blood underneath a woman's skin because Jean-Claude had been sitting beside me when he thought of it. It had been too much for me, so I'd fled to a friendly psychic who was teaching me how to shield myself metaphysically from the boys. I did okay, as long as I stayed the hell away from both of them.

Watching Jean-Claude move like he was wed to the music, to the room, to the energy, anticipating not just the music but the movements of the woman who was in his arms, made me want to run screaming, because what I really wanted to do was march over there and grab her by her long hair and punch her out. I didn't have that right; besides, they were only dancing. Sure.

But if anyone would be able to tell me who was about to bring Amy Mackenzie over to be the undead, it would be Jean-Claude. I needed to be here. I needed the information, but it was dangerous, dangerous in so many ways.

The music stopped for a few seconds, then a new song came on, just as fast, just as demanding. Jean-Claude kissed the woman's hand and tried to leave the dance floor.

She took his arm, obviously trying to persuade him to have another dance. He shook his head, kissed her cheek, and managed to extract himself, leaving her smiling. But as she watched him walk toward me, the look was not friendly. There was something familiar about her, as if I should have known her, but I was almost certain I didn't know her. It took me a second or two to realize she was an actress, and if I ever went to movies I would have known her name. A photographer knelt in front of her, and she instantly went from unpleasant to a perfect smile, posing, choosing another partner. A second photographer followed after Jean-Claude, not taking pictures, but alert for a photo opportunity. Shit.

I had two choices. I could either stand there and let him take pictures of Jean-Claude and me, or I could flee to the back office and privacy. I wasn't news, but Jean-Claude was the vampire cover boy. The press had been amused that the woman the other vamps called the Executioner, because she had more vamp kills than any other vampire hunter in the country, had been dating the Master of the City. Even I could admit it was nicely ironic, but being followed around by paparazzi had gotten old very fast. Especially when they tried to take pictures of me while I was working on preternatural murders for the police. For the American media, if you stood next to the gruesome remains, they wouldn't air the pictures or print them, but European papers would. Some of the European media make American media look downright polite.

When I stopped dating Jean-Claude, they drifted away. I was not nearly as photogenic, or as friendly. I didn't have to worry about winning the press over; there wasn't a bill in Washington that was trying to get me killed. The vamps needed the good press, and Jean-Claude was tagged as the one to get it for them.

I decided not to watch Jean-Claude walk toward me because I'd seen what my face looked like when I did—in color on the front of the tabloids. I'd looked like some small prey animal, watching the tiger stalk toward it; that explained the fear, but the fearful fascination, the open . . . lust, that had been harder to see in print. So I kept my eyes on the circling photographer and tried not to watch Jean-Claude glide toward me, as I leaned against the far wall, right next to the door that would lead into the hallway that led to his office.

I could have fled and avoided the press, but it would have

meant I would be alone with Jean-Claude, and I didn't want that. All right, truth, I did want that, and that was the problem. It wasn't Jean-Claude I didn't trust, it was me.

I'd been concentrating so hard on not watching him come toward me that it was almost a surprise when I realized I was staring into the red satin of his shirt. I looked up to meet his eyes. Most people couldn't meet the gaze of a vampire, let alone a master one, but I could. I was a necromancer and that gave me partial immunity to vampire powers, and I was Jean-Claude's human servant whether I wanted to be, or whether I didn't, and that gave me even more immunity. I wasn't vampire-proof by any means, but I was shut up pretty tight to most of their tricks.

It wasn't vampire powers that made it hard to meet those midnight-blue eyes. No, nothing that . . . simple.

He said something, and I couldn't hear him over the beat of the music. I shook my head, and he stepped closer, close enough that the red of his shirt filled my vision, but it was better than meeting that swimming blue gaze. He leaned over me, and I felt him like a line of heat, close enough to kiss, close enough for so many things. I was already flat against the wall; there was nowhere else to go.

He had to lean his mouth next to my face, a fall of his long hair moving against my mouth, as he said, "*Ma petite*, it has been too long." His voice, even over the noise, caressed down my skin as if he'd touched me. He could do things with his voice that most men couldn't do with their hands.

I could smell his cologne, spicy, exotic, a hint of musk. I could almost taste his skin on my tongue. It took me two tries to say, "Not nearly long enough."

He laid his cheek against my hair, very lightly, "You are happy to see me, *ma petite*, I can feel your heart trembling."

"I'm here on business," I said, but my voice was breathy. I was usually better than this around him, but three months of celibacy, three months of nothing, and being around him was worse. Damn it, why did it have to be worse?

"Of course you are."

I'd had enough. I put a hand on that satin-covered chest and pushed. Vampires can bench-press small trucks, so he didn't have to let me shove him, but he did. He gave me some room, then his mouth moved, as if he were saying something, but I couldn't hear him over the music and crowd noise.

I shook my head and sighed. We were going to have to go back into the office so I could hear him. Being alone with him was not the best idea, but I wanted to find Amy Mackenzie and the vampire she was going to get executed. I opened the door without looking at him. The photographer took pictures as we went through the door. He had to have been taking pictures when Jean-Claude had me practically pinned to the wall, I just hadn't noticed.

Jean-Claude shut the door behind us. The hallway was white, with harsher lighting than anywhere else in the club. He'd told me once that he had made the hallway plain, ordinary, so if a customer opened the door they'd know instantly that it wasn't part of the entertainment.

A group of waiters, vampires all, came out of the left-hand door, wearing vinyl short-shorts and no shirts. They'd spilled out of the door in a cloud of excited talk; it stopped abruptly when they saw us. One of them started to say something, and Jean-Claude said, "Go."

They fled out the door without a backward glance, almost as if they were scared. I'd have liked to think it was Jean-Claude that they were afraid of, but I was the Executioner, their version of the electric chair, so it might have been me.

"Shall we retire to my office, *ma petite*?"

I sighed, and in the silence of the hallway, with the music only a distant thrum, my sigh sounded loud. "Sure."

He led the way down the hallway, gliding ahead of me. The pants were black satin and looked as if they'd been sewn on his body, tight as a second skin. A pair of black boots graced his legs. The boots laced up the back from ankle to upper thigh. I'd seen the boots before; they were really nice boots. Nice enough that I watched the way his legs moved in them rather than the way the satin fit across his butt. Very nice boots, indeed.

He started to hold the door for me, then smiled, almost laughed, and just walked through. It had taken me a while to break him of opening doors for me, but I'd finally managed to teach a very old dog a new trick.

The office was done in an Oriental motif complete with framed fans around a framed kimono. The colors in all three ran high to reds and blues. A red lacquer screen had a black castle sitting atop a black mountain. The desk was carved wood that looked like ebony and probably was. He leaned against that desk, long legs out in front of him, ankles crossed, hands in his lap, his eyes watching me as I shut the door.

"Please, be seated, *ma petite*." He motioned to a black and silver chair sitting in front of the desk.

"I'm fine where I am." I leaned against the wall, my arms crossed under my breasts, which put my hand comfortably close to the gun under my arm. I wouldn't really shoot Jean-Claude, but the gun being close made me feel better. It was like a small, lumpy security blanket. Besides, I never went anywhere after dark unarmed.

His smile was amused and condescending. "I do not think the wall will fall down if you cease to lean against it."

"We need to figure out who the vamp is that's been doing Amy Mackenzie."

"You said you had pictures of the girl. May I see them?" The smile had faded round the edges, but his eyes still held that amusement, faint and condescending, which he used as a mask to hide things.

I sighed and reached into the pocket of my leather coat. I held the two pictures out toward him. He held his hand out for them but made no move to come to me.

"I won't bite, *ma petite*."

"Only because I won't let you," I said.

He gave that graceful shrug that meant everything and nothing. "True, but still I will not ravish you because you stand a few feet in front of me."

He was right. I was being silly, but I could taste my pulse in my throat as I walked toward him, the new leather coat sighing around me, the way new leather always does. It was a replacement coat for one that a vampire had ripped off me. I held the pictures out to him, and he had to lean forward to take them from me. I even sat down in the chair in front of the desk while he looked at them. We could be civilized about this. Of course we could. But I couldn't stop looking at the way his bare shoulders gleamed against the scarlet cloth, the way the high collar made his hair a pure blackness almost as dark as mine. His lips looked redder than I remembered them, as if he were wearing a light lipstick, and I wouldn't have put it past him. But he didn't need makeup to be beautiful, he just simply was.

He spoke without looking up from the pictures. "I do not recognize her, but then she could come here occasionally and I would have no reason to." He looked up, meeting my eyes, catching me staring at his bare shoulders. The look in those eyes said he knew exactly what I'd been looking at. The look was enough to make me blush, and I hated that.

My voice came out angry, and I was pleased. Anger is better than embarrassment any day. "You said on the phone that you could help."

He laid the pictures on his desk and clasped his hands back in his lap. The placement of his hands was utterly polite, but they also framed a certain area of anatomy, and the satin was very tight, and I could tell that other things were tight as well.

It made me blush again, and it made me angrier, just like old times. I'd have liked to be a smart alec and say something like, *That looked uncomfortable*, but I didn't want to admit that I'd noticed, so out of options that were polite, I stood up and turned away.

"None of my vampires would dare bring over anyone without my permission," he said.

That made me turn around. "What do you mean?"

"I have ordered a . . . how will you say . . . hiring freeze, until that nasty bill in Washington is defeated."

"*Hiring freeze*," I said. "You mean none of your vamps can make more of you until Senator Brewster's law goes down in flames?"

"*Exactement.*"

"So you're sure that none of your vamps is doing this?" I said.

"They would not risk the punishment."

"So you can't help me. Damn it, Jean-Claude, you could have told me that over the phone."

"I called Malcolm while you were en route," he said.

Malcolm was the head of the Church of Eternal Life, the vampire church. It was the only church I'd ever been in that had no holy objects displayed whatsoever; even the stained glass was abstract art. "Because if it's not one of your vamps, then it's one of his," I said.

"*Oui.*"

Truthfully, I had just assumed it was one of Jean-Claude's vampires because the church was very strict on when you brought your human followers over to the dead side, and the church also checked backgrounds thoroughly. "The girl's friend said she'd met the vampire at a club."

"Can you not go to church and go to a club on the weekends?"

I nodded. "Okay, you've made your point. What did Malcolm say?"

"That he would contact all his followers and give strict orders that this vampire and the girl are to be found."

"They'll need the picture," I said. My beeper went off, and I jumped. Shit. I checked the number and it was Ronnie's cell phone.

"Can I use your phone?"

"Whatever I have is yours, *ma petite*." He looked at the black phone sitting on the black desk and stood to one side so I could walk around the desk without him leaning over me. Considerate of him, which probably meant he was going to do something else even more irritating.

Ronnie answered on the first ring. "Anita?"

"It's me, what's up?"

She lowered her voice to a whisper. "Your detective friend convinced Barbara that if Amy got herself killed, she'd be charged with conspiracy to commit murder."

"I don't think Zerbrowski could make that stick."

"Barbara thinks he can."

"What did she tell you?"

"The vampire's name is Bill Stucker." She spelled the last name for me.

"A vamp with a last name. He has to be really new," I said. The only other vamp I'd ever met with a last name had been dead less than a month.

"Don't know if he's old or new, just his name."

"She have an address for him?"

"No, and Zerbrowski pushed her pretty hard. She says she's never been there, and I believe her."

"Okay, tell Zerbrowski thanks. I'll see you Saturday at the gym."

"Wouldn't miss it," she said.

"Oh, and thanks to you, too, Ronnie."

"Always happy to save someone from the monsters, which reminds me, are you with you-know-who?"

"If you mean Jean-Claude, yes, I am."

"Get out of there as soon as you can," she said.

"You're not my mother, Ronnie."

"No, just your friend."

"Good night, Ronnie."

"Don't stay," she said.

I hung up. Ronnie was one of my very bestest friends, but her attitude toward Jean-Claude was beginning to get on my nerves, mainly because I agreed with her. I always hated being in the wrong.

"The name Bill Stucker mean anything to you?" I asked Jean-Claude.

"No, but I will call Malcolm and see if it means something to him."

I handed him the phone receiver and stepped back out of the way, i.e., out of touching distance. His side of the conversation consisted mainly of giving the name and saying "Of course" and "Yes." He handed the phone to me. "Malcolm wishes to speak to you."

I took the phone, and Jean-Claude actually moved away and gave me some room. "Ms. Blake, I am sorry for anything my church brethren may have done. He is in our computer with his address. I will have a deacon at his doorstep within minutes."

"Give me the address and I'll go down and check on the girl."

"That will not be necessary. The church sister that is attending to this was a nurse before she came over."

"I'm not sure what Amy Mackenzie needs is another vampire, no matter how well-meaning. Let me have the address."

"And I don't believe that my vampire needs the Executioner shooting down his door."

"I can give the name to the police. They'll find his address, and they'll knock on his door, and they may not be as polite as I would be."

"Now that last is hard to imagine."

I think he was making fun of me. "Give me the address, Malcolm." Anger was tightening across my shoulders, making me want to rotate my neck and try to clear it.

"Wait a moment." He put me on hold.

I looked at Jean-Claude and let the anger into my voice. "He put me on hold."

Jean-Claude had sat down in the chair that I'd vacated; he smiled, shrugged, trying to stay neutral. Probably wise of him. When I'm angry I have a tendency to spread it around, even over people who don't deserve it. I'm trying to cut down on my bad habits, but some habits are easier to break than others. My temper was one of the hard ones.

"Ms. Blake, that was the emergency line. The girl is alive, but barely; they are rushing her to the hospital. We are not sure if she will make it. We will turn Bill over to the police if she dies, I give you my word on that."

I had to take his word, because he was a centuries-old vampire and if you could ever get them to give their oath, they'd keep it.

"What hospital, so I can call her mom?"

He told me. I hung up and called Amy's mother. One hysterical phone call later I got to hang up and now it was my turn to sit on the edge of the desk and look down at him.

My feet didn't touch the ground and that made it hard to look graceful. But then I'd never tried to compete with Jean-Claude on gracefulness; some battles are made to be lost.

"There was a time, *ma petite*, that you would have insisted on riding to the rescue yourself, questioning the girl's friend, and refusing to bring in the police at all."

"If I thought threatening Barbara with violence or shooting her would have made her talk, I'd be perfect for the job. But I'm not going to shoot, or hurt, an eighteen-year-old girl who's trying to help her best friend save her leg, if not her life. Zerbrowski could threaten her with the law, jail time; I can't do that."

"And you never threaten anything that you cannot or will not do," he said, softly.

"No, I don't."

We looked at each other. He at ease in the straight-backed chair, his ankle propped on the opposite knee, fingers steepled in front of his face so that what I mostly saw of him were those extraordinary eyes, huge, a blue so dark it treaded the edge of being black, but you never doubted his eyes were pure, unadulterated blue, like ocean water where it runs achingly deep and cold.

Ronnie was right, I should leave, but I didn't want to leave. I wanted to stay. I wanted to run my hands over his shirt, to caress the naked surprise of those shoulders. And because I wanted it so badly, I hopped off the desk, and said, "Thanks for your help."

"I am always willing to be of assistance, *ma petite*."

I could have walked wide past his chair, but that would be insulting to both of us. I just had to walk by the chair and out the door. Simple. I was almost past the chair, almost behind him, when he spoke, "Would you have ever called me if you hadn't needed to save some human?" His voice was as ordinary as it ever got. He wasn't trying to use vampire tricks to make the words more than they were and that stopped me. An honest question was harder to turn my back on than a seductive trick.

I sighed and turned back to find him staring straight at me. Looking full into his face from less than two feet away made me have to catch my breath. "You know why I'm staying away."

He twisted in the chair, putting one arm on the back of it, showing that flash of bare shoulder again. "I know that you find it difficult to control the powers of the vampire marks when we are together. It was something that should have bound us closer, not thrust us farther apart." Again his voice was as carefully neutral as he could make it.

I shook my head. "I've got to go."

He turned in the chair so that he leaned both arms on the back, his chin resting on his hands, his hair framing all that red cloth, that pale flesh, those drowning eyes. Less than two feet apart, almost close enough that if I reached a hand out I could have touched him. I swallowed so hard it almost hurt. I balled my hands into fists, because I could feel the memory of his skin against my hands. All I had to do was close that distance, but I knew if I did, that I wouldn't be leaving, not for a while anyway.

My voice came out breathy. "I should go."

"So you said."

I should have turned and walked out, but I couldn't quite bring myself to do it. Didn't want to do it. I wanted to stay. My body was tight with need; wet with it, just at the sight of him fully clothed, leaning on a chair. Damn it, why wasn't I walking away? But I wasn't reaching for him either; I got points for that. Sometimes you get points for just standing your ground.

Jean-Claude stood, very slowly, as if afraid I'd bolt, but I didn't. I stood there, my heart in my throat, my eyes a little wide, afraid, eager, wanting.

He stood inches away from me, staring down, but still not touching, hands at his sides, face neutral. He raised one hand, very slowly upward, and even that small movement sent his fingertips gliding along my leather coat. When I didn't pull away, he held the edge of the leather in his fingertips inside the open edge of the coat at the level of my waist. He began to slide his hand upward, above my waist, my stomach, then the back of his fingers brushed over my breasts, not hesitating, moving upward to the collar of the coat, but that one quick brush had tightened my body, stopped my breath in my throat.

His hand moved from my collar to my neck, fingers gliding underneath my hair until he cupped the back of my neck, his thumb resting on top of the big pulse in my neck. The weight of his hand on my skin was almost more than I could take, as if I could sink into him through that one hand.

"I have missed you, *ma petite*." His voice was low and caressing this time, gliding over my skin, bringing my breath in a shaking line.

I'd missed him, but I couldn't bring myself to say it out loud. What I could do was raise up on tiptoe, steadying myself with a hand on his chest, feeling his heart beat against the palm of my hand. He'd fed on someone, or he wouldn't have had a heartbeat, some willing donor, and even that thought wasn't enough to stop me from leaning my face back, offering my lips to him.

His lips brushed mine, the softest of caresses. I drew back from the kiss, my hands sliding over the satin of his shirt, feeling the firmness of him underneath. I did what I'd wanted to do since I saw him tonight. I passed my fingers over the bare skin of his shoulders, so smooth, so soft, so firm. I rolled my hands behind his shoulders, and the movement let our bodies fall together, lightly.

His hands found my waist, slid behind my back, pressed me against him, not lightly, hard, hard enough that I could feel him even through the satin of his pants, the cloth of my skirt, the lace of my panties. I could feel him pressed so tight and ready that I had to close my eyes, hide my face against his chest. I tried to keep my feet flat to the floor, to move away from him, just a little, just enough to think again, but his hands kept me pinned to his body. I opened my eyes then, ready to tell him to let me the hell go, but I looked up and his face was so close, his lips half parted, that no words came.

I kissed those half-parted lips almost as gently as he'd kissed me. His hands tightened at my back, my waist, pressing us tighter against each other, so tight, so close. My breath came out in a long sigh, and he kissed me. His mouth closing over mine, my body sinking against his, my mouth opening for his lips, his tongue, everything. I ran my tongue between the delicate tips of his fangs. There was an art to French-kissing a vampire, and I hadn't lost it; I didn't pierce myself on those dainty points.

Without breaking the kiss, he bent and wrapped his arms

around my upper thighs, lifted me, carried me effortlessly to the desk. He didn't lay me on it, which is what I half-expected. He turned and sat down on the desk, sliding my legs to either side, so that he was suddenly pressed between my legs with only two pieces of cloth between us. He lay back on the desk, and I rode him, rubbing our bodies together through the satin of his pants and my panties.

His hands rubbed up my leg, tracing my thigh, until his fingers found the top lace of the thigh-high hose. I pressed myself into him hard enough for his body to arch, spasming our bodies together. And there was a knock on the door. We both froze, then Jean-Claude said, "We are not to be disturbed!"

A voice I didn't recognize said, "I am sorry, master, but Malcolm is here. He insists that it is urgent."

Evidently Jean-Claude did know the voice, because he closed his eyes and cursed softly under his breath in French. "What does he want?"

I slid off Jean-Claude, leaving him lying on his desk, with his legs dangling over the end.

Malcolm's smooth voice came next. "I have a present for Ms. Blake."

I checked my clothing to make sure it was presentable; strangely it was. Jean-Claude sat up, but stayed on the edge of his desk. "Enter."

The door opened and the tall, blond, dark-suited figure of Malcolm walked through. He always dressed like he was a television preacher, conservative, immaculate, expensive. Compared to Jean-Claude he always looked ordinary, but then so did most everyone. Still, there was a presence to Malcolm, a calm, soothing power that filled every room around him. He was a master vampire and his power was a thrumming weight against my skin.

He tried to pass for human, and I'd always wondered if the level of power he gave off was his version of toned down, and if this was the toned-down version, then what must his power truly be like?

"Ms. Blake, Jean-Claude." He gave a small bow of his head, then moved from the door and two vampires in the dark suits and white shirts of his deacons came through carrying a chained vampire between them. He had short blond hair and blood drying on his mouth, as if they'd chained him before he'd had time to clean himself.

"This is Bill Stucker; the girl, I am sorry to say, passed over."

"She's one of you, then," I said.

Malcolm nodded. "This one tried to run, but I gave you my word that he would be punished by your law if she died."

"You could have just dropped him off at the police station," I said.

His eyes flicked to Jean-Claude, to me, to my leather coat forgotten on the floor. "I am sorry to interrupt your evening, but I thought it would come better if the Executioner delivered the vampire to the police rather than us. I think the reporters will listen to you when you say we did not condone this, and you are honorable enough to tell the truth."

"Are you saying the rest of the police aren't?"

"I am saying that many of our law enforcement are distrustful of us and would be only too happy to see us lose our status as citizens."

I'd have liked to argue, but I couldn't. "I'll drop him off for you and I'll make sure the press knows you delivered him."

"Thank you, Ms. Blake." He looked at Jean-Claude. "Again, my apologies. I was told that the two of you were no longer dating."

"We aren't dating," I said, a little too quickly.

He shrugged. "Of course." He looked back at Jean-Claude and gave a smile that said more than anything that they didn't quite like each other. He liked interrupting Jean-Claude's evening. They were two very different kinds of vampire, and neither really approved completely of the other.

Malcolm stepped over the struggling, gagged form of the other vampire and went out the door with his deacons. None of them even looked back at the vampire chained on the floor.

There were a flock of waiters and waitresses in their skimpy uniforms huddled in the doorway. "Take this vampire and load him in *ma petite*'s car."

He looked at me, and I got my keys out of the leather coat and tossed it to one of the vampires. One of the women picked the chained vamp off the floor and tossed him over her shoulder like he weighed nothing. They closed the door behind them without being told.

I picked my coat off the floor. "I have to go."

"Of course you do." His voice held just a little bit of anger. "You have let your desire for me out and now you must cage it again, hide it away, be ashamed of it."

I started to be angry, but I looked at him sitting there, head down, hands limp in his lap, as dejected as I'd seen him in a while, and I wasn't angry. He was right, that was exactly how I treated him. I stayed where I was, the coat over one arm.

"I have to take him down to the police station and make sure the press gets the truth, not something that will make the vampires look worse than they already do in all this."

He nodded without looking up.

If he'd been his usual arrogant self, I could have left him like that, but he was letting his pain show, and that I couldn't just walk away from. "Let's try an olive branch," I said.

He looked up at that, frowning. "Olive branch?"

"White flag?" I said.

He smiled then. "A truce." He laughed, and it danced over my skin. "I did not know we were at war."

That hit a little too close to home. "Are you going to let me say something nice, or not?"

"By all means, *ma petite*, far be it from me to interrupt your gentler urges."

"I am trying to ask you out on a date."

The smile widened, his eyes filling with such instant pleasure that it made me look away, because it made me want to smile back at him. "It must have been a very long time since you asked a man out; you seem to be out of practice."

I put on my coat. "Fine, be a smart alec. See where it gets you."

I was almost to the door when he said, "Not a war, *ma petite*, but a siege, and this poor soldier is feeling very left out in the cold."

I stopped and turned around. He was still sitting on the desk trying to look harmless, I think. He was many things: handsome, seductive, intelligent, cruel, but not harmless, not to body, mind, or soul.

"Tomorrow night, pick a restaurant." One of the side effects of being his human servant was that he could taste food through me. It was the first time he'd been able to taste food in centuries. It was a minor power to share, but he adored it, and I adored watching him enjoying his first bite of steak in four hundred years.

"I will make reservations," he said, voice careful again, as if he were afraid I'd change my mind.

Looking at him, sitting on his desk all in red and black and satin and leather, I didn't want to change my mind. I wanted to sit across the table from him. I wanted to drive him home and go inside and see what color of sheets he had on that big bed of his.

It wasn't just the sex; I wanted someone to hold me. I wanted someplace safe, someplace to be myself. And like it or hate it, in Jean-Claude's arms I could be perfectly who and what I was. I could have called Richard up and he'd have been just as glad to hear from me, and there would have been as much heat, but Richard and I had some philosophical differences that went beyond his being a werewolf. Richard tried to be a good person, and he thought I killed too easily to be a good person. Jean-Claude had helped teach me the ultimate practicality that had kept me alive, helped me keep others alive. But the thought that Jean-Claude's arms were the closest thing I had to a refuge in this world was a sobering thought. Almost a depressing one.

He slid off the desk in one graceful movement as if his body were pulled by strings. He started to glide toward me, moving like some great cat. Just watching him walk toward me made my chest tight. He grabbed each side of the leather coat and drew me into the circle of his arms. "Would it be pushing the bounds of our truce too far to say that it is hours until dawn?"

My voice came out breathy. "I have to take him to the police and deal with reporters; that will take hours."

"This time of year dawn comes very late." He whispered it as he bent to lay his lips against mine.

We kissed, and I drew back enough to whisper, "I'll try to be back before dawn."

* * *

IT was four days before Christmas, an hour before dawn, when I knocked on Jean-Claude's bedroom door underneath the Circus of the Damned, one of his other clubs. His voice called, "Come in, *ma petite*."

An hour. It wasn't much time, but time is what you make it. I had stopped by the grocery store on the way and picked up some ready-made chocolate icing in one of those flip-top canisters. He could taste the chocolate while I ate it, and if it just happened to be on him while I was eating it, well . . . The silk sheets on his bed were white, and we laughed while we covered him in chocolate and stained the sheets. But when every inch of him that I wanted was covered in thick, sweet chocolate, the laughter stopped, and other noises began, noises even more precious to me than his laughter. Dawn caught us before he could take a bath and clean himself of the sticky sweetness. I left him in a pile of chocolate-smeared white silk sheets, his body still warm to the touch, but his heart no longer beating. Dawn had found him and stolen his life away, and lifeless he would remain for hours; then he would wake, and he would be "alive" again. He truly was a corpse. I knew that. But he had the sweetest skin I'd ever tasted, candy-covered or plain. He had no pulse, no breath, no movement, dead. It should have made a difference, and it did. I think the siege, as he called it, would have been over long ago if he'd been alive, or maybe not. Being a vampire was too large a part of who Jean-Claude was for me to separate them out. It did make a difference, but I laid one last icing-coated kiss on his forehead, and went home. We had a date tonight, and with the feel of his body still clinging to mine, I could hardly wait.

COPYRIGHT INFORMATION